Life in
Bits

HARPER BLISS
T.B. MARKINSON

OTHER HARPER BLISS BOOKS
The Pink Bean Series
The French Kissing Series
A Swing at Love (with Caroline Bliss)
Once Upon a Princess (with Clare Lydon)
In the Distance There Is Light
The Road to You
Far from the World We Know
Seasons of Love
Release the Stars
Once in a Lifetime
At the Water's Edge

OTHER T.B. MARKINSON BOOKS
A Woman Lost Series
Confessions Series
The Miracle Girl Series
The Chosen One Series
Marionette
Claudia Must Die
Girl Love Happens

To all our readers. Merry Christmas!

CHAPTER ONE

Eileen attempted to raise her shoulder to secure the battered army-green bag, which was slipping down a little with each step. At the same time, she kept her left hand on the handle of the massive rolling luggage, which was jam-packed with the necessary pieces of her life. The rest of her belongings still resided in her London apartment, which Eileen hadn't decided what to do with: keep or sublet.

This thought, along with the thousands of others racing through her mind, wrenched a deep sigh from Eileen. For forty-nine years she'd been a woman of action, but lately, she'd been immobilized by... what? Fear? Exhaustion? Betrayal? All three, perhaps.

Despite Eileen's best efforts, the bag continued to slide precariously off her shoulder. Ever since the event and subsequent hospital stay, simple tasks had become arduous, much to her dismay and frustration.

"Eileen!" Julia, her younger sister by four years, smiled and waved as soon as Eileen cleared the final door of the soul-sucking customs area of Boston's Logan International Airport.

"Here, let me take your bag." Julia reached for the shoulder bag, but Eileen pulled back.

"I've got it, thanks." Eileen ignored the bead of perspiration snaking its way down her face.

Julia's gaze fell briefly to Eileen's stiff right arm cradled under her chest. A silent wave of anger surged through Eileen. Pity was one emotion she couldn't stomach.

Wrapping one arm around her sister's right shoulder, Julia took the opportunity to nudge the bag back into place on the good one. "How was your flight?"

"Delayed, cramped, and customs took over two hours due to the complete incompetence of allowing four international flights to land at once." Despite Julia's efforts, the bag slipped off Eileen's shoulder completely this time. Eileen crooked her elbow to stop it from plummeting to the floor, but she couldn't hoist it back into place without the use of both arms.

The rigid right arm remained in the same spot, where it'd rested the past three weeks.

Without saying a word, Julia eased the bag off Eileen's arm and tossed it effortlessly over her right shoulder.

"I need a shower," was all Eileen said. She was grateful to be relieved of the bag, but too strong-willed to say thank you out loud.

Julia nodded, seeming to understand. "The car's this way." She led her sister to the parking garage without talking, much to Eileen's relief.

After stowing the bags in the back of the SUV, Julia settled behind the steering wheel. "Let's head to my place since you don't have keys to your apartment yet. I've arranged for the key exchange on Monday morning at nine. You can shower at my place and have time for a nap before heading to dinner with the parents."

Eileen groaned, shoving her head into the padding of the seat.

"It's not high on my list of things I wanted to do on a snowy Saturday night either, so don't even start." Julia cranked the heat on. "It'll take a minute to warm up."

"I don't know if I'm ready... for mom." Eileen looked out her side window at the BMW parked next to Julia's vehicle. It was much like the type her mom drove. Her dad, a New Englander to the core, abhorred drawing attention to his wealth and more than likely still had his beat-up Ford with only three hubcaps.

"You've never known how to handle her." She paused and took a deep breath. "I've learned—to the point where we have a semi-decent relationship." Julia, with one hand on the back of Eileen's headrest, checked to see if it was all clear before backing out of the spot and heading for the exit ramp.

"*Semi-decent*," Eileen mocked. "Mom has always been hard on me, blaming me for everything that's gone wrong in her life." Her mom had never been shy about reminding Eileen at every possible chance that she'd given up her dreams when she fell pregnant with Eileen.

"Please." Julia's knuckles whitened on the steering wheel as she guided the smoke-gray Range Rover around the tight curve of the parking garage ramp, the tires squealing on the cement despite the low speed. "She's just as hard on me. Even more so when you weren't around."

"You didn't have to stay, you know," Eileen said, her jaw tightening, becoming acutely aware of her sweaty back from carrying one bag that didn't compare to the weight of her camera equipment when on assignment.

Julia, seemingly unperturbed by Eileen's tone, pressed on. "It's not that simple. Mom and Dad are getting older. I have to remind them to take their medication. Mom can't drive at night. Now that Dad's retired, he doesn't know how to entertain himself without driving Mom bonkers. I feel like a referee half the time. I have my hands full. I'm glad you're home and can help some."

Eileen rubbed her right hand with her left. "And you think that's possible? I'm currently struggling to open any bottles and I can't drive. Not just because my driver's license expired two years ago." Eileen sensed Julia quickly glancing at her immobile arm before returning her gaze to the road.

"Those aren't the only tasks I need help with. You're not useless, Ellie. Besides, I've missed my older sister. You have a niece and nephew who look up to you, but they don't actually know you. It took... this for you to come home for the first time in five years. And I've lost count how many years it was before this visit."

"Are you going to lecture me the entire drive to Derby?" Eileen yawned, setting the side of her head against the seat, fatigue settling in.

"Close your eyes. You must be exhausted." Vivaldi was playing in the background and Julia fiddled with the stereo volume to turn it down. "It's nice to have you home. Really, it is."

Eileen opened one eye and appraised her sister whose hair had grown grayer than her natural mousy brown since they'd last seen each other. It must rankle their fastidious mother. That was one quality Eileen actually shared with her mom. Although, she'd hadn't highlighted her own hair to cover the gray since leaving the hospital. "I never meant to stay away for so long this time. The days just slipped by. How are Isabelle and Michael?"

"Nearly grown. Michael's graduating high school this spring. Belle the following. It'll be weird when they're gone, although I hardly ever see them now. Teenagers have little time for their mothers, apparently."

"I remember those days," Eileen's voice was soft, infused with sleep. "And James?"

"He hasn't changed one bit. Still works too much, but he does his best to be a great father."

"Your children are lucky to have him. And you." Her exhaustion made the words sound much more perfunctory than Eileen intended.

Julia nudged the volume up a notch, indicating conversation could wait for when Eileen wasn't half-dead to the world. Ironic, considering, just twenty-one days ago, Eileen had thought for sure she was a goner. And since surviving, a part of her wished she hadn't. Not in this current state.

Eileen, with eyes closed and seconds from nodding off, feared she'd made a mistake coming home. Would she become yet another burden to her only sibling, who'd been left keeping the family together when Eileen absconded at the age of twenty-two, so many years ago?

Her parents' house hadn't changed much since Eileen's childhood. Still massive, with a curved, carpeted staircase situated to the right as you entered the house. Mahogany antique furniture, oriental vases, bronze sculptures of Greek gods and goddesses occupied every nook and cranny, making the house more museum-like than a family home.

"We're here," Julia called, stepping into the house right on Eileen's heels.

Eileen's gaze traveled the expanse of the black and white tiled foyer. A crystal chandelier shone overhead. In the center of the space was a round table with a flower arrangement and statue of Nike, the Greek goddess of victory. What stood out the most was the absence of dust. The spotless, but cold space made Eileen long for her cozy apartment in London, overlooking a private garden. The home suited Trudy Callahan's

5

personality, however: beautiful on the outside, cold and empty on the inside.

"There you are. I was expecting you two twenty minutes ago." Her mom's perfectly colored hair, in contrast with Julia's, once again reminded Eileen to make an appointment at a salon sooner rather than later. Eileen took in her mom's gray duster-length cardigan with a matching turtleneck underneath and black trousers. A necklace fashioned with tortoiseshell disc beads dangled past her plentiful bosom, the opposite of Eileen's modest breasts. Her mom drifted across the tile, her arms out, pulling the much taller Eileen into an awkward embrace. "How lovely of you to visit."

Julia met Eileen's eyes as if persuading her not to point out the obvious. Not within minutes of her arrival at least. Her parents were fully aware of the reason for Eileen's return.

Their father, Bruce, a dead ringer for James Garner, shuffled into the entryway in his dark brown leather deck shoes, Vineyard Vine plaid button-up, and chinos—his go-to outfit no matter the season.

Eileen smiled, tickled this aspect of her dad hadn't changed over the years, despite her mom's harping that he should dress in suits or formal jackets, even for a family meal in his ancestral home. "Hello, Dad."

His heartfelt hug comforted her for the first time since...

"It's good to have you home," his voice had a wisp of old man to it.

Eileen, stunned by how much he'd aged since her last visit, leaned into him briefly and then pulled back, cognizant that her mom stood two feet away. "It's good to see you." She hastily added, "Both of you."

"Would you like a drink before we sit down for dinner?" Her mom picked some lint off Eileen's right shoulder.

Eileen turned her body slightly, protecting her right flank.

Her mom continued, "It's so nice just to have the two of you over for dinner. The four of us, back together again."

Julia, biting her bottom lip as if trying to curtail a brusque remark, said, "I'd like sparkling water. Sound good to you, Ellie?"

"Sure. Thanks." A headache was starting to form behind her eyes, and Eileen chalked it up to not drinking enough water.

Their father cheerfully dittoed, rolling back onto his heels, digging his hands into his pockets.

Her mom, with a wounded look, said, "But I decanted a bottle of 2001 Vietti Barolo Villero Riserva for this special occasion."

"I'm driving tonight," Julia countered in a tone that closed the matter. "And, we should have dinner sooner rather than later. I need to get to bed early." Her stare fell on Eileen.

Eileen worried the fatigue from her travels would make it impossible to mask her mounting frustration dealing with her mom and a simple reminder, such as not drinking, only highlighted how much her life had drastically changed, adding to her irritation. The doctors had been clear alcohol should be avoided, especially during the first few weeks of her recovery. Julia, who'd flown to London the moment she'd heard, knew all the do's and don'ts relating to Eileen's recovery firsthand. Granted, a few weeks had already passed, but knowing the ever-cautious Julia, having a glass of wine to ease the tension wouldn't be permissible. Clearly, their mom, not surprisingly, was opting to ignore medical opinion along with Julia's disapproving glare. Or had her mom blocked out the knowledge of Eileen's medical issue, since that would acknowledge weakness?

Their father feigned a yawn. "This old man prefers early bird specials for a reason."

"Besides their being early, you mean? They're cheap." Julia

said, laughing, patting his cheek. "How much is Maggie charging for tonight's feast?"

He guffawed over the joke. It wasn't the first time Julia had cracked it.

"Fine. I didn't know I was surrounded by old fogies." Their mom gestured they might as well retire to the dining room. "I'll let Maggie know we're ready for dinner, *tout de suite*. It's not even six." She tutted. "Such an uncivilized time for dinner. In Europe—"

"Hey, girls." Their father cut off his wife. "If you're American in the living room what are you in the bathroom?"

Both Eileen and Julia playfully groaned, responding in unison, "European."

"Or Russian." Their father laughed at his own joke. Standing on Eileen's left, he crooked his arm for his eldest daughter to thread her good arm through, and then proffered his other elbow to Julia. "It's not often I'm flanked by two beauties."

The French oak table with its parquet top had all the leaves removed, so it sat four comfortably. Usually, when the whole family gathered, there were double the attendees or more if the far-flung members joined them.

This piece had always been one of Eileen's favorite items in the house and secretly she hoped she'd inherit it simply for the parquet top. Although now, her mom's crocheted tablecloth covered the surface. The lacy masterpiece had taken her half a decade to make and it only saw the light of day for special occasions. Eileen suspected Maggie had set the table, not her mom.

Each took their seat, Julia sitting to Eileen's right and her father on her left.

Maggie, significantly grayer since Eileen had last seen her, and slightly stooped, served everyone a grapefruit, walnut, and feta cheese salad. She placed Eileen's plate last, saying, "I made this just for you."

Eileen smiled. "Thanks, Maggie. I haven't had one since the last time you made it for me."

Maggie departed and the Callahans tucked into their salads, no one talking. She returned briefly to pour wine, but her mom was the only one who assented with a curt nod. Maggie left once again.

Eileen grasped a salad fork with her left hand, awkwardly piercing a grapefruit slice and piece of butter lettuce.

"That's new," her mom's gaze zeroed in on Eileen's use of her left hand. "Living in Europe all these years has added sophistication to your etiquette. Maybe you can teach your sister. It's never too late to better ourselves."

Julia glugged her water.

"Have you been following the Pats?" her father asked.

"Not this season. Is Brady still their quarterback?" Eileen managed to get a walnut onto the tines of the fork, but fumbled it at the last second, only ending up with lettuce in her mouth.

He nodded, chewing.

"You know what you should take up while on vacation? Knitting or crocheting." Her mom tapped the tablecloth. "I made this when I sat around waiting for your dance lessons or soccer practices to end. It helped pass the time and look at the final outcome—something I can hand down to one of you."

Eileen blinked, and Julia blanched.

Her father cleared his throat. "I have an extra ticket to next Sunday's Pats game if you want to go, Eileen. Julia still has zero interest in football and James said he has to work." He placed his fork in the five o'clock position indicating he was done, although he'd only eaten a third of the salad. Unusual for the rotund man. Or had his eating habits changed over the years?

"Maybe. I'll check my schedule." Eileen, like her sister, loathed football, but appreciated her father's diversionary attempt.

"It's so hard supporting the sport now with all the docu-

9

mentation about brain damage." Her mom sipped her red wine. "So many of them end up as vegetables. I always thought, Eileen, you would have made an excellent brain surgeon. Steady hands and wicked smart. Instead you chose to gallivant around the globe from one war zone to another. Running has always been your thing, which is ironic since I was the one who dropped out of college and gave up my dreams of medical school to have you."

Peeved, Eileen had to marvel at how her mom had seamlessly worked this into the conversation this evening in record time.

"Where's Maggie? I'm ready for the next course." Her father patted his belly, eyeing the door.

Never too far away, Maggie appeared. She quietly cleared the salad plates and returned with the main course.

"Another favorite of yours, Eileen," her mom said. "Garlic parmesan chicken with brussels sprouts."

Julia's thinning lips indicated to Eileen her sister had requested the meal.

Unlike the other plates, Maggie had cut Eileen's chicken breast into bite-size pieces, much to Eileen's relief. Julia nodded her appreciation, leading Eileen again to believe her sister had made a great effort to arrange everything this evening for Eileen's homecoming. The wine kerfuffle had probably ruffled Julia's mother-hen ways.

"And in case anyone wants more brussels sprouts, there are more in this dish." Maggie placed it at Julia's side.

After Maggie had left via the service door, her mom asked, "What are your plans while you're home, Eileen?"

"Can you pass the brussels sprouts?" Her father asked.

Julia handed the dish to Eileen, her face paling when she realized her mistake at the last second.

Eileen had reached across her chest to grasp the dish with her left hand, but juggled it when Julia released her hand, spilling three sprouts, one rolling to the center of the table, leaving a grease stained path.

"Look at what you've done to my tablecloth. You've ruined it!" Her mom's lips drew back into a snarl.

"I'm sure Maggie can get the grease out." Her father dabbed the mark with his blood-red linen napkin.

"Stop that, Bruce! You'll make it worse." Turning her attention to Eileen, she said, "You did that on purpose."

"W—what?" Eileen spluttered.

"It was my fault, mom. I let go of the dish too soon." Julia plucked the sprouts from the tablecloth, putting them onto her own plate. "I'll have it professionally cleaned."

"Stop covering for Eileen. She's had it in for me since the day she was born."

"Jesus, Mom! You know Eileen isn't home on vacation. She had a stroke and can't use her right arm and you want her to crochet and berate her for fumbling a dish!" Julia's chest heaved up and down indignant at her mother's words.

Eileen, tight-lipped, looked over to her dad, then to Julia, and finally rested her gaze on her mom. Fighting back tears, she rose from the table, her napkin slipping onto the floor, and walked out of the dining room toward the exit.

CHAPTER TWO

Naomi held the hospital door open for Kelly, then closed it behind them. The cold November air whipped her in the face. Naomi reveled in its iciness. She was used to it. Whereas most people loathed the heavy gray clouds hanging in the air this time of year, she loved them, because it meant that the holidays were soon approaching.

She grabbed her friend's arm. "Let's do something special for the kids this Thanksgiving. For just one day, let's try to make them forget where they are and why they're in hospital."

"There's time," Kelly said.

"Not that much," Naomi insisted.

Kelly stopped in her tracks. "You do know you say the exact same thing every year." She grinned at Naomi.

"Because I want it to be special for them every year," Naomi replied.

"Are you sure that this year in particular you're not over-compensating?" Kelly turned toward her.

"Oh, please." Naomi rolled her eyes.

"I just want you to know that I'm here for you if you want

to talk. Whenever you need to. Okay?" Kelly put a hand on Naomi's upper arm.

"How many times do I need to repeat myself?" Naomi said. "I'm fine."

"Jane cheated on you." Kelly squeezed Naomi's arm now. "You don't have to pretend you're fine when you're with me."

Naomi shook her head. "How did we go from Thanksgiving plans to this?" She pretended to shiver and dug her hands deep into her coat pockets.

"I'm just trying to be a good friend." Kelly's gaze found Naomi's.

"I appreciate that, but you bringing it up all the time isn't really helping. I'm just getting on with my life. Spending time with the kids in there." She nodded her head in the direction of the hospital. "Trying to replace all the negative vibes of a break-up with some positive ones."

"Maybe I'm the one who's still angry at Jane," Kelly said. "For the way she treated you." She shook her head. "And I must admit I'm a little baffled at your lack of utter rage."

"Whereas I wish you'd have started this conversation while we were still inside," Naomi said, even though it wasn't the cold bothering her. "Obviously things weren't meant to be between Jane and me. She wasn't the one for me. That's how I'm choosing to look at it." She took a deep breath. "No one, not even my ex who cheated on me, is going to mess with my holiday cheer." She shot Kelly a wide grin, hoping to lay this conversation to rest. Not that Naomi had anywhere pressing to be, or anyone waiting for her at home. She just didn't want to talk about Jane any longer.

"Don't I know it." Kelly injected some lightness into her voice. "Naomi Weaver will have an outstanding Thanksgiving and the merriest of Christmases no matter what."

"Thank you. Now am I allowed to get into my car?"

"Yes. I'll see you tomorrow." Kelly didn't move. "And call me if you need anything."

"Will do." Naomi gave her friend a quick wave and hurried to her car, a hand-me-down from her brother. Every time she got in and it started from the first turn of the key, she considered it a small miracle.

On the way home, Naomi wondered if she hadn't been too hard on Kelly who was, after all, only trying to help—even though she could be a bit subtler about it.

It was only a ten-minute drive from the hospital to her apartment and, instead of ruminating more about what Kelly had said, Naomi turned to Spotify, found the song she was looking for and put it on repeat. "What doesn't kill you makes you stronger," she sang along loudly, tapping the steering wheel with her gloved fingers, all the way home.

Naomi was still humming the Kelly Clarkson tune when she turned the key in the lock of her front door. It snapped open after one turn. Had she forgotten to double lock the door again? It surely wouldn't be the first time. In fact, most days, Naomi simply let the door fall shut behind her, much to Jane's chagrin when they were still living together.

"You don't have to make it easy for burglars to get in," Jane would repeat endlessly. These days, Naomi could leave her front door unlocked guilt-free, without having to deal with some harsh words from her partner. Because she didn't have a partner anymore.

When she swung the door open, Naomi noticed she must have left the lights on as well—oh, the things Jane would have to say about that. She quickly closed the door only to find, when she turned around, that Jane was standing right in front of her.

"What the—" Naomi tried to regroup quickly. "What are you doing here?"

"I wanted to see you," Jane said. "I miss you." She painted a soft smile on her lips.

"You can't just be here when I come home." Naomi held out her hand. "I'd like your key, please."

"Will you sit with me for a minute?" Jane pleaded. "So we can talk?"

"There's nothing to talk about. It's over." Naomi took a step back. She had no intention of sitting as long as her ex was in *her* apartment.

"Come on, babe," Jane pleaded. "This doesn't have to be the end of us."

"It very much does." Naomi brought her hands to her hips. "Now, I'd like you to leave and give me your key."

"I'm so incredibly sorry for what happened," Jane said. "You must know that. I've told you about a million times now."

"It's not about how sorry you are." While it was distressing to find Jane in her home unannounced, Naomi had no trouble at all playing this cool. "In fact, you cheating on me was the best thing that could have happened. For both of us. If anything, it showed us that we're not right for each other."

Jane scoffed. "You're such an annoying glass half-full person." She inched closer toward Naomi. "I know I hurt you and you have every right to be upset. But we were together for almost three years. Don't you think because of that alone we deserve another chance?"

"I clearly don't," Naomi said coldly.

"I came clean to you. I explained why I did what I did. You know I never meant to hurt you. The whole thing didn't even have that much to do with you."

"You didn't hurt me as much as you made me see that you're not the person I want to spend the rest of my life with. Something I'm really glad I found out."

"Christ, Naomi. Can you be any harsher?"

"Can *you* be any more delusional?" Naomi took a step closer to her ex. "I made it very clear what I wanted from this relationship. I distinctly remember using the words *monogamy* and *marriage*. Quite often, actually. And what was your response? Falling into bed with the first woman you came across, and for what? To simply prove that you could?"

"I'm not the marrying kind, Naomi. I never, ever made a secret of that." Jane shrugged. "What's marriage, other than a silly piece of paper, anyway?"

"Which is exactly why you and I shouldn't be together anymore." Naomi stepped to the side. She spotted Jane's coat hanging over a chair. She reached for it and handed it to her. "Please, give me the key and find someone else to string along. I'm sure there are plenty of women out there who don't want to be married. Maybe… what's her name? Petra, was it? Maybe she'll be up for that sort of thing."

"What I don't understand," Jane pulled her coat from Naomi's hands, "is how, when we were together, you could even bring up marrying me when us breaking up doesn't seem to bother you all that much?"

"That's easy." Naomi finally shrugged off her own jacket. She was beginning to sweat in the heat of the apartment. "I'm glad for what it has taught me. I know exactly what I want and, for a minute, I was fooled into thinking I wanted it with you. But now I know you're not the one for me. You made that very clear."

"You know Petra meant nothing to me. It was one night. We can't throw away three years because of one night. We'd be so foolish to do so."

"I see things very differently." Naomi tossed her coat onto an antique armchair. "From my point of view, it was the best thing that could have happened to us. We weren't happy anymore. Not like we used to be." Naomi scanned Jane's deflated face. She was starting to feel sorry for her. "We were just going through the motions. Otherwise, you wouldn't have cheated. People in happy, fulfilled relationships don't do things like that behind each other's back, Jane. I think we both know that."

"I disagree." Jane's bottom lip started trembling.

"We've been over this so many times now. You can't keep rehashing what happened. As I said, and as we both know very well, it's over." It was hard to get the next words past the growing lump in her throat. "You need to understand that. We're not getting back together. Not only because of what you did, but because we don't belong together. The sooner you realize that, the sooner you can move on." Naomi scooted closer to Jane again. They'd only broken up a few weeks ago. Jane admitting to sleeping with someone else hadn't instantly dissolved all the feelings Naomi had for her. She fought the urge to take her ex into her arms and tell her everything would be all right—because, for them, it never would be.

"We can still be friends, though?" Jane mumbled.

"Of course we can." Naomi tried to find Jane's gaze, but it kept skittering away.

"And you'll come to my photo exhibition?"

Naomi did put a hand on Jane's arm now. "I wouldn't miss it."

Jane dug her hand into her jeans pocket. "Here's the key. You won't find me in your place unannounced anymore."

"Thank you." Naomi took the key from Jane and held her hand for a few seconds, just one last time.

"I *am* sorry," Jane said.

"I know." Naomi watched as Jane fumbled with her coat.

"I'm going now." Jane finally looked her in the eye. It felt like a kind of very last resort. One last glance to see if all possibilities were truly exhausted.

"Bye," Naomi said. She let Jane walk out on her own, then

stood watching the door for a while after Jane had left. Breakups were always painful because of the shared history and all the memories of better days resurfacing at the most inconvenient times. Yet a wave of relief washed over Naomi after Jane had closed the door of the apartment they used to share behind her, hopefully for the very last time.

In her heart of hearts, Naomi knew it was the best thing for them both.

CHAPTER THREE

E ileen fumbled her iPhone with her left hand while attempting to press her right index finger to unlock the screen. It wasn't a difficult maneuver by any means, but the name on the screen had rattled her. Wedging the iPhone under her right hand, she navigated her finger to the exact spot, and then hoisted the phone to her ear. "Eileen Makenna."

Since leaving Derby when she was in her early twenties, she'd only used her first and middle name professionally, preferring the way it rolled off the tongue.

"Ellie Bean!"

Eileen stifled a groan. Her seventy-six-year-old boss had been calling her by that nickname for decades. She was almost fifty, for Christ's sake. But asking Ray Steffens to desist from using the moniker would be tantamount to career suicide. Besides, he had pet names for everyone, men and women. As far as she knew, no one appreciated them, but they all put up with them.

"Mr. Steffens. To what do I owe this honor?"

He chuckled, "The honor is all mine. How's my favorite photographer? The shoulder feeling better?"

"Getting stronger every day." She glanced at her shoulder, her gaze traveling downward to the arm pressed against her, cringing over the blatant lie to the man who'd given her a job before she'd even had a chance to prove herself. While Eileen had told her boss she needed time off, she hadn't been entirely forthcoming about the true reason, leading the higher-ups to believe it was a rotator cuff injury she'd had surgery on and that it now needed nothing more than TLC.

"Good, good. Any idea of when we can get you back in the field? Not to put any pressure on you, but another Pulitzer would be a boon for the company." He laughed, although Eileen suspected he wasn't kidding. Everyone in the company felt the pressure of going above and beyond one hundred and ten percent of the time. "Seriously though, we miss your work."

"I miss working. More than you know." She sucked her lips into her mouth, ruing the last sentence.

"I'm sure you do. I still remember when I met you fresh out of college. How eager you were to prove yourself. You've never let me or the company down. Please take all the time you need. We don't want to put you in harm's way—or more than we usually do considering the assignments you take on. I still remember the time we had to helicopter you and your team out of—which country was it?"

Eileen could picture the white-haired gentleman tapping his chin with the side of his index finger, as he usually did when he'd lost track of a thought or when he inserted a dramatic pause to grab his audience. Eileen suspected he longed for the good old days of yellow journalism. He probably dreamed sledgehammer headlines.

She didn't want him to focus on the dangers of her job. That would make it even harder for her to fight for it if need be. If her arm refused to cooperate ever again—a thought she kicked to the curb immediately—what would become of her?

Eileen steered the course of the conversation back on track.

"I should be back in a month or so. No later than the first of the year." Eileen closed her eyes, saying a silent prayer for this to come true. The London doctors had said to be patient. Recovery takes time. But they hadn't met the likes of Eileen. She'd been in war zones on three different continents. Documenting human barbarities. Capturing with her lens the suffering of the innocent caught up in geo-political tug of wars. When others turned down a dangerous assignment, she'd stepped up. Nothing scared her.

This was simply another arduous assignment that required true grit to persevere.

"Yes, I'll be back the first day of the new year," she repeated in a much more confident tone. She almost believed it.

"Glad to hear it. I hope you and your family have a happy Thanksgiving."

"Thank you, sir. Have a pint at the pub for me."

"Just for you, Ellie Bean, I'll have two."

The phone went silent.

At exactly 12:01, the church bells started to toll, alerting Eileen it was time to walk the fifty yards to the hospital for her appointment. Using her jacket as a cape, since she didn't have the patience for the struggle of jamming her right arm through the sleeve, she wondered why even after all this time the bells pealed at one minute past noon every single day of the year.

At the reception desk, Eileen did her best to stand tall. "I'm here for a twelve-fifteen appointment."

The woman smiled and said in a sing-song voice, "Okey dokey. Can I get your name?"

Eileen supplied it.

"Mack will be with you momentarily."

No, it couldn't be. Eileen swallowed. "Mack?"

"Yes. Mack Ashwell has been assigned as your physical therapist. Take a seat and he'll be here in a jiffy."

Eileen nodded, selecting a seat in the corner, next to an impressive peace lily on a plant stand. She couldn't help wondering if the plant was someone's sick joke because the last emotion surging through her at that precise moment was peacefulness. Picking up the latest edition of *Time*, she leafed through the magazine, her eyes not registering any words or photos within the pages.

"Eileen Callahan."

Eileen glanced up, getting to her feet. "Yes."

The soft brown eyes that met hers were reminiscent of her first love, Melissa. Not surprising considering she was standing in front of Melissa's younger brother.

"Follow me, please." Mack held the door with one hand and gestured with the other for Eileen to enter. "Second room on your right."

The door led to an examination room containing a bed with the prerequisite protective sheet of paper down the middle.

"Take a seat." Mack motioned to the bed.

Eileen hesitated before perching on the edge, the paper sheet crinkling under her.

"How have you been, Mack?" Might as well address the elephant in the room head on.

"Good." He smiled, his shoulders relaxing some. "I couldn't believe it when I read your name. Have you seen Melissa yet? I had dinner with her last week and she didn't mention you were back in town."

"Not yet. I just got back this weekend and with… jet lag, I haven't reconnected with anyone other than my folks."

Mack nodded with the same dubious look Melissa had worn when she'd sensed Eileen wasn't being entirely truthful, which had always been one of Eileen's coping mechanisms.

When placed in an uncomfortable situation, she would say just enough to seem like she'd explained everything, but never really cracked the surface. Many times, Eileen didn't even realize she was doing this until it was too late to take it back.

"I'm surprised you're back in Derby. Last I heard, you worked for one of the sports teams in Boston," she said.

"I missed it too much." His eyes mellowed, yet another reminder of Melissa's easy-going demeanor. "It's funny, growing up, all I thought about was escaping this small town and then when I did... I couldn't stay away." He crossed his arms. "You, though, haven't been back in how long now?"

"Nearly thirty years, aside from the occasional visit." She shrugged her left shoulder and immediately regretted calling attention to the right.

He stood. "Let's take a look at your arm." Mack eased the jacket off her shoulders.

Eileen remained quiet as he extended her arm as far as it would allow, and moved it this way and that.

After asking several questions about her medical history and getting her to reveal what she'd learned from the London doctors, he said, "We need you to extend it as much as possible. I can give you a device that'll force it into position. Prevent bent arm. How are you getting along with eating, showering, dressing...?" He mimed et cetera.

"Okay..." She didn't want to discuss this part of her life with Mack. Or anyone.

"Do you have help? Someone staying with you? Julia?"

Eileen shook her head. "I have an apartment near here."

"I see. There are devices that can help you with pulling on socks, fastening a bra, undoing your pants so you can use the toilet..." His voice trailed off, perhaps sensing her unease, or quite possibly the mention of going to the bathroom was even a step too far for him.

Eileen didn't speak or make eye contact.

Mack paused. "Come on, let's go into the treatment room and get started then."

The gym-like facility had a handful of patients with physical therapists. One woman in her thirties rode a stationary bike, presumably warming up for whatever exercises her torturer had in mind. A man in his sixties lay on a table, lifting one leg in the air.

Mack directed her to a chair. Next to it was a juvenile-sized soccer ball, which he easily palmed with his massive right hand. "I'm going to set this on your legs. Place your right hand on it and then your left hand on top to secure it." He waited for her to follow his directions. "Good. Roll the ball down to your knees and then back up."

Eileen sat perfectly still for several pregnant seconds. "Really?"

Mack encouraged her with a smile. "It does help. Eventually, the goal is for you to let go with your left hand and only use the weaker one."

Eileen started to pull her good arm away, but Mack said, "Not yet. Build up to it."

She continued to give him a steely eye, her chin held high.

"For me, for old times' sake." He pressed a palm to his chest. "Please."

She rolled the ball away from her lap, feeling silly playing this game. Then back up. Again and again.

After several minutes, Mack said, "That's a great start. Now for something different." He placed a large exercise ball in front of her. "If you could spread your legs wide…" Color speckled his cheeks.

Eileen ground her jaw, but she complied.

"If you can't bend over to maneuver the ball, you can stand at the table and do the exercises there."

"I'm fine."

"Okay, then. Put your weak arm on top. Secure it with your

26

left hand. This exercise involves moving the ball in a few directions. First, forward and back." With another encouraging smile, he motioned for her to begin. After the fifth repetition, he said, "Now to the left and back to the center. Five times." Once finished, he instructed her to move it to the right. "Like the other exercise, work up to being able to do it solely with your right hand."

They continued with other exercises, almost all of them just as simple.

"What's the point of all these?" Eileen asked as she slid a folded towel on top of a table away from her and then back.

"To get you to the point where you can reach for a glass. If you continue to cradle your arm all the time, your fingers will naturally want to make a fist." He balled up his fingers. "Conversely, the more you extend the arm, the more the fingers will extend." Mack stretched out his arm and followed up by unfurling his fingers. He reached for a jar of peanut butter on a shelf immediately to Eileen's left. "Here's an exercise you can do at home. All you need is a jar like this." He held the Skippy aloft. "I recommend a plastic one." Mack placed the jar on its side in front of Eileen and positioned her right hand on it. "You can tape your hand to it if need be. Roll it back and forth on a table. Attach a straw to it so you can see the progress."

"You've got to be kidding." Eileen bristled. "All of these… so-called exercises are ludicrous. Shouldn't I use a weight machine or something? Kick this into a higher gear?"

Mack hooked a stool with his left foot and pulled it so he could sit side-by-side with Eileen. Pressing his palms into his thighs, he said, "You had a stroke, Ellie, which is an assault on the brain. Once the swelling went down, you experienced some return of movement to your right arm. But significant damage has been done. In order to acquire more return, we need to train other parts of your brain to take over. Create different pathways for messages to travel from your brain to your arm.

You can retrain your brain. However, in order to do so, you have to use a lot of repetition." He placed his hand on her right shoulder. Massaging it, he said, "These muscles bounce back before the arm, hand, and fingers. That's why we're starting with the shoulder and we'll work down into the hand. Like I said, the goal is for you to be able to reach for a glass."

Eileen absorbed his words. "How long?"

Mack cocked his head. "For the exercises? Several minutes each."

"No. How long until I can use... my arm again?"

"I won't lie. It takes time and patience to construct new pathways."

"Weeks?" She squeaked, closing one eye, peering up at him.

"I think it would be beneficial to have you work with an occupational therapist as well. To learn ways to overcome your limited arm movement, such as new techniques for getting dressed, taking a shower, and quite possibly driving a car again. An OT can suggest ways to set up your home. Make it safer."

"You make it sound like I'll always be this way. An invalid." She patted her right arm with her left hand.

"Let's not think that way. Individuals make the most progress during the first few months. It's imperative for you to exercise every single day. If you do so, you'll see improvement. Even years later."

"Years!"

"Don't focus on a specific time frame."

"Easy for you to say."

"Ellie, like I said earlier, the muscles and nerves in your arm aren't receiving the essential messages for movement and manipulating objects. With diligent treatment and dedication, the neural linkage between the brain and arm can be repaired. I know you're eager, but it takes time. There's no way around it."

"I don't have time!" She sucked in a deep breath. "I need to be back to normal by the end of the year."

Mack lowered his eyes. "I wouldn't set that as your goal."

Too late, Eileen thought.

"I want to shoot straight with you. It's possible you may never fully recover complete use of your arm. I hope this isn't the case. I know you—your heart and dedication. If we work together, we can do everything possible to get you back to where you want to be. But you have to realize there's no magic pill to get you there." He motioned for her not to speak. "I know. You feel like you don't have time. Unfortunately, your body is telling you differently. You need to listen." He dipped his head to peer into her eyes. "Something you aren't good at, if I remember correctly."

CHAPTER FOUR

"I can't believe she showed up like that," Kelly said, giving a dismissive shake of the head.

"At least I got my key back. That's something." Naomi sipped from her cappuccino. The quality of the coffee had gradually improved since she'd started working at the hospital, first as a volunteer and since last year as a full-time social worker.

"Yeah right." Kelly pushed her cup away. According to her, the beverages at the hospital coffee shop were only getting worse with the years.

"Derby's a small town. It's important to me that Jane and I can remain friends." She cleared her throat. "We're likely to run into each other all the time and I would prefer it if we could be civil to each other."

"God, you're such a lez, Nomes." Kelly grinned at her. "Best friends with your ex, who cheated on you. Where will it end? Braiding each other's hair in the old people's home?"

Naomi chuckled. "Who knows? And I wouldn't say *best* friends. I already have a best friend." She shot Kelly a wink.

"Jane and I will probably be more like acquaintances, I guess. But I did promise I'd go to her photo exhibition on Friday."

Kelly shook her head—again. "You're too good for this world. If it were me…"

"I know," Naomi cut her off. "You'd never give her the time of day again."

"I'm just angry with her because she hurt you. You're my best friend and I want you to be happy. If Frank cheated on me, you'd be equally angry with him."

"I'd give him a very stern talking-to. You can be sure of that." Naomi cradled the coffee cup in her hands. "But it's not the same with Jane and me. We weren't made for each other like you and Frank. Now that a few weeks have passed, I feel more relieved than hurt. Like it was this very clear instance of life telling me something I was perhaps too blind to see. And it's actually working out for me instead of causing me a huge bout of heartache."

"I guess I should be glad you see it that way then."

Naomi sat facing the door and, absently, kept an eye on who left and entered. The hospital coffee shop was busy, with quite the line forming at the counter. She checked her watch. She had ten more minutes before she had to get back to work.

"I'll be just fine, Kel. Now about Thanksgi—" Derby Hospital was full of people Naomi had never encountered before, but the stranger entering the coffee shop just as Naomi looked up, stood out for some reason.

She was tall and lanky with wild, reddish blond hair tied back in a ponytail. Maybe Naomi noticed her because she looked out of place, as though she wasn't from Derby, or at least had never been to Derby Hospital before.

The woman's right arm was cradled against her chest, her brow set in furrowed determination.

"Earth to Naomi?" Kelly was waving her hand in front of Naomi's face. "You were saying?"

Naomi followed the woman with her gaze. She witnessed how the woman joined the line at the counter.

"About Thanksgiving." Naomi forced herself to look away and refocus on the conversation with Kelly. "We should…" The clatter of something falling to the floor pulled Naomi's attention away from Kelly again.

The red-haired woman had dropped some coins. Before she knew it, Naomi was out of her seat, collecting them from the floor.

"Here you go." She handed the fallen coins to the woman.

"For heaven's sake," the woman bristled. "I could have picked those up myself. I may look like an invalid, but I'm—"

Their eyes met—the woman's were a hue of bright green Naomi didn't think she'd ever come across before—and she stopped talking, holding Naomi's gaze.

"I'm sorry," the green-eyed woman said, her gaze softening. "Thank you for your help."

Naomi, used to working with people who were trying to come to grips with the new physical reality of their lives, offered a wide smile. "Don't mention it." She glanced at the woman's incapacitated arm and shoulder.

The woman turned away from her, as though wanting to hide her injured body part. "Have a nice day." She returned to the counter, the line having now shortened considerably.

When Naomi rejoined Kelly, her friend was on the phone. Naomi took the opportunity to sneak a peek over her shoulder. The woman was now ordering at the counter.

When she finished her call, Kelly got up. "Sorry to cut our riveting Thanksgiving celebrations meeting short, but duty calls. Megan claims to have found a discrepancy in the hospital budget I've only verified a million times." She rolled her eyes. "See you later."

"Tell Megan she has a hundred percent track record of

being wrong when it comes to questioning your calculations," Naomi said.

"Will do." Kelly shot her a quick smile and bounded out of the coffee shop.

Naomi glanced behind her again and noticed the woman she'd just helped looking around for a table. She scooted out of her chair and waved at her. "There's room here."

The woman eyed Naomi's table as if it was the least appealing spot for her to sit, but then seemed to cave, her gaze softening again.

"Thanks. Again." She sat down and deposited her cup on the table.

"My pleasure. I'm Naomi." Naomi thought better of holding out an outstretched hand, foreseeing annoyance when the other woman wouldn't be able to hold out her own.

"Eileen Makenna. I hope I didn't chase away your friend." Eileen shuffled in her seat and shrugged her coat off her shoulders. "You'd think half of Derby is sick with how busy it is in here." She gave a half-smile, then turned away slightly, as if wanting to mask her weak shoulder and arm.

Naomi decided not to bring up Eileen's arm, nor ask her what brought her to the Derby Hospital coffee shop.

"It's that time of the year, I guess," Naomi said, instead.

"God yes, I'd forgotten how cold it can be around these parts."

"So, you're from around here?" Naomi asked.

"Used to be. I've been gone a long time, though. I guess you could say I'm home for the holidays." The smile she tried on next didn't radiate a lot of holiday cheer. "How about you?"

"I work in this hospital. I'm a social worker and I volunteer at the children's cancer ward a few times a week."

"Wow." Eileen pursed her lips together for a brief moment. "You're unlike most people then, who prefer to turn away from the darker sides of life."

34

"If you put it like that." Naomi didn't see it like that at all, but this wasn't a discussion to have with a stranger who had ended up at her table by sheer coincidence. "What do you do when you're not home for the holidays?"

"I'm a photographer," Eileen said matter-of-factly.

Naomi inadvertently snorted.

"Why is that so funny?" Eileen glanced at her with raised eyebrows.

"No, I'm sorry. It's just..." She didn't think she should mention Jane to this woman she'd just met. Besides, Jane might be exhibiting some of her photos at a local gallery on Friday, but being a photographer was hardly her profession. "Someone I know is having her first photo exhibition this Friday."

"Really?" Eileen drank from her coffee again. Naomi's cup was long empty. "This town may end up surprising me yet. Where is it? I'm always keen to spot some local talent."

"On Main Street, next to the tavern." This time Naomi couldn't stop herself from saying more than she perhaps ought to. "And I wouldn't be so sure of spotting any talent."

"Now I'm doubly intrigued." Eileen slanted her torso over the table a little, adopting a conspiratorial posture. "Tell me more. I've been away a long time. I need to be caught up on all the gossip and it seems to me I've landed at the right table with the right person." For the first time, her smile reached all the way to her eyes.

Naomi mirrored Eileen's smile, but waved off her comment. "I've said too much already. Just a cowardly quip about my ex, who happens to be the photographer in question." Naomi thought of all the hours she'd posed for Jane as she studied light and composition, deeming herself the one and only rightful heir to Annie Leibovitz.

"What's your ex's name? Will I have heard of him?"

"Her." Naomi locked her gaze on Eileen's. "And no, that's

highly unlikely." She couldn't drag her gaze away from Eileen's. God, those strange green eyes. "Her name's Jane Rodman."

Eileen nodded. "Well, Naomi, it looks like I might see you at Jane Rodman's photo exhibition on Friday then." She flashed Naomi another smile, which, just like the light that only a few seconds ago had appeared in her eyes, dimmed brusquely.

"I think I would like that." Naomi was fairly certain they had crossed over into flirting territory. Maybe that was what had stood out to her when Eileen had entered the coffee shop. Her gaydar had started pinging—not something that happened often in a town like Derby.

"I'll see you there then." Eileen emptied her cup and shoved it away from her. She cast one last glance at Naomi, then pushed herself up with one arm. "It was a pleasure to meet you, Naomi." She grabbed her jacket from the back of the chair and held it in her good hand.

"Likewise," Naomi said, with a smile.

As she watched Eileen walk off, she thought that the event she'd been dreading to go to on Friday, would now be much more interesting.

Naomi looked at the clock above the door. She had to get back to work. She carried the empty coffee cups to the counter and considered what had just happened.

Eileen-the-mysterious-photographer was intriguing and, Naomi believed—but couldn't be entirely certain—interested in women. Even so, the woman was nothing like Jane or the other women Naomi had dated. It wasn't only the obvious age difference between them that set her apart, but everything about her, really. What had stood out to Naomi most, however, was Eileen's complete refusal to acknowledge why she was at the hospital—to admit any weakness on her part.

On her way to her office, with a little tingle fluttering in the pit of her stomach, Naomi wondered if she had a date on Friday. She guessed she would only find out then.

CHAPTER FIVE

Eileen stared out her bedroom window at the falling snow. Since returning home almost one week to the day, the weather had steadily dipped closer and closer to dead-of-winter temperatures, not Thanksgiving time weather. She'd always been sensitive to the cold, something not many people knew. On nights like this, she would never leave the house without cashmere wool tights.

She eyed her right arm, and muttered, "How, though?" Getting into loose pants every day had proven challenging every morning and she'd entirely given up on her favorite pair of skinny jeans. Tights?

Maybe Mack had been right when he suggested working with an occupational therapist. It wasn't as if she could ask her girlfriend to help since she hadn't been with anyone in years. Not seriously and certainly no one she could call up and say, "I need you."

She thought back to her last substantial relationship and struggled to affix a year reference to Tami. Surely that meant it'd been some time.

Work. That was her life. And if she couldn't work, who would she become?

Shoving that thought aside, Eileen strode to her closet to select an outfit for her... what? Date? Did hanging with Naomi at a local photography exhibition even count as a date? Did women Eileen's age actually go on dates? So many questions ran through her head.

Selecting a no-nonsense pair of black slacks, she placed them on her bed. A burst of wind slashed her window, the top of the loose-fitting screen scratching the glass.

Sighing, she went back into her closet and rummaged through the suitcase on the floor. She hadn't managed to find the energy or desire to unpack, convincing herself it'd be a useless effort since her time in Derby would be short. Rooting out a pair of black tights, she made her way back to her bed, her gaze landing on the sheets. They were pure whimsy, part of a nautical collection in which the delicate paisley print turned out on closer inspection to form tiny purple whales with cheerful grins. She wondered if Julia had enjoyed a good chuckle as she'd purchased them for Eileen. Julia had told her on many occasions that Eileen took herself way too seriously, which would be impossible to do while sleeping on these.

Dropping her robe, she eyeballed the black tights. "Only one of us will survive this," she threatened, knowing it made zero sense. She envisioned the headline: "Woman Dies While Trying to put on Tights." It was the type of headline Ray Steffens of yesteryear would have enjoyed.

"Ellie? You home?" Her sister's voice echoed from the entrance.

Eileen snatched her robe from the bed and attempted to cover herself, only managing to get the robe situated on one shoulder before Julia burst through the doorway. Why had she given Julia a key to come and go as she liked?

"There you… are." Julia lowered her glance to the scratched hardwood floor. "Whatcha doing?"

"Baking chocolate chip cookies. What do you think I'm doing?" Eileen's lip curled up with displeasure.

"I meant, why are you getting dressed to go out on a night like this?" Julia gestured to the window and the tree branches blowing this way and that.

"Going to a local photography exhibition." Eileen casually tried to adjust her robe to cover herself entirely without looking like she was, but failed miserably.

"Ah." Julia nodded. "Jane's photographs. I didn't know you knew her." She helped Eileen into her robe, without acknowledging her sister's need for assistance.

"Haven't had the pleasure. I met a woman in the hospital coffee shop and she mentioned it."

Julia clapped her hands. "You've been in town less than a week and you already have a date. What's her name?"

Eileen bit her bottom lip, assessing her sister's face. "Um, it's not a date. Just two people meeting up at the same event."

Julia cupped her ear with a hand. "I'm sorry. Did you say a name yet?"

Eileen darted her glance to the ceiling, but still confided, "Naomi."

Julia's hazel eyes darkened a smidge, or so Eileen thought, but upon further inspection, they were back to their normal color. Maybe the snow outside had obscured the street lamps, playing tricks with Eileen's vision. "And you're wearing tights with your slacks so you won't freeze, even indoors. Nice to see that hasn't changed."

"I… couldn't find socks, that's all." Eileen's gaze fell to the sheets on her bed.

"Right." Julia scrutinized the tights on the bed and then Eileen. "Let's get you dressed for your non-date. Sit on the edge of the bed." She swept the opaque fabric into her hand.

Not budging, Eileen said, "It's okay. I can still dress myself."

Julia held the thick stockings out to Eileen. "Go ahead."

Eileen didn't reach for them. "I'm not going to, not with you watching. You're getting weirder and weirder with each passing year."

"How would you know? You're never around."

Eileen groaned. "Are you going to help or lecture?"

"Do you want my help?" Julia folded her arms over her chest, the tights still in her hand.

"You might as well while you're here," Eileen said in a tone that conveyed it only made sense, as if she were doing Julia a favor.

"Take a seat."

"I'm not wearing underwear." Eileen balked.

"Yeah, I noticed that earlier. You can skip that since you'll be wearing these." She raised the hosiery aloft to emphasize the point.

Eileen shook her head, appalled. "I've never left the house without underwear."

"Underwear. Right." Julia flipped around to the antique white dresser on the far side of the room. "Which drawer?"

"They're still in my suitcase." Eileen motioned to the closet with her left hand. "I forgot to unpack them earlier."

Julia rummaged in the luggage. "Oh, wow. I never..." She held up red-licorice floral lace panties and a matching bra. "I don't think I ever knew this about you."

"That I wear undergarments?"

"Sexy ones." Julia spun the panties and bra on her index finger, imitating the actions of a stripper.

Eileen gave Julia a frosty look. "Maybe this is one of the reasons why I never come home."

"Having your skeletons tango out of the closet?" Julia manipulated the garments as if they were dancing.

"Being judged."

"I'm not judging you. I'm impressed. I haven't bought anything like this in years. Too bad it's not a date, because Naomi would dig these."

"How do you know that?"

"Uh, she's a woman, right? Who likes women? Hell, I'd find these sexy if they weren't on my sister."

Eileen shivered.

"You must be freezing."

"Repulsed, you mean. My sister likes my underwear? Yuck." She made a gagging sound.

Without further comment, Julia assisted Eileen with her clothes. When Eileen was fully dressed, Julia said, "You know, a lot of women like it when others show their vulnerability."

"I never have." Eileen pressed her lips together.

"Yeah, but you're... different."

Eileen studied the electric sign in the window of the studio located on Main Street. The words The Place flashed in neon pink, eliciting an eyeroll from Eileen. It was a decent size for the likes of Derby, but Eileen couldn't help thinking if she attended an exhibit in a space like this in London, with that particular name in flamingo pink, it would have been described as overreaching on the hipster level.

"Would you like me to take your jacket?" a young woman asked Eileen.

Eileen weighed the question. The studio was warm. Much warmer than she'd anticipated. If she didn't ditch the coat now, in all likelihood she'd have to shed it soon and hold it with her good arm leaving her completely at the mercy of... oh, who knew what. On the flip side, taking off the jacket now in the presence of the woman would clue this stranger in about her useless arm.

"There you are!" Naomi appeared at her side, her jasmine perfume permeating the space. "You look fantastic." Without any prompts, Naomi eased Eileen's jacket off, taking extra care with her right side, and handed it over to the young woman, who in return gave Naomi the coat check slip. "Thanks so much for coming tonight." A grin split Naomi's face. Her stunning dark eyes, high cheekbones, flawless skin, and narrow chin were all perfectly proportioned, giving Eileen the itch to capture her image.

Alas, that wasn't possible. Casting her photographer's eye aside, Eileen said, "What do you know about the exhibit? Or is it best for me to go in cold?"

"It might be best to fill you in some. Jane's work can be..." Naomi's voice trailed off as an older bickering couple passed them on their way out. When the coast was clear, Naomi continued, "The star of the show is Bitsy, a doll."

Eileen pivoted her head to scrutinize Naomi's face and quirked an eyebrow. "That's intriguing." *Really? A doll?* Maybe the flashing signage was the least pompous part about the evening.

"Isn't it just," Naomi gushed.

Eileen couldn't gauge if Naomi's reaction was sincere or mocking. The twinkle in the woman's hypnotic eyes conveyed so many emotions, while masking a defining one. It wasn't as if they were deceptive, rather processing more thoughts than most.

Naomi briefly patted Eileen's good arm as if Eileen was in on the joke. It stirred a tingling sensation within Eileen. Naomi explained, "The show is titled *Life in Bits*."

Eileen tore her gaze from where Naomi's hand had touched briefly and stared into her sparkling eyes long enough to make a blush appear on Naomi's cheeks. "Bitsy and Bits."

She glanced to her right, seeing the first piece. The doll, with scuff marks on its plastic face and a tattered green and blue dress, lay in a pile of leaves on the side of a dirt road, as if had been left there years ago and completely forgotten. Eileen stood perfectly still, taking in the piece designated "The Forgotten."

Naomi shifted on her feet, seeming unsure how to interpret Eileen's reaction.

Eileen nodded and they moved on to the next photograph. In this shot, Bitsy, still with scratched face and torn clothing, sat in a field, with other dolls strewn about face down. Only Bitsy's face could be seen. Eileen leaned closer and detected a *tear* in the corner of one of her eyes. The title was "Refugee Child."

"Interesting," Eileen muttered.

Slowly, they made their way to the other pieces, each showing Bitsy in provocative works, including protesting outside an abortion clinic, but Eileen couldn't determine if Bitsy was for or against the cause.

After viewing the last offering, Naomi steered Eileen to a quiet corner. A waiter passed by with glasses of wine and Naomi snagged two, seeming to question her decision when she held onto both. She took a sip then asked, "What do you think?"

Eileen relieved Naomi of one of the glasses, but didn't partake. "It's interesting."

"Ha! You've said that or a variation of that statement after viewing each one. And your face has been priceless. I don't recommend you play poker." Naomi leaned closer and whispered, "Ever." Her melodious laughter tickled Eileen's ears, blunting the words.

Eileen, knowing she'd been snared by Naomi's observation, didn't mind in the least, an unusual reaction that she'd have to ponder later in solitude.

Eileen smiled then said, "It's not that I don't like portraiture. I do. It's a passion of mine, really. No matter how hard most individuals attempt to mask their feelings, more often than not, it's their eyes that can't lie. And the lines around the eyes—you can see their whole lifetime, the good and bad." Eileen paused. "I'm not saying you can determine everything that has happened to a person from their face but you get a sense of their emotions. An insight into their psyche. And, from my assignments in war zones, I've seen people enduring the worst moments of their lives. It's not easy to witness, but my job calls for me to record as much as possible for others so they can experience what's happening."

"War zones? Really? That sounds incredibly dangerous." Alarm flashed in Naomi's expressive eyes.

Eileen shrugged her left shoulder. "Adrenaline and wanting to expose the truth—that keeps me in the moment. It isn't until after the dust settles that I contemplate the danger."

"Wow." Naomi shivered. "I had no idea. I feel a bit foolish for inviting you to... this exhibit. What must you think of Bitsy?"

Eileen smacked her lips. How could she say what she truly thought? The pretentiousness of this photographer. Thinking a doll could express true human feelings. Eileen had witnessed firsthand refugees fleeing their home countries. War zones. The smells. Sounds. The sobbing. The hatred. Fear. Desperation.

To avoid making Naomi feel even worse, Eileen said, "It's always good to support art."

Naomi laughed, seeming much relieved by the answer. "If you say so." She moved closer conspiratorially, her shoulder pressing into Eileen's good arm. "Between you and me, I've never fully understood Jane's vision." She pulled away and took another sip of wine. "I only came to show my support for my ex. She's always been sensitive, especially about her work."

Before Eileen could ask how long ago the breakup was, a woman with short, spiky hair approached.

The woman tossed an arm around Naomi's shoulders and planted a sloppy kiss on her cheek. "Here's my girl."

Naomi jabbed an elbow into the woman's side. "Ex-girl, you mean." As she spoke, Naomi's glance sought Eileen's. "This is Jane, the photographer."

Eileen nodded her acknowledgment, thankful Jane didn't offer a hand to shake. Although, she didn't appreciate Jane's manhandling of Naomi, who seemed to like it even less.

Jane returned the nod, before turning her full attention back to Naomi, and gave her shoulder a squeeze. "Why do you have to say ex-girl?"

"Because it's the truth." Naomi wiggled out of Jane's grasp, nearly spilling her wine onto the white cement floor.

Eileen saw a woman waving at Jane, trying to get her attention. "I think you're needed over there," Eileen said, slanting her head toward the woman. Jane left without another word.

A hand pressed Eileen's shoulder from behind. "I didn't expect to see you here."

Turning her head, Eileen gaped at Melissa, the girl she'd left without officially ending the relationship when she'd fled Derby to pursue her photography career. Her hair was grayer, reminding Eileen once again to make an appointment to have her own grays taken care of. The inquisitive creases around Melissa's eyes attested she hadn't lost her spunk.

Standing shoulder-to-shoulder, Eileen could only think to say, "Oh, hi." What else could she say really? *Hey, I've been meaning to explain why I left the way I did but could never find the right words so yeah… you look good.*

"I didn't know you liked art like this. Back when we dated in school, you had very strong opinions," Melissa said to Eileen. "Even the Mona Lisa irritated you."

Eileen shifted slightly to block the hypocrisy of Jane the Artist trying to hawk a picture of feigned suffering, when the homeless rate in America was on the rise again. Not wanting to turn into the guest people avoided for spouting the truth, Eileen responded to Melissa's Mona Lisa comment. "She doesn't have any eyebrows and don't get me started on the smile. At first glance, it looks like she is, but then it's hard to determine."

Melissa laughed, turning her attention to Naomi. "How are you, *dear*?"

"Good. And you?"

Eileen watched their greeting, remembering that in Derby everyone knew everyone else. And, she picked up on Melissa's emphasis of dear, as if to alert Eileen to Naomi's younger age.

Melissa turned her focus back to Eileen. "You always did see things in black and white terms. I thought of you, when was it, gosh… it's been years." Melissa tapped her fingers against her forehead. "Anyway, I read a news article that explained the Mona Lisa did originally have eyebrows, but over the centuries they've completely faded. As for the smile, the Italians have a word for it: *sfumato*. It means blurry, ambiguous, and leaves things to an individual's imagination."

Eileen's posture stiffened. "Are you implying I lack imagination?" Her eyes skittered over another one of Jane's pictures, wondering if that was what counted for imagination in Derby.

"What?" Melissa placed a hand on her chest. "Not at all. Just defining the term." Melissa's phone rang, bringing a frown to her face when she glanced at the screen. "Would you excuse me?" She gave Eileen's shoulder a squeeze and exited via the back door of the studio.

Naomi stared at Eileen, a smile slowly forming on her face. "Well, we got that out of the way. Both of us bumping into our exes and being put on the spot." She laughed. "I don't know about you, but I've had enough *culture* for one evening. Would you like to head back to my apartment for a drink? Or tea or coffee?" Naomi's eyes fell to the glass in Eileen's hand, still untouched.

CHAPTER SIX

"Drink?" Naomi asked. She leaned against the kitchen counter as Eileen struggled out of her coat. "Wine? Beer? Water, perhaps?"

"Sure." Eileen managed to dispose of her coat and, one-handedly, draped it over a chair. "It's not as if I'm driving anywhere tonight." She gave Naomi a hint of a smile.

Naomi remembered Eileen's untouched glass of wine at the gallery. She was also amazed that Eileen had so easily accepted her invitation for a nightcap. Yet, part of her had also expected her to say yes. Something in the glint of her eyes had predicted it—had, perhaps, even given Naomi the courage to ask.

"I'll have a beer, please," Eileen said, briefly glancing at Naomi before casting her gaze about Naomi's living room again.

"Coming right up." Only the other day, Jane had been pleading for Naomi to forgive her, right where Eileen was standing now. It was strange to have another woman in her home so quickly.

Eileen was inspecting the antique silver teapot that stood in the middle of the dining table.

47

"Here you go." Naomi walked up to her and offered her the bottle of beer.

Eileen turned to her with her good arm and accepted it. She held up the bottle and Naomi clinked her own against it.

"What are we toasting?" Emboldened by the very fact that Eileen was having a beer in her apartment, Naomi looked her straight in the eye.

"Good question." Eileen smiled, then averted her gaze. "I love your place. It's so cozy."

"Thanks." Naomi headed to the couch. "Are you staying with your family while you're in town?" She leaned back and watched Eileen, who apparently didn't much feel like sitting down.

"Goodness, no. I wouldn't survive two days in the same house as my mom, let alone two months. I've rented an apartment close to the hospital so I can get to my physical therapy sessions easily." She tilted her head back, exposing her long, delicate neck, and swallowed a tiny sip of beer.

Naomi reached for her phone and turned on Spotify. She glanced up at Eileen and searched for the song that had been playing in her head ever since she'd learned her name.

When the first notes started to play, Eileen turned toward her, a crooked grin on her face. "Ah, that song. The very bane of my existence." She finally sat in the armchair opposite the couch. "Isn't 'Come on, Eileen' from way before you were even born?" She fixed her green eyes on Naomi.

Naomi returned her gaze. She knew what Eileen was really asking. "Some songs are timeless classics."

Eileen chuckled. "How old are you, Naomi?"

"Twenty-seven." Naomi rose from the couch.

"Twenty-seven," Eileen repeated and gave a throaty laugh. "I was correct. That song came out quite a few years before you were a twinkle in your parents' eyes."

"That may be so." Naomi reached for her phone again and

turned up the volume. "But that doesn't make it any less great for dancing." She rose from her seat and swayed her hips.

Eileen shook her head. "Twenty-seven-year-olds do have funny ideas in their heads these days."

"Come on," Naomi reached out her hand, *"Eileen."* She swung her hips gently from left to right. "Dance with me."

"I'm not much of a dancer. Besides," Eileen said, "I'm trying to think of a song with Naomi in the title so I can avenge myself later."

"No need for that." Naomi jigged a little closer to Eileen, her hand still outstretched. The chorus of the song started again and Naomi sang along, coaxing Eileen to get up again.

At last, Eileen allowed herself to be pulled out of the chair. She stood still for a moment, getting rid of the bottle of beer, of which she had barely taken a sip, before starting to sway to the music along with Naomi.

Naomi had disclosed her age, but she still had no idea how old Eileen actually was. Definitely somewhere in her forties, Naomi guessed, but she would only know for sure if she asked her. But first, more dancing—because what did it matter, anyway?

The song was about to end. Naomi inched a little closer to Eileen, their hips softly bumping together.

Eileen lost her balance and her right side landed against Naomi's chest.

Reflexively, Naomi wrapped her arms around Eileen to steady her as well as to regain her own balance.

The song ended and they stood face-to-face in the silence that followed. Naomi didn't think. She just did what came naturally now that she had this gorgeous woman in her arms. She leaned in and planted her lips on Eileen's. Her arms drew Eileen a little closer and soon she felt Eileen yield in her embrace.

Their lips opened as the kiss grew more fevered, and

Naomi brought a hand to Eileen's cheek. They broke their lip-lock for an instant, gazing into each other's eyes, only for their lips to meet again in another passionate kiss.

Eileen's left arm snaked up Naomi's shoulder, caressing her neck. Then Naomi felt Eileen stiffen in her embrace.

Eileen had a funny look in her eyes. "I'm forty-nine," she said. "Which makes this a bit ludicrous." She took a step back, breaking all physical contact between them.

"Does it, really?" Naomi asked. "Because I don't think so."

"You kissed me before you knew my age." Eileen leaned against the armrest of the chair she'd sat in earlier.

Naomi shook her head. "I would have kissed you either way."

"Easy enough to say." Eileen narrowed her eyes.

With Eileen in front of her like that, her delicious lips a little swollen and a pink flush on her cheeks, Naomi couldn't care less that Eileen was almost twice her age. She just wanted to kiss her again—as quickly as possible.

"Well then, now that I know, why don't I kiss you again?" Naomi drew up her eyebrows.

Eileen's lips curved into a wide smile. "I'm not sure. I feel like I should be the wiser one."

"This has nothing to do with wisdom or age or anything like that." Naomi scooted closer, gently putting a hand on Eileen's shoulder. "This is just two women meeting and... giving in to the desperate urge to kiss each other. Again and again." With that, she slanted forward and first kissed Eileen on the cheek. She planted another light kiss just above the corner of her mouth, then found her lips again.

Eileen's lips opened up to hers eagerly, not displaying any of the doubts she had just put into words.

Naomi pressed herself against Eileen, feeling her warmth radiate onto her body. She could kiss Eileen for a good while longer, but she wanted to check in with her first. "Just to clarify, that was me kissing you knowing exactly how old you are." She kept her hips pressed against Eileen's.

Eileen chuckled briefly only to break out into a deep sigh. Her cheeks were still flushed but the eagerness had left her eyes.

"We don't have to kiss. We could just talk," Naomi said, but didn't move an inch.

"Look, Naomi, my life's very complicated. And I'm just passing through Derby. I have no intention of staying here— and certainly not of starting an affair with a twenty-seven-year-old." She shook her head.

Naomi did step back now. She tried to ignore the sting of rejection. "I just figured you could do with someone to talk to." She looked around for her previously discarded bottle of beer.

"I certainly don't need your pity," Eileen snapped.

"Good thing I'm not the type to pity people then."

"Ha, says the girl who volunteers at the children's cancer ward."

"That has absolutely nothing to do with pity. Those kids are the most courageous people I've ever met." Naomi fixed her gaze firmly on Eileen. "In fact, they could teach you a thing or two."

"Excuse me?" Eileen pushed herself up. "Who are you to tell me I'm not brave?" She walked over to where her coat was hanging. "What does a twenty-seven-year-old who has spent her entire life in Derby know about bravery?"

Naomi ignored Eileen's snide remark. "You haven't even had the guts to tell me what happened to you. What happened to your arm?"

"Maybe that's because I only met you about two minutes ago." Eileen snagged her coat off the chair.

"It sure was long enough for you to let me kiss you though." Naomi regretted her harsh words instantly.

"That was clearly a mistake." Eileen looked at her.

To Naomi's surprise, it wasn't only frustration that she saw in her glance.

Naomi hurried toward Eileen. She didn't touch her, just stood close enough to get her point across. "I may only be twenty-seven and have never left the country, but I've been through a thing or two. You don't have to leave Derby to witness how cruel life can be—nor to see how strong and courageous even little kids can be."

Naomi scanned Eileen's face, hoping against hope.

"You're a nice girl, Naomi. And I like you, but this—" She shrugged. "This can't be a thing. Do us both a favor, and forget about that kiss. Pretend it never happened. That's what I'll be doing." Eileen turned around and walked out.

For the second time that week Naomi stood watching her front door close. She ignored the lump in her throat and the unmistakable knot that started coiling in her stomach. She could see Eileen's pain—it was obvious—but clearly the woman didn't want to be helped. And maybe she was right. Maybe Naomi should forget about that kiss as soon as she possibly could.

But Eileen's perfume still hung in the air, and the bottle of beer she'd drunk from still stood on the table.

"Snap out of it," Naomi told herself. Eileen certainly was right about one thing, they had only met about two minutes ago. For that reason alone, that lump in her throat was ridiculous. A good night's sleep was all she needed. And tomorrow, she'd get started on the Thanksgiving decorations at the hospital.

She picked up Eileen's almost-full beer bottle and knocked back its contents. Then she tossed it in the bin and swiftly got rid of the last reminder of Eileen.

CHAPTER SEVEN

The church bells started to clang at six in the morning and Eileen groaned and yanked a down pillow over her head. The most infuriating part was they didn't ring six times to mark the hour, but eighteen. Half a dozen intrusions wouldn't be such a hard thing to ignore. But eighteen tolls every time the clock struck six in the morning, noon and six in the evening were intrusive. She couldn't stop herself from fully waking. And once awake, Eileen wasn't the type who could roll over and drift back into dreamworld.

She didn't have anywhere to be until many hours later and after last night's restless sleep, after a handful of nights of barely sleeping, she'd hoped to stay in bed until at least eight. The same hope she'd had every morning all week, but the bells had other ideas. The goddamned bells.

She was supposed to be convalescing after all and wasn't sleep supposed to be important to the healing process? Someone needed to tell the priest. Or God.

Even though the bells had stilled minutes earlier, the sound still reverberated in her mind. She clicked the Spotify app on her iPhone, not caring what song played, just as long as it wasn't church music.

Propped up on her back with the covers yanked up almost to her chin, she contemplated her agenda for the day and deflated when she could only conjure up one pressing appointment: physical therapy with Mack. There was no way she'd miss that, even if the man insisted on asinine exercises that Eileen couldn't decide were helping or not. At least they gave her a purpose. Something to channel her mind on and not...

Eileen shifted her mind like a car from first to second gear to contemplate what had become of her. For as long as she could remember, she'd always dashed from one assignment to the next, cursing there were never enough hours in the day and not enough days in the week. And now all she had to do that day was a thirty-minute physical therapy appointment that wouldn't even cause her to break into a sweat. How had this happened?

"You got old, that's what happened," Eileen said aloud, her voice echoing in the darkness of the room.

Maybe not too old, because Naomi had shown an interest in her.

Or, perhaps the young woman simply pitied her and trying to seduce Eileen was her good deed for the holidays. Naomi had said she didn't do pity, but how could Eileen trust someone so young whom she barely knew?

Was that why Eileen had put on the brakes, sensing what she thought was Naomi's true motivation? Had Eileen suspected it would only be a pity fuck, but couldn't bring herself to call that out? Instead she'd drawn attention to the bigger elephant in the room, so laser-focused on the obvious, in order to stop what could have happened.

What *could* have happened, though?

What would it be like to feel Naomi's skin against her own? She groaned, mentally kicking herself. What forty-nine-year-old in her right mind wouldn't want to sleep with a much younger gorgeous woman?

Would it have been so bad to jump into bed with Naomi no matter her reasons? Who cared if it had been a pity fuck? It would have made Eileen feel alive again, which was something missing from her life, not only since the event.

Naomi clearly had wanted to. But, even if it hadn't been a pity fuck for her, it still wasn't a good idea. Twenty-somethings hadn't learned enough about life to know it was best to tread carefully before bounding into the unknown and messing with affairs of the heart. It'd never worked all that well for Eileen in the past and frankly, she'd given up on relationships. Way too much trouble. Yes, she'd been right to stop things before *it* got out of hand.

Before another thought could ping-pong through her mind, the song "Come on Eileen" started on her phone.

Eileen groaned once again.

How could she stop thinking about Naomi if everything made Eileen think of her?

Unlike Naomi, Eileen had real-world problems. Those always stopped frivolous things in their tracks. *The woman has silk flowers in an antique silver teapot as a centerpiece on her table. Who does that?*

She should get out of bed. Right this second. *Stop dillydallying, Eileen Makenna.*

Was Naomi still in a warm bed? Eileen ran a finger over her lips. Naomi's were so soft. Sweet. Sensual.

Was it wrong for Eileen to want to get to know Naomi more before… anything happened? What drove her? Made her tick? Turned her on? Eileen's hand traveled down her front, stopping at the waistband of her pajama bottoms. This was a bad idea. Horrendous, even.

Eileen had come home to recover, not to get involved with

a woman. Even a casual fling could distract her from focusing on her recovery, threatening her livelihood.

Besides, after last Friday, Naomi probably never wanted to see Eileen again.

"Get your lazy ass out of bed!" Eileen yanked the covers away with a swoop of her left hand. Sitting on the edge of the bed, she straightened her right arm as far as it would go, trying to wiggle the fingers. Eileen found Mack's exercises silly, but she understood the need to create a new pathway to get them to cooperate.

She should apologize, at least, to Naomi for the way she'd stormed out. Then again, Naomi had started something she shouldn't have. Eileen had been right in stopping them from making a mistake. Someone had to keep her wits about her.

In the bathroom, standing in front of the sink, she smacked her lips and focused on the task at hand. Morning breath was one of her least favorite things, and she wasn't the type to have a sip of coffee or bite of food until after brushing her teeth and gargling with mouthwash. Even on remote assignments with no bathrooms within miles, she'd always carried a travel size toothbrush, toothpaste, and Listerine. Nothing would stop her from having minty-fresh breath.

Eileen reached for her toothbrush with her left hand, and sighed. It was such a simple thing she did at least twice a day—usually three. Again, she attempted to straighten her right arm out completely but failed. "But no, you have to complicate the shit out of it."

Was she losing her grip on reality? Talking to her useless arm as if it was alive with a mind of its own?

She placed her toothbrush, with the head dangling over the edge of the sink, secured it with a folded towel to stop it from rolling to the side or turning over completely. Using her good hand, she flipped open the cap of the toothpaste, and applied a dollop onto the bristles. It had taken her some time to work out the mechanics of this routine. Julia had come up with the bright idea of pouring the Listerine into a container with a loose-fitting stopper that was easily yanked out with one hand.

Eileen hated the everyday rituals that were now a burden. How had this happened to her? One step from being a helpless invalid and she wasn't even fifty yet? Close enough, though.

Naomi's words about the children in the cancer ward being the bravest people she'd met rattled in her mind. It was commendable, really, that Naomi volunteered. Unlike Jane who pretended to have an understanding about tragedies in the world.

Her thoughts flitted to the children in remote places around the globe she'd photographed in the worst of situations, the children desperately trying to stay alive in war zones. Did they even have toothbrushes?

Eileen stared at her reflection in the mirror. "You hate pity, so stop feeling so fucking sorry for yourself, Eileen Makenna."

Over an hour later, Eileen nursed her third cup of coffee at the table by the window overlooking the hill. Some trees still had red, orange, and yellow leaves, with a speckling of snow. Clapboard houses were randomly tucked into the foliage, much like you'd see on a thousand-piece puzzle depicting a charming town along the East Coast. But this wasn't a puzzle. This was where Eileen lived now or at least where she was staying until... *if* she recovered. Mack had said it was possible to still see improvement years from now, which he'd meant as good news. Eileen could only focus on the *years* part of the statement. Years...

The main street was nearly deserted. To her right she had a view of the town square, where two stooped-over ladies shuffled around the perimeter of one of the oldest parks in Massachusetts. It was possibly one of the smallest as well.

The front door creaked open. "Ellie?" her sister called out.

"Kitchen," Eileen answered, straightening in her seat.

"Please tell me you have coffee on." The bags under Julia's eyes had a life of their own. "We had to entertain a couple of James' clients last night and I'd forgotten how much finance people like to drink."

"Help yourself." Eileen nodded to the coffeemaker on the metal cart next to the sink. Her temporary housing had limited counter space. Not that Eileen had the abilities or patience to cook with only one arm.

Julia set her bulging mom bag on the stove top, promptly fixing a cup. She took a lustful chug of the hot liquid before she slipped into the blue and white striped upholstered chair opposite Eileen. "So, tell me about your date?"

Eileen shook her head. "It wasn't a date. I already told you that. And the event was a week ago. Done and dusted."

Julia scrunched her brow. "That sounds so very British. Are you doing your best to keep calm and drink coffee?"

"Please. You're insinuating last Friday rattled me or something. I assure you, nothing happened. I went to the exhibit, if you can call something featuring a doll named Bitsy that. Then I left. End of story." She waved her left hand dismissively in the air.

"You're neglecting to mention a key detail. You left with Naomi and the two of you walked in the direction of her car."

Eileen flinched. "How do you know that?"

"London may have more cameras recording people than any other city, but Derby has the best type of intel: people with nothing more to do than gossip."

"And these gossips include my baby sister." Eileen feigned a yawn.

"If you're trying to shame me into silence, it won't work. What happened?" Julia's eyes were wide with anticipation.

"Nothing," Eileen said through gritted teeth. "She's twenty-seven, Jules. Would you let something happen with someone that young?"

Julia nodded. "If I wasn't married, I absolutely would."

"Some of us aren't so impetuous." Eileen sipped her coffee.

Julia examined her face. "Something happened."

"According to whom?" Had Naomi spilled her guts? Would that be something someone so young and inexperienced with the way the real world operated would do?

Julia circled a finger in the air. "According to you. The darkness in your eyes gives you away." She leaned her forearms on the table. "Talk to me, Ellie. It's been so long since we had sisterly chats. It'd do you some good to let me in because from the way you're grinding your teeth, you're about to explode."

Eileen massaged her eyes. "When did we ever have sisterly chats? And, I don't explode. Or talk. What did you tell me last week? I'm different from other women?"

"Ah, I get it. She shot you down." Julia placed a supportive hand on Eileen's arm. "It happens to the best of us."

"She didn't shoot me down." Eileen pulled her left arm away. "I shot her down."

"And now you regret it?" Julia pushed, seemingly thrilled she'd found the right button to get Eileen to admit something she normally wouldn't.

"Why in the world would I regret not sleeping with Naomi? She's... she's... twenty-seven."

"Is that the only reason you didn't?"

"Oh my God!" Eileen stressed each word. "Is this all people in Derby have to do? Talk about sex. I for one have... lots to do."

Julia made a show of checking out her sister's bathrobe. "Tell you what. I'm going to make a proper pot of coffee because this"—she hoisted her cup in the air—"is crap. And then you and I are going to talk. Or..." she left the rest unsaid.

"Or what?"

Julia rose. "I'll tell Mom you slept with Melissa."

"That makes zero sense!"

"Would you rather I told her you slept with Naomi?" Julia dumped the used coffee filter and grounds into the trash.

"I didn't sleep with either last week. I haven't slept with anyone in years!" Eileen banged her left palm onto the table.

Julia, with a heaping scoop of coffee grounds hovering in the air, said, "Oh, Ellie. You really do need to talk. Get whatever it is you're dealing with out. Because that isn't right. Not at all. Jesus, I was joking earlier that you were about to explode, but now I know. You're one step away from kaboom!"

The church bells started to toll and Eileen glanced at the wall clock over the oven. "Shit, I'm going to be late for my appointment."

"Look at that. It's one minute after noon. For someone who claimed she didn't need to talk, you've been spilling your guts for hours."

"Whatever! Are you going to help me so I don't miss my appointment?"

After hastily tossing on clothes with Julia's assistance, Eileen dashed out of her apartment.

As she approached the hospital elevator, two nurses engrossed in a conversation exited from it, allowing Eileen to slip in and press the button for the fifth floor. There was still a small chance she'd make the appointment in the nick of time.

Just as the doors were about to shut, a hand impeded their progress, and they started to reopen. Begrudgingly, going by the grinding sounds.

Eileen swore under her breath and then turned her wrath onto the intruder. "Who do you think you are? This is a hospital. People have emergen—Oh, it's you," Eileen said when she saw it was Naomi.

"I'm sorry. Are you in the midst of an emergency?" Naomi

looked her up and down, and then glanced around the massive space.

"What? No? I wasn't expecting it to be you."

"It was bound to happen, us running into each other, since I work here and you have appointments. As the older and wiser one, I would have thought you would have been able to see this eventuality playing out during your stay at least once." Naomi leaned on her hands which were gripping the edge of a cart. "If you don't mind, since you aren't dying or anything, I would like to come inside. I also have things to do today."

Eileen moved out of the way. "Yes, of course. Let me help you." With her good arm, she steered the cart into the elevator.

Naomi pressed the button for the fourth floor, initiating the doors to slide shut. Excruciatingly slowly.

The wheels and pulleys of the old elevator jerked to life, but apparently they were in no rush to reach their destination. What if someone truly had an emergency? They'd die before reaching the second floor.

Eileen eyed the contents of the cart. Wanting to drop the tension between the two of them down several notches, she attempted to be cordial. "What is all this... stuff?" Cordial, apparently, wasn't her forte.

"Thanksgiving decorations. Usually I don't take the elevator, preferring the stairs to reach my daily goal of fifteen thousand steps, but it wouldn't be fun to lug all this upstairs. Hence why you're stuck with me. The last person you wanted to bump into, probably." Her shrug and crossed arms seemed to imply tough noogies.

"I never said that." Eileen eyed the four-foot inflatable turkey wearing a black pilgrim's hat and green vest.

Naomi followed her gaze. "What?"

"That you were the last person I wanted to see."

"Oh, you made it clear when you stormed out of my apartment that I didn't do it for you." Naomi's arms tightened around her chest, perhaps accidentally shoving her cleavage upward in an extremely hard-not-to-notice way.

Eileen forced her stare downward, letting out a sigh. "That's not true."

"So, I do do it for you." Naomi stumbled over the repetition of the word *do*, a blush rising to her cheeks, her arms falling to her sides.

Exasperated, Eileen said, "I can't win with you."

"Like you've even tried," Naomi spat out.

"To think I'd considered apologizing to you. But you should be apologizing to me."

Naomi's head whipped back. "For what? Liking you? That's the most ridiculous thing I've heard all week. All year, maybe."

Eileen had to dig deep for something believable. "F-for implying I'm not brave."

Naomi stomped her boot on the floor. "I did no such thing! I do remember saying the kids I work with are the bravest people I know. I didn't say you weren't brave."

Eileen countered, "Maybe I'll find out on my own."

Naomi raised both hands in the air. "What are you talking about?"

"Volunteering with the kids. What would you say to that?"

Naomi tapped her forehead with an index finger. "I don't get you."

"There's nothing to get."

"Clearly."

"So, you don't want me to volunteer?" Eileen asked.

"I encourage everyone to," Naomi responded with bite.

"Is that the only reason you think I should?"

Naomi blinked.

Eileen poked the pilgrim hat on the ridiculous turkey, making it tilt to the side before popping back upright. "On Thanksgiving. I'm volunteering that day. In the morning."

"I'm volunteering that morning!" Naomi exclaimed.

"Meaning no one else can?"

"Fine! We can volunteer together," Naomi said.

Both of them stared at the other, breathing heavy.

The elevator doors opened on the fourth floor and Naomi started to maneuver the cart into the hallway.

Before exiting completely, Naomi released a slow breath, and said with sincerity, "It might do you a world of good to do something for someone else. Show you haven't been beaten."

Eileen stopped herself from her first sarcastic response, settling on, "I've heard the kids on the fourth floor can teach me a thing or two."

"No doubt." Naomi furrowed her brow as if taking extra time for the statement to sink in. "Wait... I said that to you."

"You did." Eileen peered into Naomi's softening eyes.

Naomi's expression transformed into the kindness Eileen had witnessed on their first meeting. "Is this your way of apologizing?"

"I have nothing to apologize for."

Naomi groaned, but there was a hint of a smile. "You are so stubborn."

"I don't think we should continue to hold up the elevator. This is a hospital, you know." Eileen had meant to sound like she was joking, but the words came across much harsher than she intended.

"So, I've been informed." Naomi shoved the cart out of the elevator completely, but as the doors started to close, she looked over her shoulder, "I can be just as stubborn. And I expect to see you on Thanksgiving morning. No take backs."

Eileen craned her neck to watch the twist of Naomi's hips as she walked down the hallway, until the doors blocked the view.

CHAPTER EIGHT

Naomi arrived early at the children's ward on Thanksgiving morning. She wasn't only spurred on by wanting to make the kids forget where they were for a few hours. A different kind of excitement had taken hold of her. She might as well admit to herself that she was looking forward to seeing Eileen again.

She hadn't been able to get Eileen out of her head after that evening in her apartment. Those brilliant green eyes turned out to be hard to forget.

Today was hardly a date—volunteering with kids too sick to be at home on Thanksgiving wasn't the most romantic of circumstances—but a few stubborn butterflies held court in Naomi's stomach regardless.

She had just donned a silly turkey hat when she heard rustling in the hallway. She peeked out and watched Eileen lug a heavy plastic bag with her good arm.

"Let me help you." Naomi rushed over to her.

Eileen dropped the bag and took a breath. "Whew. I'm more out of shape than I thought." She glanced down at the bag. "If I'm having trouble transporting a bunch of disposable cameras,

I can't imagine what it will be like carrying my actual equipment again."

Naomi sneaked a peek into the plastic bag. Disposable cameras? What on earth was Eileen talking about?

She bent and took one out of the bag. She held it in front of her face to examine it further. Naomi guessed that it looked like a camera because it had a lens on one side and a tiny hole to look through on the other, but where was the screen?

"What's this?" she asked.

Eileen brought her arm to her hip. "Please tell me you're kidding?"

Naomi turned the camera around in her hands and gave it a good once-over. "This must be a relic from the very distant past." She glanced up at Eileen with amusement in her eyes.

"Watch it, you." Eileen stood smiling at her. She nodded at the hat on Naomi's head. "This should make a good shot." She took the camera from Naomi's hands, brought it to her eye with her left hand, and pressed the button at the top. The camera made a clicking sound.

"That's the first picture of the day taken." She grinned at Naomi. "And no, you can't see what it looks like on some magic screen. These are actual disposable cameras and you have no idea how hard it was to find two dozen of them in Derby."

"Two dozen?"

"I should have asked you how many children are in the hospital," Eileen said. "I wanted them all to have one."

"That's so sweet." This was definitely the sweetest side to Eileen she had witnessed so far. Or maybe she had spotted this before, hidden beneath that thick shield of hers, below that guard that was always up.

Eileen shrugged. "I always used to take a couple of instant cameras with me on assignment. Trust me when I tell you that you aren't the only one baffled by the sight of a non-digital camera." She slanted her head. "Of course, the kids I gave them to are too young to have dated an amateur photographer." She stood there grinning again.

"I truly doubt Jane would know what these are." Naomi reached into the bag again and picked out another camera. "You have way too many so I can only assume you brought one for me as well." She brought it to her eye and looked through the viewfinder. Through it, she saw Eileen's face. Her wavy red-blond hair was tied into a high ponytail again. Naomi focused the center of the viewfinder on Eileen's eyes and took a picture.

"Hey. I didn't sign a release for that," Eileen protested. She burst into the widest grin Naomi had seen on her, and she felt compelled to take another picture.

When she pushed the button, it wouldn't go all the way down.

Eileen shook her head. "You, millennials," she said. "You don't know anything anymore." She held up the camera she had in her own hand. "You have to turn this wheel here before you can take the next picture." She tried to show Naomi how to do it, but clearly it wasn't an easy feat to accomplish with only one fully functioning hand.

"Christ, what kind of an antiquated item have you brought in here?" Naomi said as she helped Eileen turn the wheel on the camera. "You can't see the result of what you're taking a picture of and then you have to fiddle with this thing before you can take the next one."

"It's part of the charm. Imagine going to pick up the prints? The thrill of the surprise."

"Pick up the prints?" Naomi drew up her eyebrows. "Good luck finding a place in Derby that can develop these."

"Don't you worry about that." Eileen collected the bag. "I believe some children are waiting to be introduced to the wonder of disposable cameras."

Naomi thought better of helping Eileen with the bag and

led the way to the ward. If this was Eileen's true personality, she thought, she didn't stand a chance against those butterflies in her stomach—they were already starting to cause a riot.

Eileen's disposable cameras were a hit with the kids, although most of them, just like Naomi had done, inquired where they could see the instant result of their picture-taking efforts—unlike their parents, who looked at the cameras with nostalgia in their eyes.

Naomi decided not to put too much thought into what this said about the age difference between her and Eileen. Yes, they were from different generations, and when they were in Tyson's room, a thirteen-year-old boy who would be leaving the hospital soon after Thanksgiving, Naomi felt much closer in age to him, than to his parents or Eileen. But what difference did it really make?

Tyson, in particular, was mesmerized by the camera. After Eileen showed him how to use it, he swiftly started giving instructions to his parents on where to stand, taking the light from the window into consideration, so he could take the best shot.

"I want to take one of you two as well," Tyson said to Eileen and Naomi.

"It would be my honor to be photographed by you, young sir." Eileen glanced at his parents. "That's a future Pulitzer winner right there." She held out her good arm to Naomi. "Come on then. Let's freeze this moment in time."

Naomi stepped into Eileen's unexpected embrace. But it was Thanksgiving and Eileen volunteering had been a big hit—something Naomi hadn't been so sure of beforehand—and she was just glad that Eileen seemed so happy to be spending time with her and the kids. So, Naomi took the opportunity to lean into Eileen's side, pushing herself against Eileen and feeling the warmth of her again, the way she had done only ever so briefly last week.

To Naomi's welcome surprise, Eileen responded by rubbing the side of her hip slightly against Naomi's.

"You take your time to get the best shot, Tyson," Eileen said. "Naomi and I are very comfortable here."

"I'm not going to hear the last of it if you don't come back for Christmas," Naomi said when they stood outside.

"Christmas?" Eileen said. "I'll be back much sooner than that." She lifted the bag. "I need to bring them the prints, remember."

"Right." Naomi snickered. "Do you have any other tricks from the days of yesteryear up your sleeve?"

"We'll see." Eileen's eyes narrowed. "Best not put too much pressure on me to surprise you again." She sighed contentedly. "It was just great to see the smiles on their faces and, more self-ishly, for me to have a camera in my hands again—no matter how small or quaint."

"How about the same time again next week?" Naomi responded to Eileen's expression of contentment with a big smile.

"That would be nice." Eileen sucked her bottom lip between her teeth.

"Unless…" Naomi caught Eileen's glance.

"Yes?" Eileen rubbed her hand over her jeans.

"Unless… you want to have dinner this weekend? After the Thanksgiving family madness has subsided and we can think of having food again?"

Eileen stood there glancing at her, as though this question needed some serious pondering.

"Why not?" she said, at last.

Naomi burst into an even wider grin.

"How about I pick you up? So you don't have to walk in this weather?" Naomi asked. "We could go to the grocery store together, if you like. You can pick some things up for yourself. It must be hard walking everywhere, let alone carrying grocery bags."

"I've got my sister…" Eileen started saying, then paused. "Actually, that would be nice."

"Saturday night?" Naomi asked.

Eileen nodded, something glittering in her eyes. Something that told Naomi she might already be looking forward to Saturday evening as well. Or maybe it was just the reflection of the low November sun—Naomi really shouldn't get ahead of herself like that. If it really was the difference in age between them that had Eileen fleeing her apartment last week, then that was an issue that could never be resolved. But Naomi's business in life was dealing with people's emotions, and interpreting what they couldn't always say in words. She might be young, but she had experience in reading people, and what she saw behind all the words Eileen didn't say, filled her with hope.

"It's a date then." Naomi inched closer to Eileen, and gave her a quick kiss on the cheek, before going to find her car.

CHAPTER NINE

Eileen gave a timid wave with her good hand as Naomi pulled out of the parking lot. While she wanted to see the young woman off, Eileen worried she was proclaiming herself *an old fogey* by ensuring Naomi's car, which may be older than the driver, started and made it out of the parking lot. Did twenty-somethings still do that in this day and age? Or would they keep their eyes glued to their phones, waiting for a message stating: Car started. On way home. Or would the message solely consist of abbreviations and emojis?

Naomi's car disappeared around the corner and Eileen set about arranging her own transportation. Something about having to catch a cab to go to Thanksgiving at her family's seemed desperate. If she was in London, it wouldn't have occurred to her. But in her hometown, it seemed odd at best.

Julia had offered to pick her up, but Eileen had refused for two reasons. To show her independence and she didn't want to explain that she was volunteering that morning and wouldn't be ready when Julia wanted to leave. Her sister would question Eileen's motives for volunteering, because Julia questioned absolutely everything. If Eileen said she preferred red over green grapes, Julia would insist on having a twenty-minute dialogue about why and if the color red signified something about her childhood or some psychobabble bullshit like that.

Complications. Eileen was surrounded by them and she didn't need to invite more, especially not the Julia kind.

She dialed a local cab company. A woman answered on the fifth ring, not a good sign. Eileen requested a driver.

"You want a cab now? Today?" Her raspy voice sounded as if she had a pack a day habit.

Eileen pictured the woman with a cigarette dangling from her bottom lip. "If possible."

"Uh…" There was some rustling on the other end of the line, as if she was covering the mouthpiece. "Would an hour from now work?"

"Does Derby have Uber? Or Lyft?" Eileen scanned the empty street, hoping a lone taxi would pass by, but there wasn't a car in sight.

"How would I know?" The woman's defensiveness made it clear she did.

"Because you're in the transportation business."

"We're professionals. Not some random dude with a ratty car who may or may not get you to your destination. Or murder you. Roll of the dice, really, with *those* people," she hissed.

Eileen chomped down on her bottom lip. Getting into a quarrel with a woman on the other line wouldn't solve her problem.

"Do you still want a car or not?" the woman barked.

Eileen looked at the clock in the middle of the town square. She'd still arrive well before the family would officially sit down for Thanksgiving dinner, at least. And, honestly, would a delay be so bad considering it meant less time with her mom? "Yes, please."

They finalized the details, with Eileen providing her number.

Maybe she'd grab a coffee or go for a walk. Option three was to get a coffee and then go for a walk. She'd been staying inside her apartment quite a bit. Too much, frankly. While her right arm was mostly incapacitated, her legs weren't. It would do her good to get some exercise considering how winded she'd gotten earlier, lugging the bag with disposable cameras. And if she truly planned to get back to work in the new year, she couldn't let herself go. She had to snap out of this funk. Pronto.

Today would be the first day of... her new life.

Eileen laughed at the absurd thought.

Maybe it was Naomi's influence. The thought of their date on Saturday. Naomi's smile and piercing dark eyes. The type that could penetrate deep inside someone's soul.

Or perhaps it was Tyson. Here was a young man in a hospital bed on Thanksgiving. Yet, when given the disposable camera, he was full of life. A wonderful mix of excitement, sweetness, and raw talent. Naomi had been right about learning a thing or two from the kids.

Not knowing if any places would be open on a holiday, Eileen trekked back into the hospital and grabbed a cappuccino to go from the coffee shop. Back out in the parking lot, she walked in no particular direction.

The sun hung overhead in the brilliant blue sky, although there was a nip in the air and when the wind kicked up, it cut right through Eileen's clothes.

Even this brought a smile to her lips. To feel the wind on her cheeks. To feel alive.

She passed an art gallery and from a cursory glance through the window the offerings consisted of oil paintings of lighthouses. Her mind wandered back to high school. When she and

Melissa would go for drives so Eileen could take photos of the coast and, of course, lighthouses.

Did Derby offer any photography classes? A child like Tyson would truly benefit from lessons. Eileen set her coffee on the ledge of the window so she could get her phone out and pull up Google Maps to search for local photography classes. The nearest was twenty miles away. Which wasn't that far by American standards. Practically everyone living outside of Boston owned a car. But this particular part of Massachusetts didn't have easily accessible buses and no subway system. Basically people like her, not to mention kids, had no way of getting around on their own.

Eileen tucked her phone back into her pocket and retrieved her coffee cup to continue her journey. She stopped at the new-looking white wooden Welcome to the Town of Derby Incorporated 1850 sign. Next to it was a yard sign announcing the Christmas tree lighting ceremony in the town center on December first. Part of her had missed this aspect of living in Derby. The sense of community. Pride.

Taking a sip of her cappuccino, she wondered if it would be difficult to set up a photography class in town. And what was the likelihood of finding instructors? The only other photographer she'd met since her return was Jane. While Eileen wasn't overly impressed with the subject matter of the Bitsy show, the photos themselves showed a modicum of skill. Thirteen-year-old boys didn't need more than that to inspire them to pursue photography in life.

Eileen walked past the hardware store, then paused. Sitting on the sidewalk were pumpkins for sale, Christmas decorations, and other odds and ends that one may need from a hardware store this time of year, like snow shovels, bundles of wood, and bags of rock salt. Was it open on Thanksgiving? Eileen squinted to see inside, but the lights were off and no one stirred. They left this stuff outside all the time? Upon further inspection, she noticed none of it was secured. Didn't they worry about theft? Not that pumpkin crime was rampant in America, but what about teenagers who might find it funny to smash them?

Her phone rang and she tossed her half-empty cup into the trash so she could answer it. "Yes?"

"Your ride is on the way," the grumpy woman from earlier instructed.

"Thank you very much and I hope you have a wonderful holiday!" Eileen shook her head, confounded by her own cheerfulness.

The cab pulled up outside Eileen's childhood home and she paid the driver.

The front door opened before Eileen had a chance to knock. Had she really intended to knock? How peculiar to feel like such a stranger on the doorstep of the home she grew up in.

"I would have picked you up." Julia, in faded jeans, gray sweater, and red and black checkered wool socks, embraced her.

"I can still get around on my own." Eileen crossed the threshold, noticing the quiet. "Where is everyone?"

"Mom and Dad are in the library. Michael and James are playing football with the neighbors. You remember Old Man Grover's annual Turkey Football Bash? His son has kept the tradition alive and well. They'll be here later when there's actually food on the table. Belle is beefing up her college application by volunteering at the shelter. She's been doing that every holiday for… Oh, I don't remember really. She wants to go into social work. Oh to be young again, and to think you can change the world."

Eileen thought of Naomi, but shoved her beautiful image from her mind before Julia picked up on some weird mental sibling wavelength and wanted to probe every angle. "You don't watch the game anymore?" Eileen asked.

Julia waved a hand leading Eileen towards the library. "Mom balked and really, it's just a bunch of boys and some fathers who still haven't given up the ghost they could have played professionally. We can go watch, though, if you want to."

Eileen shook her head.

"We never were very sporty, were we? Much to Dad's dismay."

"True. Making me a double let down."

Julia narrowed her eyes. "What does that mean?"

Eileen cursed herself for letting her guard down yet again with Julia. "Oh, you know. Dad always wanted a son. And I'm not a sporty dyke. It was just a joke, really. No need to dissect it."

Julia glanced over her shoulder, with a knowing smile. "Someone's feeling vulnerable after spilling her heart out last Friday."

Eileen rolled her eyes.

They entered the library.

"There you are. I was about to send out a search party." Her mom rose from the leather wingback chair and air-kissed Eileen's right cheek.

"Am I late?" Eileen looked to her father, who motioned for her not to pay any attention to his wife.

"Dinner isn't for another hour, but I would have thought you'd want to spend time with your family on Thanksgiving. After such a long absence." Her mom wore a gray cashmere turtleneck with gold sequins forming snowflakes, black slacks, and two-inch heels.

Her father sported his typical chinos, plaid shirt, and like Julia, he was in socks. "You look well. Your cheeks are rosy."

"I went for a walk," Eileen explained.

"You didn't walk here, did you? Is that why you're so late?" her mom asked.

"What can I get you to drink?" her dad got to his feet.

"A tea would be lovely."

"So very British of you." Her mother smiled fondly.

Her dad left the room, more than likely to instruct Maggie to make a pot of tea.

Her mom took a seat on the cherry-red leather couch and patted the spot next to her. "Sit next to your mom. Let's chat."

Eileen sat, inwardly regretting not coming up with an adequate excuse to skip Thanksgiving entirely. Maybe she could fake food poisoning halfway through the meal. No one wanted to be around that. Not even family members.

Her mom placed a hand on Eileen's thigh. "Guess who I bumped into yesterday?"

Julia met Eileen's eyes as she sat across from her on the opposite couch. Their father returned empty handed confirming Eileen's suspicion that he'd handed off the order, and took a seat next to Julia.

Perhaps sensing the tension, he asked, "What'd I miss?"

"Nothing dear. I was just telling Eileen I bumped into Melissa yesterday and we ended up having lunch." She swiveled her head to Eileen. "She's doing so much better. Can you believe it's been two years since her partner died?" Her mom made a mournful tsking sound, before her eyes lit up. "But I do believe she's ready to date again."

"Oh, Mom. You didn't actually ask, did you? She was with Susan for over twenty years." Julia sipped her white wine.

"Of course not." She laid a hand over her heart. "As a woman and mother, I could tell." To Eileen she said, "Melissa said it was good to see you at the photography exhibition. You should call her. Do you have her number?" She ran a hand through Eileen's hair. "Before you see her again, I should make you an appointment to get your hair and nails done. What conditioner do you use? It's so limp."

Eileen didn't bother telling her mom the struggle she had simply shampooing her hair. Conditioning was out of the question at the moment.

Maggie entered the library with a tray, arranging a silver teapot with a matching sugar and creamer set on the table.

"Thank you, Maggie." Eileen leaned forward, but Maggie waved for her to relax while she poured her a cup.

"Two sugar cubes and a splash of milk?" Maggie asked.

Eileen smiled. "Your memory astounds me."

"I'll take a cup," her mom said.

"Of course," Maggie said.

"I didn't know you liked tea?" Eileen asked her mom while accepting the cup from Maggie with a gracious smile.

"Who doesn't like tea?" she said, avoiding her daughter's eyes.

When Maggie closed the library doors, her mom said, "What were we talking about? Oh, yes. You inviting Melissa for lunch or dinner. Shall we go shopping for some new clothes?" Her mother eyed Eileen's slacks and loose-fitting sweater.

Eileen, ignoring her mom's barb, blew into her tea, the steam momentarily blurring her vision. "Dad, do you still have connections with anyone at the community center? I would like to talk to someone about starting photography lessons for children here in town."

"So they can run away from home at their first opportunity like someone else I know?" Her mom's forced laughter was anything but mirthful. She set her teacup down on a coaster on the end table, not bothering to take a sip.

Eileen swallowed a mouthful of scorching tea to prevent

the words tumbling from her mouth— she'd never felt welcome in her mom's life.

Her dad cleared his throat, his eyes landing on his wife briefly before answering, "I can place a few calls."

"Will you teach a course?" Julia asked.

"Me?" Eileen squeaked. Recovering, she continued, "No. I was thinking of Jane."

"Jane!" Julia's eyes shot upward and she pitched one hand into the air. "She'd be terrible with children."

"And you think I'd be better?" Eileen blunted out the memory of seeing Tyson's smile earlier. As far as her family was concerned, Eileen didn't like children. Period.

"I do. Not only because you've won awards. Your passion for photography—"

"I can't hold a camera!" Eileen closed her eyes and sucked in a cleansing breath. "Sorry."

Julia wasn't deterred. "You'll be instructing others how to hold the camera."

"You're forgetting, *Julia*, I won't be around after the holidays." Eileen spoke slowly for the words to sink in.

Julia stared at Eileen. "You don't know that for sure. I happen to know your apartment is available to rent from the new year."

"I've told work I'll be back in January."

"That's wonderful." Her mom picked up her teacup, brought it to her lips, but set it back down without sampling the drink. "Derby has always been too small for you." Her tone implied the town wasn't big enough for the two of them and Eileen was of the same opinion.

"Ellie, are you sure that was wise?" Julia appeared to go out of her way to avoid looking at her sister's rigid arm.

"I need to work, Jules." Eileen locked her eyes on Julia's.

"Surely you have money saved. Not to mention sick leave. You've been with the company for years. They'll understand."

"You don't expect Eileen to stay in town teaching photography lessons, do you?" Her mom glared at her youngest daughter. "What kind of life would that be? After everything?"

There it was again. The not-so-subtle hint her mom gave up her life for Eileen's. She turned her gaze to her dad. "Is there a game on today? I haven't watched the NFL in years."

Julia leaned forward, her eyes skipping past their mom and landing on Eileen. "You have told your employers about your stroke?"

Eileen remained mute her silence confirming the unanswered question.

"Oh, Ellie. Why are you so stubborn?" Julia supported her forehead with her fingertips.

"Unlike you, I don't like people in my business." Again, she asked her dad if there was a game on.

He nodded, but didn't get up.

"Guess I'll watch it on my own, then." Eileen fled the library, muttering, "Joyous family time," once she was out of earshot.

CHAPTER TEN

"I'll drive," Eileen said, and put a hand on the shopping cart. "I miss driving an actual car, so the least you can do is give me control over this vehicle." She had a relaxed smile on her face. "You can fill this baby up."

"Happy to hand the steering wheel over to you." Naomi pulled up the shopping list she'd made on her phone earlier. "Do you want me to put something on the list for you?"

"I'll just be inspired as we go along." Eileen pushed the cart in front of her with one arm. It veered to the right immediately.

Instinctively, Naomi reached for it to bring it back on course.

"I've got it," Eileen said. "Mack says I need to start using my other arm more, so that's what I shall do."

Naomi watched how Eileen, with a grimace on her face, put her other hand on the bar of the shopping cart. She started moving it forward again and it didn't veer so much to the right now, although it hardly followed a straight line either.

"Where did you get your driver's license?" Naomi joked.

"Or are you from the generation that had it handed to them without having to take the test?"

Eileen shot her a look, then refocused on pushing the cart forward. "What's for dinner, wise-ass?"

"You'll see."

"Well yes, I am in charge of the shopping cart." Eileen stopped and turned to look at Naomi. She seemed a little tired underneath the harsh glare of the supermarket lights, but her eyes shone just as brightly. "Either way, I've been having mostly take-out, so I won't be a difficult customer."

"Customer?" Naomi cleared her throat ostentatiously. "And here I was, roaming this supermarket, on the look-out for the best ingredients, under the impression that you were my date."

"Right." Eileen nodded. "I might have lived in Britain for too long, though. A country where it's not customary to go to the supermarket together to start off a date." She shot Naomi a wink.

If anything, Eileen had brought her sense of humor with her. She seemed much more relaxed than on their previous attempt at a date—although perhaps Naomi had been a bit quick classifying it as such.

They'd reached the produce section and Naomi stopped. They could banter for the next half hour, but it wouldn't fill their shopping cart.

She caught Eileen gazing longingly at a bag of lettuce.

"What does that lettuce have that I don't?" she asked.

Eileen burst out laughing.

Naomi loved it when Eileen's lips curved all wide like that.

"You try having pizza from Jimmy's and burritos from that place around the corner of the hospital as your main sources of sustenance for a few weeks. I dare say you'd be making eyes at some lettuce as well."

Naomi grabbed a bag and put it into the shopping cart. "It's there for the taking, you know. I'm not sure how they did things in London, but this is how it works over here." Naomi just wanted that smile to reappear on Eileen's face.

"Even making—" Eileen didn't smile, nor did she finish her sentence—she didn't have to. She looked at her right hand sitting limply on the shopping cart.

"Look what else we have on display here." Naomi waved her hand dramatically along the shelf. "All the ingredients to make your own salad." She grabbed a bag of chicken strips and placed it in the cart. Then proceeded to do the same with packets of matchstick carrots, beets, and already peeled hard-boiled eggs. "You're back in America, where we make things very easy for you." She pointed at the products in the cart. "That's tomorrow's lunch right there."

"Easy?" Eileen said. "Lazy you mean. I should fit right in, then."

"Don't be so hard on yourself," Naomi said. "It will only keep you from moving forward."

"You know," Eileen said, "for a twenty-something, you do seem to have all the wisdom." She started pushing the cart, away from the produce section.

"Hold up." Naomi grabbed some broccoli and put it in the cart.

"And of course, you would enjoy eating broccoli," Eileen said.

Naomi suspected the smile wouldn't be back for a while, but at least Eileen was back to grinning at her—albeit rather sheepishly at the moment.

"Please, do reserve your judgment until you've tasted my dish."

"Yes, chef," Eileen said. "From here on out, at least for the rest of this date, I shall put my trust in you and your culinary skills."

"What's my job?" Eileen asked, once they were at Naomi's apartment.

"Sit on that chair and keep me company." They had unloaded the groceries and Naomi had separated the ingredients for Eileen's salad into a bag and stored it in the back of the fridge.

"Can't I even pour us some of that wine we just bought?" Eileen had almost outmaneuvered Naomi at the cash register and slipped the woman at the checkout her credit card to pay for all the shopping. It was only after some heavy debating—in front of the baffled cashier—that Eileen allowed Naomi to split the bill for the groceries for tonight.

"Can you manage that?" Naomi looked up from the broccoli she was chopping.

"That's why I chose a bottle with a screw top." Eileen grabbed the bottle from the counter. "Behold my skill, young Naomi," she said theatrically reaching for the bottle.

Naomi stopped chopping and focused all her attention on Eileen. She was wearing jeans and a loose shirt and somehow managed to look completely scrumptious in it.

Eileen propped the bottle between her thighs and unscrewed the top with her left hand. She tossed the screw cap onto the counter and held up the bottle of wine with a triumphant grin on her face. "*Voila.*"

"Goodness me. I'm utterly blown away by your dexterity," Naomi dead-panned. "Best keep it up and impress me with your pouring skills after the dazzling display you just made of unscrewing that bottle."

"Where are your wineglasses?" Eileen deposited the bottle onto the table.

"Behind me. Top shelf," Naomi said.

"On it." Eileen moved behind her, but Naomi's kitchen was small, and Eileen briefly put a hand on Naomi's hips as she turned to face the cupboard.

The sudden touch took Naomi straight back to the few minutes they had danced in the living room, their hips crashing together—preceding their first kiss. How would tonight end? A shiver ran up Naomi's spine at the thought—at the possibility of it.

A few minutes later, when Eileen was safely back on the other side of the kitchen counter, she presented Naomi with a substantial glass of wine.

"Grocery shopping makes me thirsty," Eileen said.

"It's a thirst-inducing business." Naomi sipped from the wine, which had been Eileen's choice.

"You still haven't told me what you're preparing." Eileen didn't sit, but leaned over the kitchen counter. "I might have the world's biggest dislike of broccoli."

"And you only tell me now? You were right there when I bought it!"

"There's always take-out, I guess," Eileen joked.

"Or you can make us a salad," Naomi said.

"Thanks to you, I actually could." Eileen's voice softened. "And I actually don't mind broccoli that much."

"When I'm done with this," Naomi gazed into Eileen's eyes, "you'll barely notice it's broccoli you're eating."

"In that case, I can hardly wait." Eileen had stopped moving and even though there was a kitchen counter between them, she stood very close to Naomi. Almost as close as when they'd kissed.

"The secret's butter." Naomi swallowed hard.

"Butter's the secret to many a tasty dish," Eileen said.

Naomi wasn't sure they were still talking about butter. She smelled the aroma from the wine in Eileen's glass, but on top of that, she could also make out Eileen's perfume. It was fruity and light and Naomi had to stop herself from leaning over and inhaling more of it.

Her gaze was drawn to the hollow of Eileen's neck, where it

was exposed at the opening of her pale-blue shirt. She was beginning to regret not ordering take-out. This dish would take at least another half an hour to prepare, and already Naomi was having great trouble keeping from kissing Eileen.

But first, she needed to figure out whether Eileen was up to being kissed again. A repeat of what had happened last time would end things once and for all for them. They hadn't suddenly miraculously closed the age gap between them, just because Eileen had successfully volunteered alongside Naomi at the hospital once. But it had, at the very least, brought them closer together again. And created the opportunity for this date.

Eileen was the first to pull back. She shot Naomi a quick grin and, at last, sat, taking her wineglass with her.

Naomi melted some butter in a pan before adding the broccoli, all the while keeping her back to Eileen.

They had all night to have a much-needed conversation about what this was exactly. Naomi turned to glance at Eileen, who seemed to be greatly enjoying the wine. Enjoy this date, she told herself, then see what happens. Because taking in the sight of Eileen like that, Naomi was damn certain she wanted something to happen.

CHAPTER ELEVEN

While Naomi busied herself putting the finishing touches on their dinner, Eileen asked, "Would it be okay for me to use your bathroom?"

"First you make me do the grocery shopping. Then cook you dinner. And, now you want to use my bathroom. Geez Louise, give you an inch and you take a mile." Naomi laughed, sparking a sexy twinkle in her eyes.

"If I remember correctly, I did drive the shopping cart. No one appreciates the skill involved in looking like you're contributing when doing the least amount of work."

"Yeah, that's the image that comes to mind when I'm with you. What's the opposite of determined?" She arched a playful eyebrow.

"Lazy and we've already established I am with the ready-made salad ingredients."

"Determined, stubborn, and frustrating. Those are the top three words that come to mind when I think of you." Naomi chewed on her bottom lip, her long lashes fluttering, drawing even more attention to her stunning dark eyes.

Warmth pooled inside Eileen, but it was too soon to... "I sound challenging."

"I love a challenge." The slight twist of her lips was intoxicating. "The bathroom. Second door on the left." Naomi jerked her head toward the hallway.

"Right. That's how we started. Bathroom." Eileen hesitated, watching Naomi watch her. "I should take care of that now."

"I do appreciate women who are potty-trained."

Eileen laughed. "And I like a woman with spunk."

"Very good news for me. Now scoot or I'll ban you permanently if you piddle on the floor." She shooed Eileen away.

In the bathroom, Eileen was nearly struck dumb by the effort Naomi put into decorating a space that most would consider as purely functional. There was a lavender towel on a hook labeled *hers* in fancy painted script, and from the hole in the wall, Eileen gathered there had been another hook at one point. Jane's perhaps. On an antique chest there were two soap dishes with homemade bars still wrapped in beautiful floral paper. A wire corset that bowed out was secured on a corner and one of Naomi's bras dangled teasingly from a hook.

It wasn't a bathroom, but a refuge from the daily grind. Eileen's eyes found Naomi's bra once again. Silk. Fire-engine red. Sexy as hell. She reached out with her left hand, but withdrew it before making contact. Not like this, Eileen thought. It would be better to wait to touch...

On the way back to the kitchen, flickering lights in the front room beckoned Eileen.

The scene brought another smile to her lips.

The silver teapot with flowers had been moved from the center of the table to a teacart off to the side. In its place was a candlestick, which wasn't a candlestick in a traditional sense. Instead, it was an aluminum octopus, holding three glass lanterns with its arms while the remaining five limbs supported the body. Inside each lantern was a tealight. On the mantel of the fireplace was a cheerful wooden whale, with its tail curved upward supporting a small rowboat with yet another lit candle.

Naomi approached from behind, setting the plates down on the table. "Ah, I see you've found your way."

"Hard not to with this little guy guiding me to port." She patted the octopus on the table, staring deeply into Naomi's beguiling eyes.

"I'm glad to hear it, because I thought you'd fallen in or something and I would have to rescue you." Her wicked smile worked wonders on Eileen.

Not wanting to be outdone by the younger woman, Eileen decided to give her a taste of her own medicine, so to speak. "It takes time to go through someone's medicine cabinet." Eileen placed a hand on Naomi's shoulder. "It's okay. Everyone stocks up on anti-fungal products, lube, wart medicine, prescription-strength deodorant, lice shampoo, and anti-stink foot powder."

Her face reddened. "I don't have any of that... well, maybe lube... but that's because... it prevents my nipples and inner thighs from chafing."

Eileen's jaw dropped.

Naomi's face reddened further.

"I'm learning so much about you tonight," Eileen chuckled.

"It's not what you think." Naomi seemed to regroup. "Every year I run the Boston Marathon to raise money for the children's cancer ward. As it happens, lube is wonderful for preventing chafing."

Eileen nodded. "Ah, I should have known it would be for something like that."

With a hand on her jutted hip, Naomi demanded, "What does that mean?"

Eileen raised her left hand and mimed waving a white flag. "Don't shoot, please. I didn't mean it in a negative way. It's just everything about you screams goodness." The memory of the bra flooded her mind. Maybe not everything.

The corner of Naomi's mouth quirked up. "You know, you can be adorable sometimes in a cranky old person kind of way."

Eileen grinned. "I deserved that one, but you did toss in adorable so…" She shrugged her left shoulder as if saying she'd take advantage of the backhanded compliment.

"So…?" Naomi inched closer.

A wave of nervousness washed over Eileen. Her right arm felt heavier, and she bought some time by saying, "We should eat this beautiful dinner you prepared."

Much to Eileen's relief, Naomi seemed to comprehend the source of Eileen's sudden shyness. "It would be rude to cook a delicious meal and not let you sample it."

"I do love eating… dinner that is." It was Eileen's turn to blush.

Neither of them moved to take a seat at the table, the palpable desire building with each thundering heartbeat in Eileen's chest.

Finally, Eileen said, "We shouldn't let it get cold. Not after all of your effort to cook me a meal. For which, I'm truly grateful." She placed a hand over her heart.

Naomi pulled out Eileen's chair. "Please sit, madam." She made a sweeping gesture with her arm that rivaled a waiter in a three-star Michelin restaurant.

Eileen wanted to sweep Naomi into her arms, or arm rather, and kiss her deeply. Instead, Eileen took her seat and crossed her legs to tamp down the fire that was building below.

Naomi plopped onto her seat, pulling one leg underneath.

Her pose was charming and fit the personality of a woman with an octopus light fixture. "I love the nautical theme you have going."

Naomi, with wineglass in hand, smiled sheepishly. "I'm a sucker for whimsical. Honestly, though, I don't understand why anyone would surround themselves with serious things. Life's short. Live it while you can, dammit. That's my motto. And, if having a little guy like this brings a smile to my face all the better."

You'd hate my parents' house.

Naomi picked up her fork, seeming to struggle for the right words to fill the emptiness. "Now, for tonight's feast of salmon and buttered broccoli."

"Who doesn't love something fishy on a date?" Eileen winked.

Naomi groaned playfully. "You're terrible, you know that."

"You aren't the first woman to say that to me." The salmon was succulent and easy to fork with her left hand, which Eileen suspected Naomi had hoped for.

Naomi watched her take her first bite, her eyes momentarily focusing on her non-dominant hand. "Do you ever plan on talking about it?"

"Are you referring to sex?" Eileen waggled her brows. Naomi's impressive overly exaggerated eye roll spurred Eileen to say, "Careful. It'd be a true shame if your eyes got stuck in the top of your head denying me the pleasure of staring into them."

The flecks in Naomi's dark eyes shone with desire. "While I do appreciate a sweet talker, I'm not that easily thrown off track."

"Of course, you aren't. You wouldn't be you, if you were." Eileen sighed. "There's not much to talk about really. I had... a stroke, which you've already probably guessed."

"Yes. I've worked with a few people at the hospital who held one of their arms in the same way."

Eileen glanced down at her arm. "I try not to focus on it. In my line of work, I've seen so much and honestly, a useless arm isn't such a big deal when compared to a child who's lost a limb from a landmine."

Naomi nodded her head. "I know it's not the same, but when I'm having a truly horrendous day, I'll pop down to visit the kids to get some perspective. It's the look in the parents' eyes that truly reminds me I'm blessed."

"I admire your dedication to the kids. When people learn about all my assignments in war zones and how I've witnessed firsthand refugees attempting to escape, many claim they'd love to get involved. But their idea is to toss money at the problem." Eileen shifted in her seat. "Look at Jane's exhibit. While I understand her desire to raise awareness of the harsh realities in this world in an artistic way, I sincerely doubt Jane's ever witnessed a tenth of the turmoil she tried to depict."

"It's hard to picture you in a war zone." Naomi's eyes widened and she added, "Not because of your arm. It's just hard to see anyone doing something like that. The bravery involved. I'm in awe of your determination to showcase the atrocities so many want to ignore because it's painful to see. I think you're giving Jane too much credit saying she's seen ten percent of the tragedies she wanted to portray with the doll. She absolutely refused to volunteer at the hospital with me and didn't even once step inside to say hello to the kids."

Eileen boosted an eyebrow. "Really? Part of me is surprised given your passion and part of me isn't." And that meant Julia was right, Jane wouldn't be a suitable candidate to teach a photography class for kids. Back to the drawing board on that issue. "What inspired you to volunteer in the first place?"

Naomi's gaze fell to her plate and she traced the tines of her fork in her broccoli. "It's always been a passion of mine. Wanting to help. It's why I studied social work in college even when everyone kept telling me I'd never have more than two pennies to rub together." She raised her chin. "I've managed to survive, though." Her eyes shone with pride as her gaze skimmed the quirkiness of her cramped one-bedroom apartment. "I love to scour consignment shops for just the right pieces to add to my eclectic collection."

"Going back to the nautical theme, it's funny, really." Eileen pointed at the octopus and then jerked her thumb over her shoulder to the items on the mantel. "My sister set up my apartment before I arrived and she purchased sheets with tiny paisley whales on them—"

Naomi burst into laughter. "Did she do that on purpose?"

Eileen laughed along, nodding her head. "At first, I was like what the fuck was she thinking."

"And now?" Naomi leaned forward in her seat, her voice was soft and sweet.

"I'm kind of fond of them. They're cute." Eileen shrugged.

Naomi propped her chin on folded hands. "There's hope for you yet."

Eileen mulled this over. "Isn't that what all of us want? Or cling to? A glimmer of more, because there's so much in reality that's soul-crushing. But then when you least expect it... something happens to make you believe in... oh, I don't know. I'm talking nonsense, now." Eileen laughed nervously.

Naomi reached across the table and threaded her fingers through Eileen's. "It's not nonsense at all."

CHAPTER TWELVE

Naomi looked down at their intertwined fingers. No matter the profound direction their conversation had taken, Naomi knew that the time for more talking had passed. She swept her thumb over Eileen's palm and glanced up again, straight into her luminous eyes.

Eileen didn't smile, but there was something else going on in her gaze. Naomi hadn't come face to face with desire like this in a very long time. The longing in Eileen's eyes was so fierce and acute, Naomi rose from her chair, making sure her fingers remained curled in between Eileen's, and stood next to her.

She lifted their joined hands, turned over Eileen's, and planted a kiss on her wrist. This spurred Eileen on to get up.

"You're a truly remarkable twenty-something," Eileen said. "And I can't seem to stop myself from doing..." She inched closer, her face so near, their lips almost touched. "This."

Up close, Eileen's lips were tantalizingly sexy. Naomi held her breath as she anticipated the moment she'd been waiting for—probably since Eileen had fled her apartment the last time she was there.

Naomi had tried to push away the memory of the kiss they'd shared then, but the image of Eileen leaning in, of the desire in her glance, kept popping up in Naomi's mind at the most inopportune times. But now, here they stood. This time, there was not a hint of hesitation in the expression on Eileen's face.

Eileen bridged the last tiny gap between them and kissed Naomi softly on the lips. Naomi tightened her grip on Eileen's hand, pulling her as near as she could.

Eileen made a soft groaning sound in the back of her throat as she kissed Naomi over and over again, pressing her body against hers.

In response, Naomi widened her lips and let in Eileen's tongue, starting a slow, sensuous dance when their tongues met. With her free hand, Naomi cupped the back of Eileen's head, twirling her fingers through her curly hair, which she wore loose tonight.

Naomi wanted to march Eileen straight into the bedroom as soon as they broke from this delicious kiss, but her instincts told her to let Eileen take the lead. Not that she suspected Eileen had much experience making love with one arm barely functioning—in fact, it was a miracle she was even kissing Naomi.

But something happened—a change in the air— when they were together. Eileen allowed her defenses to go down and Naomi responded to that by moving past her ever-present urge to help, to be of assistance, to try to make people feel better and, in turn, to allow herself to indulge in the emotions this woman had ignited in her from the very first time they'd met.

They broke from the kiss but Eileen didn't retract her head very far. Instead, she kissed Naomi on the cheek, then trailed a path down to her neck. The kisses there, on that sensitive patch of skin, unleashed a fire within Naomi, and she feared she might soon start tugging Eileen into her bedroom regardless of wanting to be understanding of her situation.

She wanted her with a force so big, like a ferocious heat bubbling beneath her skin, it was almost a welcome break when Eileen pulled herself away from Naomi's neck and gazed at her for an instant.

Naomi took the opportunity to catch her breath and take a small step in the direction of her bedroom. Eileen followed, then stopped.

"I don't want to kill the mood by bringing up logistics, but this is the reality when you bring an older woman into your home." She shot Naomi a sly grin.

"That's the price I have to pay." Naomi tilted her head, a smile on her lips.

"I'll try to make it worth your while." Eileen stepped closer. "But I may need a little help."

"That's what I'm here for." If anything, the conversation they were having was increasing the intimate vibe between them. For Naomi, Eileen admitting she needed help was much more intimate than her pretending nothing was wrong—and trying to shrug out of her clothes on her own.

"Let me start with this." Naomi kissed Eileen on the cheek, then found her lips again. God, those intoxicating lips. She could not get enough of them—either to press her own against, or when they curved up into a warm smile the way Naomi knew they could. She wanted to see that smile on Eileen's face again as soon as possible, and she'd do everything she could tonight to make it reappear.

"That's extremely helpful," Eileen said, when their lips broke apart.

"I got distracted by the hot cougar in my apartment," Naomi said.

Even though Eileen gave a small shake of the head, she had a twinkle in her eye.

"Shall I help you take that off?" She tugged gently at the hem of Eileen's top.

"Sure." Eileen lifted her right arm away from her body a fraction.

Naomi noticed the grimace on her face. "Does it hurt?" she asked, as she started hoisting Eileen's top over her head.

"Not really, it's just annoying," Eileen said. "But don't worry." That twinkle in her eye reappeared again. "I can do many things with my left hand these days."

Naomi chuckled nervously. She stole a quick glance at Eileen's left hand. The hand she'd grabbed hold of at the table earlier.

"I want you... so much," Naomi said. "But if you feel uncomfortable or in pain at any point, will you let me know?"

"I will," Eileen said in a much more serious tone than Naomi was expecting. Maybe Eileen sensed that this was very important to her. It made Naomi want her even more. Because she'd already learned that Eileen could be stubborn and uncommunicative about her stroke, but she said the right things when it really mattered.

After Naomi helped Eileen get her top off completely, she stood in front of her again and brought her hands to Eileen's sides, touching her warm skin. She wondered how Eileen managed on her own—it must be all that willpower she saw brimming in her eyes all the time.

"I'm afraid I can't really lend you a hand," Eileen said. "Looks like you'll have to undress for me all on your own."

"You sure know how to woo a girl," Naomi joked.

"Is this not how it's done anymore?" She leaned against the side of the table. "You'll have to inform me about the millennial way of doing this. Or better yet. Show me."

"Come here." Naomi grabbed Eileen by the hand and led her to the couch. "Why don't you sit and let me show you what I've got."

Eileen sat on the edge of the couch, glancing up at Naomi. She didn't appear to have a comeback to that.

Naomi wasn't planning on stripping in a sexy fashion. It wasn't her style at all. She just wanted to get some clothes off as quickly as possible so she could feel Eileen's naked skin against hers. She swiftly pulled her blouse over her head and threw it behind her.

She locked her gaze on Eileen's, stepped closer to the couch, and straddled her. She pushed Eileen's back against the couch and leaned into her again. She cupped Eileen's chin in her palms and kissed her delicious lips over and over again—until she felt Eileen's hand fumble with the clasp of her bra.

"Damn it," Eileen said. "I was hoping I could still do this with one hand, but my left hand isn't dexterous enough yet." She had a half-smile on her face.

"Hold on." Instead of helping Eileen get her bra off, Naomi brought her hands to Eileen's shoulders and guided down the straps of her bra. Then she slipped her hands behind Eileen's back and unhooked her bra.

"That's hardly fair," Eileen said. "Now you're just taking advantage of the situation."

"I think I might do so for a good while longer." Only then did Naomi dispose of her own bra.

She found Eileen's glance again and saw something else burning in it now.

Lust.

With her lips slightly parted, Eileen brought the back of her hand to Naomi's belly and caressed it. She slowly dragged it up to her chest, where she cupped Naomi's generous breast.

Naomi was entranced by the combination of Eileen's glance and her hand, now squeezing gently, on her breast. She'd never in her life encountered a look like that in someone's eyes. It was more than lust. It showed glimpses of the life Eileen had lived and the health scare she'd been through and how, at this moment, she could put all that behind her. With Naomi looking at her like that. With her hands cradling Naomi's breast.

Naomi brought one of her own hands to Eileen's chest. She had to glance away from Eileen's eyes because she wanted to see her hand envelop Eileen's breast. Then, with her own lust having flickered to new heights, and not wanting to wait any longer, Naomi flicked the button of her jeans open, sat up a little straighter and wriggled them off her hips and pushed them down as low as they could go.

Overcome by a desire that could only be quenched in one particular way, she cupped her right hand over Eileen's left one, and pushed it downward, inside her panties.

They had the rest of the night for whatever may come after, but this was what Naomi wanted now.

Judging from the look in Eileen's eyes, bright green and brimming with the same fire Naomi felt burning inside of her, she wasn't acting too quickly at all.

Naomi's clit pulsed as Eileen's fingers drew closer. She leaned over because she wanted her lips on Eileen's when those fingers met her clit.

When she let her tongue slip inside Eileen's mouth, Eileen's fingers eased down, past her clit, and briefly dipped inside the wetness that had gathered between Naomi's legs.

Naomi pinched Eileen's nipple between her fingers and pressed her lips harder against Eileen's, her entire body anticipating the touch of Eileen's fingertip on her clit. Then it happened. The first touch was so gentle, so light, Naomi barely registered it. The second was more brazen, more slippery, more insistent, until the subsequent circles Eileen drew with her fingertip turned into a blur of pleasure and heat inside Naomi's panties.

When the heat grew so fierce inside her, she withdrew her lips from Eileen's, because Naomi wanted to look her in the eye when the orgasm overtook her; before she closed her own eyes in ecstasy, she wanted to see the look in Eileen's eyes first.

Eileen's face was a study in concentration—a more distilled version of the expression she usually wore. Eileen Makenna was nothing if not utterly determined—and, quite clearly, as Naomi had expected, not someone to let a half-paralyzed arm stand in the way of giving Naomi the ultimate pleasure.

"I—I'm…" Naomi groaned, and then she had to close her eyes, because a wave of pleasure crashed over her. But even with her eyes closed, all she saw was Eileen's face. Her luscious lips. Her brilliant meadow-green gaze. And how she had, so willingly now, given herself to Naomi.

CHAPTER THIRTEEN

Eileen woke when a streak of sunlight splashed across her face. Sunlight? The bells usually clanged well before sunup. Had she slept through them? For the first time since her arrival?

Opening and closing her eyes she attempted to jostle the sleepiness from her brain.

She reached for her water glass on the nightstand, but it wasn't there. Neither was her old-fashioned silver alarm clock. The one that ticked quietly, keeping her company when she couldn't sleep.

Rolling onto her back, massaging the confusion from her eyes, the memory of the night before suddenly seeped into her brain.

As if on cue, Naomi's arm wrapped around her stomach.

Eileen released a contented sigh, nestling into the warmth of the blankets and Naomi. How long had it been since she'd woken up with a woman? Actually, best not to think about that. Live in the now. With Naomi, who was deliciously naked, snuggled up close to Eileen. Squinting with one eye, Eileen determined Naomi was still asleep. She held her with her left arm, trying to let her mind go blank, to enjoy the sensation of their flesh pressed against the other.

It was odd to think how much she missed being touched by another human. Since she hadn't been with anyone for... years, perhaps she'd either forgotten the wonderful sensation of human touch or had blocked it out of her mind entirely. Knowing her, it was probably the latter. It had always been so easy in the past for Eileen to block out the negative and press forward with the positive.

And for years, the positive had been her career.

She sucked in a deep breath, a surge of unease washing over her.

"Good morning," mumbled a sleepy Naomi.

Eileen relished hearing the smile in Naomi's voice. "Morning."

"How'd you sleep?" Naomi tightened her grip on Eileen, making it clear she wasn't in a rush to get out of bed.

"Surprisingly well. Didn't even hear the bells." Eileen yawned into her own shoulder.

Naomi propped her chin on a bent elbow, keeping her free arm on Eileen's stomach. "What bells?"

"The church bells." Eileen's eyes widened. "You've never noticed the church bells at six every morning?"

Naomi's face scrunched. "Sometimes I hear them later in the day, but I'm so used to it, I probably don't really register their intrusions as much as you." She traced her finger along Eileen's skin. "Is that one of the reasons you've been grumpy since your return? Not getting enough sleep?" Naomi tickled Eileen's side.

Eileen laughed. "You're acting like we've known each other forever."

"After last night, it kinda seems that way. Are you implying that being grumpy is your perpetual state?" Her eyes shimmered with mischievousness.

"How would I know? Grumpy people aren't great at introspection." Eileen pressed Naomi's button nose.

"So, you do admit you're a grumpster?"

"Doesn't that come with age?"

"You aren't that old." Naomi blew some wisps of hair off her forehead.

"True, but I am looking forward to reaching the age when I can let out obnoxious tirades and have people think I'm a cute old lady."

"Wow. That's an interesting ambition to strive for. You know, most people will think you're the bitchy old lady to avoid at all costs."

"Even better!"

Naomi gently slapped Eileen right above the belly button. "I happen to know you don't shun all human contact."

"Is that right? On what grounds do you know this?"

"I'm a fan of hands-on knowledge." Naomi pinched Eileen's left nipple.

"You young people today always—"

Naomi took Eileen's nipple into her mouth, biting down briefly. "Oh, sorry. You were about to bash young people. Please proceed." She waved Eileen on.

"Uh, what? My mind went blank. You can proceed." Eileen eyed her nipple with a hopeful expression.

"You old people today." Naomi sucked the nipple back into her mouth causing Eileen's breath to hitch.

"I prefer it when you call me a hot cougar instead of... well, an old person."

Naomi climbed on top of Eileen. "Is that so? What else do you prefer?"

"You proved last night you innately understand my preferences."

"Oh, no. That's not how this works. You're a grown woman,

you can use your words to tell me what you like." Naomi arched one brow, waiting.

"You know, back in my day, there was a lot less talking involved."

"You mean when you knocked a woman over the head with your club and dragged her back to your cave."

"Please, I'm not that old."

"But just as stubborn." Naomi went limp on top of Eileen, her arms spread out on the soft pink sheet. "Not moving until you tell me something. Anything."

"Interesting form of punishment you've chosen. Complete torture having a naked twenty-something lying on top of me while I'm also naked. Earlier, I was thinking about how much I've missed this."

Naomi's head popped up again. Resting her chin on Eileen's breast she said, "Define *this*." She added, "Please."

Eileen ran her hand down Naomi's backside. "This. Touching. Feeling someone's skin against my own."

"Has it been a while?" Naomi's expression didn't show any trace of jealousy. It wasn't even curiosity. Concern perhaps. That was the emotion Eileen detected in the recesses of Naomi's penetrating eyes.

"Good question. I've been so wrapped up in my life, which has revolved around work, that I honestly can't put a finger on the number of years." Eileen sighed. "It sounds absurd saying that, and to you of all people."

Naomi's head snapped up. "Why me?"

"Besides the obvious?" Eileen winked.

Naomi flared her nostrils.

"It's hot, really, when you get frustrated with me." She tweaked Naomi's adorable earlobe.

"Still waiting for your answer."

"You seriously don't give up. Fine. You're a people person.

Sweet. Caring. Always thinking about others. And, I'm..." Eileen's eyes dropped.

Naomi lowered her head to stare into her eyes. "Dedicated. Talented. Not to mention trying to save the world by searing images of the terribleness of war into the public's mind."

Eileen ran a hand through Naomi's hair. "I guess we both have causes we're fighting for." It wasn't the time to bring up Eileen's assignments, which typically occurred halfway around the world.

Naomi's eyes darkened. Had the same thought flickered through her mind? But the grinding of her hip into Eileen erased that concern.

"You still haven't told me what you prefer," Naomi said.

Eileen cupped her cheek. "Who knew tenaciousness was such a delectable quality."

"I would like to add, it works in your favor as well. Let's compromise. Tell me one thing. And it can't involve your nipples, because I already know what you like there." For emphasis, Naomi licked one.

Eileen groaned. "Not fair, changing the rules."

"Are you really complaining?" Naomi stroked the nipple with her tongue.

"Seems like a foolish thing to do in the moment."

"And you're never foolish?"

"I don't know about that."

Naomi pulled away from Eileen's aroused nipple.

"Kissing. I like kissing you. Your soft lips. The way you taste." Eileen traced a finger over Naomi's full lips.

Naomi's gaze pierced Eileen's. She didn't speak. Didn't move.

The craving between them seemed to intensify with every intake of breath.

From the intensity of Naomi's stare, she clearly wanted

Eileen. And the yearning Eileen was currently experiencing was further proof of their connection.

Their lips inched closer. Their eyes didn't break contact.

Eileen placed her hand behind Naomi's head guiding her exactly where she was urgently needed.

The kiss started off soft, their lips brushing against the other's, neither in a hurry to get from point A to Z. Eileen couldn't help but think how amazing living in the now was. It was becoming pretty clear she hadn't done so in a long while. If ever. The day had barely begun and neither of them had anywhere to be. They could kiss for hours and it'd be sexy as hell. Not to mention satisfying.

Eileen nearly laughed. How was it that this young woman was showing her how to appreciate the little things in life?

Naomi's tongue penetrated her mouth, pulling Eileen further into her orbit. Naomi deepened the kiss even more.

Eileen moaned, fisting Naomi's luxuriant hair, the dark strands binding around Eileen's fingers like a favorite pair of gloves providing warmth and protection.

Down below, Naomi continued rubbing her hips into Eileen's ever-increasing wetness. Eileen smiled knowing Naomi would take her on an earth-shattering journey, bringing them closer together. God, she wanted that.

Eileen wrapped one leg over Naomi's buttocks.

Naomi nipped Eileen's bottom lip. "I like that particular move of yours."

"Which?" Eileen panted.

Naomi angled her top half to allow Eileen a better view. "The leg over me."

"Oh, that. It just happened on its own. I didn't even know I had that in me, really."

"What happens when I do this?" Naomi kissed Eileen's chin, not staying for long, her mouth leaving a trail of soft kisses downward, her tongue licking the hollow of her throat, as she veered to Eileen's right nipple.

Eileen dug her head into the pillow.

"Ohh... I like that reaction." Naomi teased the nub into her mouth, sucking it hard.

"Again, it just happened."

"That's the best part. Getting you out of your head and into the experience. Don't overuse your brain. Let me do what I want to do to you. Your job, since you like to think that way, is simply to enjoy." Naomi's hand snaked down Eileen's side, bringing to life thousands of goosebumps.

"A tough ask," Eileen teased.

"Like I said last night, I love a challenge. And the one I plan to tackle right now is to rock Eileen Makenna's world so she turns into a gooey pile after having an out-of-this-world orgasm."

Eileen beckoned Naomi with her left index finger and then tapped her lips. Naomi, with a crooked grin and shimmering eyes, kissed Eileen. Hard. Sensual. Naomi pulled away and whispered in Eileen's ear, "That's the last command I'll obey for now. I'm in control from here on out."

Eileen started to speak, but Naomi silenced her with another explosive kiss.

This time, when Naomi started her trek downwards, she didn't stop at either nipple, her tongue trailing down to right above Eileen's belly button, peppering the soft flesh with kisses. Eileen, slightly ticklish, writhed underneath Naomi, which only spurred her to continue her torture of Eileen.

Not that Eileen was complaining.

Naomi's mouth continued its trek, her teeth grazing Eileen's pubic hair. When she reached Eileen's pussy, Naomi inhaled deeply. "I love your smell. Truly intoxicating."

Naomi didn't stay, though. Instead she moved to Eileen's thigh, teasing the skin, working down her leg.

"Oh, God," Eileen muttered. How was Naomi driving her this insane simply by kissing the inside of her thigh? Every touch, kiss, lick, nip was driving Eileen mad with desire as if every nerve ending in her body was aflame.

Naomi worked her way back up from Eileen's ankle on her other leg, taking her time exploring.

"You're killing me." Eileen's breathy tone implied she wasn't at all dissatisfied.

Naomi sank her teeth into Eileen's inner thigh. "Something tells me you're enjoying this manner of death." Her finger skimmed Eileen's pussy lips which were wet with wanting. "This, my dear, is hard to deny."

"I'm not trying to. Take me, please."

Naomi released a throaty laugh. "I meant it's hard to hide how much you want me. And I thought I told you, I'm in control. Although, hearing your plea… that deserves a reward." Her tongue split Eileen's swollen lips, dipping inside for a taste.

Eileen's hand fisted the sheet.

Naomi worked her way up to Eileen's clit, teasing it with a flick of her tongue, and then took it into her mouth. Circling it with her tongue, Naomi eased a finger inside.

Eileen's body shuddered.

Naomi added another finger, moving slowly in and out, while her tongue languidly lapped at Eileen's bud.

It amazed Eileen how the younger of the two wasn't in a hurry, and was appreciating the fine art of making love. Because right then, Eileen wanted Naomi to take her quickly and hard.

As if in tune with Eileen's inner thoughts, Naomi quickened the pace of her fingers, going in deeper and curling her fingers upward. And her tongue was working wonders all on its own.

Eileen's feet pressed into Naomi's thighs, allowing her to arch her back off the mattress.

Naomi kicked her efforts into an even higher gear, her

fingers and mouth working in unison to deliver on her promise of an extraordinary orgasm.

The first wave of Eileen's bliss confirmed Naomi would exceed her pledge.

Eileen reached for the other pillow, chomping down on the corner, right when Naomi drove her fingers in deep. The second wave crashed over Eileen causing all of her muscles to spasm.

When Naomi triggered Eileen's G-spot with her fingers, the third wave sent Eileen over the edge. "Holy fuck!" Her back arched up and her body shuddered. "Holy fuck, holy fuck, holy fuck," Eileen chanted.

CHAPTER FOURTEEN

On Monday evenings, Naomi's mother usually met her for a quick bite between the end of Naomi's workday at the hospital and the couple of hours she volunteered afterward.

When they'd first started their Monday evening tradition, Naomi had told her mother about the cozy coffee shop inside the hospital, but her mother refused to set foot inside unless there was something life-threateningly wrong with herself or any member of her family.

"Why would I go inside a hospital voluntarily if I have no reason to be there?" she'd said. "They're such cold, morbid places. I don't understand why you spend all your time there when you don't have to."

But of course, her mother understood. Naomi knew that much. Just as she knew that she shouldn't push her mom to meet her there. Especially today—on that particular day of the year.

Naomi had been telling her mother about Tyson, who would be released from the hospital tomorrow. This would make him miss the delivery of the disposable camera pictures. Because of Thanksgiving weekend—and Eileen being some-

HARPER BLISS & T.B. MARKINSON

what otherwise occupied—she had admitted to Naomi that finding a place to develop the pictures was proving harder than she'd first thought.

Naomi had assured Tyson that as soon as she had the prints, she would bring them to his home. It would be a good activity for her and Eileen to do together, actually. Eileen had really lit up—

"Naomi," her mother said. "You seem miles away today."

"Sorry." Naomi tried to refocus on the conversation, but it was hard when images of Eileen kept slipping into her mind. "So, yeah, Tyson gets to go home."

"He's one of the lucky ones then," her mother said.

"I guess he is, although it's much more than just a matter of luck." Naomi sipped from her soda.

"You know what I mean." Her mother's voice trembled a fraction as she spoke.

"I do." Naomi tried to shoot her mother a warm smile.

"I just can't help picturing what a handsome man Joey would have grown up to be." A few tears gathered in her mother's eyes, but they didn't spill.

Naomi hadn't even been born when her brother had died of leukemia. She did, however, remember her parents' grief. Even though her mother called Naomi her miracle baby, who had helped her overcome the despair of losing a child, the grief was still a big part of their lives even now.

All Naomi knew to do at a moment like this, and there had been many over the years, was to try and cheer her mother up. For a brief moment, she considered telling her mother that she'd met someone, but it was too soon for that.

Having to tell her about her break-up with Jane had been hard enough. Because it was as though, as a result of one of her children dying, Sophia couldn't bear the slightest bout of unhappiness in any of her other children's lives. Even though

Naomi had tried to tell her time and time again: unhappiness is as much a part of life as happiness.

Besides, Naomi didn't want to get the third degree from her mother. *How old is she?* That would surely be one of the first questions Naomi would be faced with, and today was not the day to have that conversation with her mother. Come to think of it, no day would ever be that day.

"What's different about you?" her mother asked before Naomi had the chance to come up with something uplifting to say. "You can't fool a mother's intuition about her daughter."

Naomi chuckled. Her mom was much more perceptive than Naomi was willing to admit. "I had a nice weekend, that's all."

"Really? Who with?" Her mother narrowed her eyes. "Not with Jane, I hope?"

Naomi had not been able to keep the cause of their break-up from her family. In a town like Derby, things like that soon became common knowledge.

"God no," Naomi said. "That's well and truly over."

"She and what's-her-name didn't take up together," her mother said matter-of-factly. "And I've heard she still loves you."

Naomi arched up her eyebrows. "Who told you that?"

"It doesn't matter who. The only thing that matters is that she hurt you and, for that reason alone, she has no business going around town proclaiming how much she still loves you. It's not right."

Naomi shrugged. "I'm very lovable." This brought another image of Eileen into her mind. After they'd showered and gotten dressed on Sunday—after the church bells had chimed many more times—Naomi had admired the ingenious trick Eileen had devised of single-handedly gathering her hair into a ponytail.

"You don't have to tell me that, darling." Her mother smiled. "Don't get me wrong. Your love life is your business and if you told me that, despite everything, you knew in your heart that Jane was the love of your life, I would accept that, of course." She put a hand on Naomi's wrist. "You do know that, don't you?" Her voice had gone solemn.

"Yes." *Wait until I bring a forty-nine-year old woman home.* But, in her heart of hearts, Naomi knew that, in the end, if Eileen made Naomi happy, her mother would accept it. However, she was getting way ahead of herself again. If Eileen stuck to her plan, Naomi would never have to introduce her to her family. She was just passing through. She'd be gone after Christmas. Naomi pushed that thought from her mind as quickly as she could. "That's good to know, Mom, it really is, but Jane truly is out of the picture."

"You take some time to gather yourself then." Her mother patted her wrist and then withdrew her hand. "You're still so young. You could still do anything you want with your life."

"And yet here I am, already doing what I love most."

Her mother just nodded.

Naomi looked at her watch. "Kelly will be expecting me soon."

"I know you love what you do, darling, and I admire you for it. But these days, people don't stay in the same job their entire life any longer. Times have changed."

Naomi knew that her mother worried about her spending so much time at the very hospital where her brother had died. "You should really come with me some day," she said. "Meet some of the kids at the hospital. They're so unbelievably... resilient."

Her mother shook her head. "I know you mean well, but I don't think that's going to happen any time soon." She shot Naomi a small smile, then looked around for the waiter. "Let me get the check."

❄

"Ready to go home tomorrow?" Naomi asked Tyson. He looked like he could do with some cheering up.

"You haven't heard?" Despite his illness, Naomi had seen his eyes bright with joy and laughter—there was none of that sparkle in his gaze today.

"Heard what?" Naomi curled her fingers around the bed frame.

"I can't go home tomorrow. My last lab tests weren't clear."

"Oh no. I'm so sorry, Tyson."

He was sitting up and he didn't look sick at all. He shrugged. "It sucks."

"What did the doctor say?" Naomi walked to the side of the bed and sat on the chair next to it. She'd be sticking around a while.

"Same old shit," Tyson said. He looked away, but when he glanced back at Naomi, his eyes lit up briefly. "When's that photographer lady coming back?"

Good question, Naomi thought, while she tried her very best not to blush. "I'll be sure to ask her that soon."

"Because I've had some ideas for pictures. Like detailed shots of larger things." He reached for his phone. "I've been practicing and I would like to show her."

"Tell you what," Naomi said. "I'll give her a call tonight and see if she can stop by tomorrow."

"What's wrong with her arm?" Tyson asked, in the direct manner only children had. "She never uses her right arm."

"You can ask her all about that tomorrow." Naomi wondered how Eileen would feel about being questioned about her health by this boy. Perhaps she'd find it easier to open up to someone like him—someone so disarming and to the point.

Naomi accepted Tyson's phone. As she glanced at the pictures he had taken, most of them from the confines of his hospital bed, a smile grew on her lips. Eileen clearly didn't know the kind of energizing effect she could have on people—on these kids who needed it most of all.

"These are wonderful. Eileen will be so thrilled." She gave Tyson back his phone. "One visit from Eileen and you already want to be a photographer." Naomi couldn't help but swell with pride.

"I typed 'Eileen' and 'photographer' into Google and easily found her. She won a Pulitzer." He pronounced it Puh-litzer. "That's a big deal."

"It is." What got Naomi most of all when she worked with kids around Tyson's age was how they would mimic how their parents spoke, but could never hide, be it in tone or pronunciation, that they were still very much kids.

"It's so great that she came to see us," Tyson said.

"I'll make sure she stops by again soon."

"Thanks." Tyson leaned back. He suddenly looked tired.

Naomi made a mental note to check with the doctor whether his prognosis had changed or they were just keeping him a few days longer for further observation. Just because these kids might be the bravest of all, they still didn't belong here. In that respect, her mother was right.

"How about you go to sleep and I'll call Eileen." She got up and touched her palm softly to his upper arm.

Tyson nodded and, even as she was still walking out of his room, Naomi was already reaching for her phone.

CHAPTER FIFTEEN

The bell on the diner door announced Eileen's entrance and three heads slowly pivoted to scrutinize the new arrival. However, one lone person at the counter didn't take note.

Eileen recognized Jane's spiky hair. She held her phone in her hand, clearly absorbed in whatever was on the screen. When the waitress placed Jane's order of Eggs Benedict, not right in front of Jane's hunched body, but within reach, Jane didn't acknowledge the young woman in the slightest. The waitress didn't seem to mind Jane's aloofness, leading Eileen to believe this was how Jane usually acted in the establishment. Or possibly everywhere in town.

Two hunched white-haired ladies, the ones who walked the town park together every morning, whispered back and forth not bothering to hide the fact that Eileen was the subject of their conversation. That narrowed down Eileen's choice on where to sit to the four-seater that was tucked away in the corner by the bathroom entrance and completely out of view of the nattering nabobs of Derby.

Her eyes scanned the interior of The Early Bird Café. Every

wall, booth table, and countertop were a retina-scorching yellow as if the sun had exploded. Blinking several times, Eileen fiddled with the paper placement, covered in ads for local business. If she needed a lube job, she now knew Al of Al's Garage was a no-BS businessman. If he had to shout that he wasn't a swindler did that actually imply the opposite? Did cars still need lube? Or was Al being cheeky or talking in code?

A young woman, barely old enough to be out of high school, in black jeans and a T-shirt approached. "What can I get you?"

Eileen hadn't bothered to peruse the menu knowing every American diner would have her go-to meal. "Toast, scrambled eggs, and a double order of bacon."

The woman jotted down the items on her pad. "What kind of bread?"

With a wisp of guilt, Eileen opted for white instead of a healthier option. What was the point of whole wheat, really, when requesting a double order of bacon?

"Anything to drink?" The woman tapped her pen against the pad.

"Coffee. Black."

"From the looks of it, several cups." The woman's sincere smile, showing her youth, blunted the comment.

Eileen smiled back, knowing the true source of her exhaustion. Naomi had spent the night at her place and there hadn't been much time allotted for actual shuteye. "Stayed up late binge-watching the final season of *The Americans*," Eileen said to the woman, wondering why she felt the need to clarify anything. The lying didn't surprise her considering she was skillful in that particular field when need be.

Given this was a small town, though, maybe it wasn't all that surprising that Eileen's instincts kicked in. Everyone knew everyone's business. Hence the reason Naomi had fled Eileen's place well before the church bells this morning. True, people had seen them together at Jane's exhibition, but appearing together at a public event and leaving an apartment early in the morning—that would light up the Derby grapevine faster than Chuck Yeager's plane breaking the sound barrier.

The waitress returned with a coffee pot and flipped over the cup already on the table. "How long are you home for?"

Eileen didn't recognize the woman, probably due to the fact that Eileen had been gone for years before the waitress was born, but that didn't matter. "Oh, I'm here for the holidays. Then it's back to… work."

The woman's eyes fell to Eileen's right hand, which Eileen had forced into a flat position on the table top. "Work ruins everything," she said with an enigmatic expression in her eyes. She turned on her heel and cheerily greeted an elderly man and woman who shuffled through the door.

The only people younger than fifty, aside from the server, were Jane and Eileen and it didn't escape Eileen's recollection that she only had months until she ticked over to the big five-oh.

Eileen focused her attention on her right hand. She pivoted the hand upward, so it was perpendicular to the table with the side of her pinky still touching the table top. She flattened it again. And repeated the physical therapy exercise as she usually did whenever she had time to kill.

The days kept ticking by, bringing Eileen closer and closer to the brink of her self-imposed deadline for being back on the job.

"Oh, hey, it's you."

Eileen looked up into Jane's pinched face. "Hello."

Jane eased onto the bench opposite Eileen.

Please, Jane, take a seat.

"I was just thinking of calling you, but I don't know your number. Or email for that matter. But here you are." Jane whipped out her phone from her back pocket.

"About?" There was no way Eileen would provide any contact details. If anyone really needed to get ahold of her, they could reach her through work. But that took initiative and Jane seemed more like the type to rely on others for practical things.

"About my show." Jane quickly added, "How much you liked it."

The waitress set Eileen's plate down and Jane swiped a slice of bacon off the stack of extra crispy pieces. Just the way Eileen liked them.

Eileen, who had been living abroad and didn't have many opportunities to enjoy American bacon, controlled her urge to plunge her fork into Jane's hand.

Seeming not to notice Eileen's death stare or silence, Jane pressed on around bites of bacon. "What do you say?" A piece of bacon fell from her mouth and landed on a placemat, grease spreading out.

I'd like you to keep your grubby paws off my bacon. Still not understanding Jane's request, Eileen repeated her earlier question, "About?" There was no point in expending too much energy into the conversation.

"Giving me a line or two about how much you liked *Life in Bits*. It'd look great coming from you."

Eileen uncrossed her legs. "You want me to give you an endorsement"

"Yeah. An endorsement." Jane appeared as if it was the first time she had heard the word or truly understood its meaning.

Not a chance in hell. Eileen re-crossed her legs again, angling her left flank to Jane. "Are you going to the Christmas tree lighting in the town square tonight?"

Jane palm-slapped her forehead. "Is that tonight?"

Taken aback by her palm-slapping, Eileen said, "I'm pretty sure today is the first of December." Eileen nodded when the waitress raised the coffee pot as a way of asking if she wanted a top up. "Thank you."

"Don't mention it." The waitress buzzed over to the other patrons, topping everyone up.

"Shoot. I just made plans for tonight, but I'm supposed to take photos for *The Derby Gazette*." Jane rapped her fingertips on the table. "Can you manage it, you think?"

Eileen sputtered, "W-what?" Surely, she didn't mean the photos for the *Gazette*? Or was she still fixated on the endorsement?

Jane motioned to Eileen's hand. "What are you doing? Is that a photographer's exercise or something?"

Eileen hadn't even realized she'd continued her PT exercises while she waited for Jane to leave so she could attempt to butter her toast with one arm. "Something like that."

Jane copied Eileen's exercise with her right hand. "So, can you manage tonight?"

Eileen forked in a mouthful of eggs. Chewing slowly, she finally swallowed. "What?" Honestly, how did Naomi ever carry on a conversation with Jane?

"Can you take some photos of the ceremony tonight? I'd be indebted to you." She placed her hand over her heart. "Truly."

Eileen's gut response was to tell Jane to fuck off. But she thought better of it. "I suppose I can manage some photos. Maybe I can enlist Naomi's help." Part of her felt a twinge of guilt for tossing out Naomi's name, especially since Naomi had gone to the effort of sneaking out of her apartment this morning. But Jane needled Eileen more than Eileen cared to admit.

Jane bolted upright in her seat. "Great. I'll let the paper know. I'm sure they won't mind."

Eileen stifled a laugh, knowing the publisher, who was an old family friend, wouldn't have any objections. If she used her iPhone, tripod, and Bluetooth Remote Shutter, taking photos for the *Gazette* wouldn't be too difficult. This would never fly for her real job, but this was for a paper in a town with less than fifteen thousand residents.

"Are you and Naomi close?" Jane's expression was remarkably blank and Eileen couldn't decipher if she was attempting to disguise all traces of jealousy or if this was the amount of interest Jane took in anyone's life, including her ex.

"We attended your exhibition together, as you know." Eileen wasn't the type to provide many private details, although she had let Naomi's name slip from her lips.

"Be careful. I heard you're back in town because of a health thing or something." Jane waved a hand in the air. "Naomi has a bad habit of taking on charity cases." She laughed. "One time, when we were driving on Route 13 with five cars behind me, she screamed for me to slam on the brakes to avoid hitting a turtle that'd wandered onto the road. Then she wanted me to pull over and get it to safety. A turtle I ask you!"

"Did you run over it?"

"Are you going to eat your toast?" Jane pointed at the four untouched slices. "I'm a bottomless pit today."

In so many ways. "Go ahead."

Jane buttered one, topping it off with a glob of strawberry jam.

"So, did you run over the turtle?"

"What?" Jane shoved toast into her mouth.

Eileen waited for her to finish.

Jane swallowed. "Oh, the turtle. No, I didn't. But I wasn't going to risk my life to save it from getting squashed. It shouldn't have gotten onto the road in the first place. Naomi's soft. Always wanting to save everyone." Jane leaned over the table. "You and I both know, since we're behind the camera, how cruel this world can be. We see things others don't."

"Yes, your doll, Bitsy, has truly seen the dark side of this world."

Jane tapped the tip of her nose with an index finger and then jabbed it in Eileen's direction. "Exactly. You get it."

Eileen said a silent prayer that her Bitsy jibe wouldn't spark Jane's memory to ask again about the endorsement.

Jane finished the slice of toast. "I should shove off. Thanks again for covering for me. If you ever need me to pinch-hit for you, just give me a shout."

Yeah, sure. Eileen sincerely doubted Jane had so much as a valid passport.

The bell on the door chimed as Jane stepped out into the foggy morning, heading to God knows where. Good riddance.

The two older women shuffled by Eileen's table on their way out, both giving Eileen the once over as they passed.

Did they think Eileen was involved with Jane?

Eileen blew out a breath. "Whatever."

Let them think that as long as they stayed off the Naomi trail. Jane invited local gossip with her antics. During one of their late-night chats, Naomi had disclosed Jane's affair. Eileen had only interacted with Jane on two occasions, but both instances left a sour taste in her mouth.

What in the world had Naomi seen in Jane?

The thought of Naomi wanting to rescue a lost turtle made her smile.

That was so like Naomi.

Another less pleasant thought struck Eileen.

CHAPTER SIXTEEN

Naomi was just heading out to lunch with Kelly in the hospital coffee shop, when her phone started ringing. Her lips curved into an involuntary smile when she saw Eileen's name appear on the screen.

She picked up, her smile spreading.

"Am I a turtle?" Eileen's voice came over the phone—crisp and harsh.

"What?" *Whatever happened to hello?* Or was Eileen playing some sort of prank on her?

"Am I another turtle that needs saving?" Eileen's voice was starting to soften a little.

"Eileen," Naomi said. "This is Eileen Makenna, right? Have you started working for a very special kind of pet shop now? Making the most bizarre cold calls?"

A pause on the other end of the line, followed by a sigh. "I ran into Jane," Eileen said. "She told me about that turtle you wanted to save from getting run over on the road."

Naomi shook her head. What else could Jane have told Eileen about her? She shook off the thought. "And she made it sound as if wanting to save an animal is a bad thing?"

"It's not so much about the turtle," Eileen admitted. "It's more about me knowing if I'm just another creature for you to save."

"You didn't much look like someone who needed saving in bed this morning." Memories of the nights they'd been spending together flooded Naomi's mind.

Eileen chuckled, but then her voice sounded serious again. "Jane somehow knows exactly how to get under my skin."

"She has a knack for that." Naomi walked back to her chair and sat down. "If I ask you not to pay too much attention to her, do you think you can do that? Jane's really not that bad. She's still getting over the break-up whereas I... Well, I've kind of moved on already."

"She actually got me a job," Eileen said. "Taking pictures at the Christmas tree lighting in the town square tonight. For the local paper."

"Really?" This conversation was getting weirder by the minute. "Are you going to do it?"

"Yes. I agreed to help her out."

"Eileen Makenna, Pulitzer Prize winner, taking snaps for *The Derby Gazette*."

"I'm here. I might as well make myself useful." Eileen's tone had brightened. Maybe she was happy to be useful. "Idle hands and all that."

"Do you need help?" Naomi asked. "I can carry your equipment."

Eileen went silent for a moment. "That would be nice, actually."

Warmth bloomed in Naomi's chest.

"I won't be taking a lot of equipment. I'll just use my phone and take a tripod."

"Switching on the Christmas tree lights isn't exactly the social gathering of the year, but it does draw a bit of a crowd," Naomi said. "Are you sure you want to go together?"

"I am," Eileen said, no hint of doubt in her voice. "I'll be taking pictures so you'll need to resist my charms until I finish."

Naomi burst into a smile again. "As long as I get to carry your equipment all the way home and have my way with you then."

"I guess I need to pay you for your work somehow."

"Do we, um, need to talk about this? If people see us together, there might be talk."

"People can befriend each other in this town, can't they?" Eileen said—not a hint left of the harshness in her voice at the beginning of their phone call.

"Sure," Naomi said. "We'll be discreet."

"I wouldn't want you to think I don't want to be seen with you." Eileen snickered.

"How about I come by your place after work, we can then go from there together?" Naomi could hardly wait.

"Sounds like a plan." Eileen paused. "I'd best let you get back to it."

They hung up and Naomi made her way to the coffee shop downstairs, ten minutes late for her lunch date with Kelly.

Naomi wasn't worried about anyone seeing her with Eileen, but she wasn't sure if Eileen felt the same way about being seen with Naomi.

She hurried down the stairs and put the people of Derby out of her mind. When she entered the coffee shop and caught sight of Kelly, one of her most favorite people in Derby, she figured that, at the very least, she should tell her best friend about Eileen.

But Kelly wasn't interested in the Derby Christmas tree lights—she and Frank were going to a concert in Boston tonight—and Naomi considered that, before she officially told anyone, she needed to have another conversation with Eileen.

After all, Eileen might be gone in a few weeks—and wouldn't they both be better off not having told anyone then?

Naomi could put her dalliance with Eileen down to a rebound fling—because, at the heart of it, wasn't that what it was? Eileen had told her from the start that she was only in Derby for the holidays.

Perhaps Naomi should start thinking of protecting herself, and this definitely included keeping Eileen a secret. She'd just gone through the unpleasant ordeal of sharing the news with all her friends and family that she and Jane had broken up—the information that Jane had cheated on her included. She didn't want to go through any of that again.

She sat opposite Kelly and gave her a big smile that she hoped would camouflage how she was feeling.

When they approached the town square, Naomi carrying Eileen's tripod, she feared they might look quite conspicuous. But, as it turned out, Naomi and Eileen blended in perfectly, because, these days, every single person had a smartphone to take pictures and considered themselves an amateur photographer. A handful even had tripods of their own.

The whole thing was over in fifteen minutes, yet Naomi had witnessed another side of Eileen. She wasn't playful, as she'd been with the kids at the hospital, even though her passion for the camera had shone through then as well. Tonight, she'd been focused and professional. Even though she was shooting with a phone, just like everyone else, she tried out a dozen different angles, and had Naomi move the tripod just as many times.

Eileen had only nodded in recognition at a handful of people. A few decades away from Derby could, apparently, erase most people from your memory—at least from Eileen's. And whenever Naomi had asked Eileen about her family, she'd shut the conversation down pretty quickly, claiming that, apart from her sister, she wasn't close to them at all. Naomi hadn't pressed Eileen for more information, sensing that the time for that had not yet come. They had plenty of other, much more pleasurable, activities to engage in when they were together.

On the way back to Eileen's apartment, Eileen said, "I guess this means Christmas is right around the corner."

"Indeed, with all the lovely family gatherings that come with it," Naomi replied. She was still carrying Eileen's tripod.

"That's what I came back for. If you can believe it. I must be a real sucker for punishment."

Naomi had to stop herself from grabbing Eileen's hand. "Aren't we all this time of year?"

"Look around you, though. Derby's all lit up. It's like they've not only switched on the lights, but given the start sign for all the fake merriment that comes with it."

"That sounds a bit glum, even coming from you." Naomi walked a little closer to Eileen.

Eileen chuckled. "I think I know what would cheer me up."

"I can probably guess what you're thinking, but it's a bit cold outside. Let's wait until we get to your place," Naomi joked.

Eileen stopped and turned to her. "I may have given you reason to believe so, but I really don't have a one-track mind like that." She inched closer to Naomi. "My mom throws a big Christmas party the first weekend of December every year. How about you be my date and make the whole ordeal infinitely more bearable for me?"

"You want to take me to your family Christmas party?" Naomi's eyes grew wide.

"It's just a pre-party and there will be loads of people. It won't be an intimate affair at all. Quite the opposite, actually."

"Of course I would love to be your date," Naomi blurted out

before she could reason herself out of accepting the invitation. "It's about time I find out where you come from."

"Don't expect to have a good time, though. In fact, just this once, you *can* look at it as treating me as a charity case." Eileen scoffed. "There will be lots of free booze, however. So, there's that."

"I've never seen you as a charity case, Eileen," Naomi said.

Eileen tilted her head. "Not even when you picked up those spilled coins in the hospital coffee shop?"

"I just thought you were hot and I made the most of the opportunity presented to me. So that makes me much more of an opportunist than you think."

It was Eileen who took Naomi's free hand in her good one. "You should fit right in with my family then." Eileen grinned at her and dragged Naomi along with her.

They walked the rest of the way to Eileen's apartment in silence, their fingers intertwined. Naomi took the time to digest everything Eileen had said, and to mentally prepare for the party.

CHAPTER SEVENTEEN

Eileen stood on the sidewalk outside her apartment, waiting for Naomi to swing by in her car so they could go to the Callahan Holiday Bash, part one, together.

Darkness had already settled over Derby, but the night sky was clear, aside from some wispy clouds and the waning crescent moon low in the sky off to her left. Eileen studied the moon, remembering some of the moments she'd taken the time to stop and look. Like her first night in Iraq during the first Gulf War. Or on a Greek shore after witnessing the arrival of Syrian migrants, and a mother's grief upon realizing her three-month daughter had died in her arms. The photo Eileen had snapped ended up winning the Pulitzer.

So many memories of terrible sadness. Fear. Guilt.

Tonight, though, standing in Derby, the sheer beauty of the moon stood out to her more than usual. Never before had she considered its presence romantic.

And she felt years younger.

Perhaps both changes were Naomi's influence. One benefit of sleeping with a twenty-something.

Eileen was still chuckling when Naomi pulled up.

After Eileen climbed into the passenger side of the beat-up Subaru Outback, Naomi, with one hand on the back of Eileen's seat, asked, "What's so funny?"

"The moon."

Naomi scrunched her brow. "Do I even want to ask?"

"Probably best not to. Hi, by the way. You millennials and your non-greeting habits," Eileen teased.

"This coming from the woman who launched into 'Am I a turtle' on the phone the other day."

"An excellent point." Eileen laughed.

Naomi scanned the street before leaning over and kissing Eileen full on the lips, her tongue forcing its way into Eileen's mouth. Pulling away many moments later, she asked, "Was that a better greeting?"

"I may have to get out of the car and get back in if that's how you plan to greet me every time you pick me up."

"I'd let you if we weren't running late."

Eileen smiled. "Oh, we have plenty of time before dinner. I don't know why my mom insists on hosting a sit-down meal considering the number of guests. She treats these parties like she's hosting a State Dinner. Absolutely ridiculous."

Naomi blinked. "Really... that... is odd."

"You okay?" Eileen placed her hand on Naomi's thigh, giving it a squeeze.

Naomi placed her hand over Eileen's. "I am now. Your touch has a healing effect on me. So, where are we going?"

Eileen provided the address.

"Do I need to enter it into my GPS or do you still remember your way home?" Naomi teased, but there was a smidge of trepidation, or something Eileen couldn't put her finger on, in her tone.

"I think I can bumble my way there. Take a left at the stop sign."

Fifteen minutes later, they pulled up outside the house.

"This is your parents' house?" Naomi leaned over the steering wheel, taking in the Victorian lakeside manor, its original clapboard siding covered in a pristine coat of apricot paint. Her eyes wandered over the cream-covered gingerbread trim on the one-hundred-fifty-year-old house. "I had no idea you're..." She let her voice trail off.

Eileen, uncomfortable with the awkward silence, tried to see everything from Naomi's perspective. The stark differences highlighted between Eileen's family home and Naomi's car that was at least a decade old. She rushed to explain, "It's not as impressive as you think. The house has been in the family for generations. Originally it was my great-grandparents' summer home, but my parents moved in permanently before I was born."

"It's not..." Naomi let out a breath and smiled awkwardly. "Do you live in Buckingham Palace when you're in the UK?"

Eileen let out a bark of laughter. "Hardly." She studied Naomi's face. "You okay? You seem a bit pale. We don't have to go inside."

"What? No. It must be the moon's effect." She swallowed. "Shall we... head in?" Without hesitation, Naomi got out of the car.

"If we must." Eileen reached across her chest to open the door.

Both outside, Eileen waved for Naomi to walk ahead of her.

"So polite." Naomi patted Eileen's cheek.

"Not really." Eileen cocked her head to fully appreciate the twist of Naomi's hips. "This is the best view of the evening."

Naomi peered over her shoulder. "Naughty."

The foyer was brilliantly lit. Strands of white lights twinkled in crisscross patterns across the high ceiling, highlighting the massive chandelier made of sparkling Irish crystal.

Naomi met Eileen's eyes with a look of mystification.

"Sadly, there isn't one octopus centerpiece in the entire

house," Eileen whispered into Naomi's ear. Although, she noted the red and green beads around Nike, the Greek goddess. Julia's touch?

"How did you survive childhood without one?"

"It was touch and go for many years." While Eileen had been joking, it was difficult to kick the thought that it really had been that way living with her mom.

Naomi helped Eileen out of her coat before a young woman quickly approached them sweeping their coats out of sight.

It was Eileen's first glimpse of Naomi's quirky sleeveless 1950s cocktail dress. It was ruby red with a full skirt, lace at the neck, and with a detailed depiction of a winter village at the hem, complete with falling snow. The outfit was finished off by black stockings with seams up the back, and three-inch heels. Eileen whispered, "You look great."

"Eileen! There you are, darling." Her mom practically floated over to Eileen, greeting her with a kiss on the cheek.

Naomi took a step to the side, giving mother and daughter some space, her dark voluminous hair falling over her face in the process.

Eileen started to introduce Naomi, but her mom interrupted, "I'll be right back. The mayor just walked in."

"I'm so sorry," Eileen said to Naomi.

"Don't be. I mean it's the mayor after all." Naomi's eyes twinkled with frivolity, as she swept the strands of hair off her face.

"Hey there, cousin." A man in a red tartan bow tie and suspenders with gray hair at his temples stuck out his hand for Eileen to shake.

"Oh, sorry. I have to be weird and shake your hand with my left arm." Eileen avoided Naomi's questioning gaze.

"What'd you do?" he asked, eying her stiff arm.

"Nothing serious. Pulled a muscle or something." She gestured it wasn't a big deal. "Philip this is Naomi."

"Nice to meet you," Philip said, squeezing Naomi's hand in a limp handshake. "Can I get you two lovely ladies a drink? Can't have my favorite injured cousin go without one."

"You've always been the gentleman. Like when you used to put snot-filled tissues into my shoes."

"Careful, Ellie. I'm in the early stages of a cold so I still may manage a few surprises. One's never too old for that practical joke." He left them, presumably on the mission of acquiring two glasses of bubbly.

"Ellie?" Naomi asked, adding, "Do you prefer being called that?"

"Professionally I go by Eileen, but those who know me well do call me that."

Naomi's eyebrows nearly reached her hairline. "Oh really. Do I know you well enough now to call you Ellie?"

Eileen whispered in Naomi's ear. "Trust me. You know me a helluva lot better than Phil."

"Naomi. I wasn't expecting to see you here." A woman in black trousers and a pastel sweater with a knitted scene of a man and woman in a sled wrapped Naomi into her arms.

"Hi, Mom."

Eileen blinked. Looked more closely at the older woman and then blinked again.

"Mom, you remember Eileen Makenna *Callahan*? Eileen, this is my mom, Sophia Weaver." Naomi's emphasis on Eileen's last name didn't go unnoticed.

Eileen nodded, mouth slightly agape. Recovering her faculties, she said, "Mrs. Weaver it's so very good to see you again."

"And you, my dear."

Mother and daughter chatted briefly, before Mrs. Weaver excused herself.

Eileen steered Naomi into a corner. "You're Mrs. Weaver's daughter? Why didn't you tell me?"

"You never asked. And, I'm just as surprised as you are

137

about all of this. I didn't start putting the pieces together until you gave me your address less than an hour ago. When I met you, you told me your name was Eileen Makenna, leaving out the key detail that would have clued me in immediately. Everyone in Derby knows the Callahan family."

"I've never used my last name, aside from legal documents, since I left. But, I... I don't remember you. How is that possible?" Eileen ran her hand over her head. "It does explain why your face lost all its color earlier in the car. You weren't about to say you didn't know I came from a wealthy family or something. You were about to say you didn't know I was a Callahan. Hence why I never say my last name because people act like the way you did in the car." Eileen circled back. "But, how do I not remember you? Naomi Weaver." She said the name as if running it through her mental computer for any sign of recognition.

"I'm the youngest of five kids and there was a huge gap between me and the sibling who is closest to my age. Mom's always called me her miracle baby. You probably left for college before my birth."

"College," Eileen echoed. So much for feeling younger dating a twenty-something. "But... our moms are friends."

"Uh, they know each other, yes. But you can say that about most moms in Derby."

"Surely you knew your mom was going to a party tonight. You didn't make the connection when I asked you?" Eileen knitted her brow.

Naomi shook her head. "Nope. I've never associated much with... your family."

From Naomi's puckered forehead she gathered the reason for Naomi's avoidance. Naomi wasn't the type to appreciate Trudy Callahan and Eileen couldn't fault her for that. Actually, she respected it.

"There you are." Phil held two glasses in his hands. After

handing off the drinks to Naomi and Eileen, he turned to his cousin. "How long are you in town for?"

"The month. You?" Eileen sipped her drink.

"I'm driving back to Connecticut tomorrow. I'll be back for Christmas or your mom will have my head on a platter. How have you avoided the wrath of Trudy Callahan all these years?"

"By living in a different country."

"Jules!" Phil called out, waving a hand about as if trying to guide a plane to a landing strip. "Get over here."

Julia, shaking her head and laughing, left James alone with the nattering nabobs from the café. "You bellowed, Probate Will Phil."

Phil, with hand over heart, said, "You deeply wound me Jules the Mule that Drools."

"Okay, I get the mule one, but Probate Will Phil? That's an odd nickname," Naomi whispered to Eileen.

"Phil's a probate lawyer, just like his dad, grandfather, and great-grandfather. He's been called that since he was three."

"What's your nickname?"

"Ellie."

Naomi shot her a *don't mess with me* glare. "If you don't tell me right now, I'll start asking every relative and family friend." Her glance bounced over all the possibilities in the room.

Eileen feigned betrayal. "You wouldn't dare."

Naomi flipped around, but Eileen corralled her with her good arm.

"Before I tell you, I want to make it crystal clear. Paybacks are hell."

Naomi crossed her arms. "You don't scare me."

"You've been warned." She let out a puff of air, but still didn't share.

Naomi tried to get Phil's attention.

Eileen lowered Naomi's hand. "Fine. Smelly Ellie."

Naomi attempted to smother her laughter with one hand

over her mouth, but it couldn't be contained, spilling through her fingers.

Eileen felt heat creeping up her neck. "No one calls me that."

"Hey, Smelly Ellie!" Phil beckoned her with a finger.

Before leaving Naomi's side, Eileen clarified, "No one who ends up in my bed."

Eileen joined Julia and Phil, while Naomi's mom returned to her daughter's side. Soon Phil drifted away to chat with James who'd somehow managed to shake the old ladies and Naomi and her mother roamed far enough away from the sisters to take in the view of the Christmas lights outside the window.

Eileen stared menacingly at her sister.

"What?" Julia hid behind her Champagne flute.

"Why didn't you tell me Naomi is Mrs. Weaver's daughter?"

"Oh, that." Julia sipped her drink, clearly stalling for time. "It… slipped my mind."

"Bullshit."

"Didn't you know Naomi's last name?"

"I may have, but I certainly didn't make the connection. It's been years since I gave a second thought to Sophia Weaver."

Julia sighed. "Does it really matter? You keep telling everyone you're leaving in a month anyway. What's a harmless fling?"

"With Mrs. Weaver's daughter."

"Why is that a big deal?"

How could Eileen confess to Julia that when Eileen was in high school she'd had a major crush on Sophia Weaver?

Julia leaned into her sister. "Have you slept with her yet?"

Eileen stiffened, momentarily thinking Julia had asked if she'd slept with Mrs. Weaver. Of course, Julia was talking about Naomi.

"Oh my. You have!" Julia clamped a hand on Eileen's shoulder. "My big sister still has game."

"You aren't off the hook, Jules. What's Mom going to say?"

Julia flinched. "Do you have to tell her?"

"We came to the party together."

"Which isn't all that unusual for old family friends. And you can't drive, so there's that excuse. Naomi was just giving you a ride and you're paying her back by riding her."

Eileen bit her lip, choosing to ignore Julia's last comment. "How do I explain Naomi offering to give me a ride in the first place?"

"How were you going to explain before you found out about Naomi?"

"I wasn't, but now it seems like I may have to. To cover my tracks."

Julia waved a dismissive hand. "You're forgetting Mom has her heart set on you getting back together with Melissa, who hails from the only other wealthy family in Derby. I doubt she'll ever make the connection that you're boffing Naomi who's half your age."

Eileen gestured for Julia to shut her trap. "Bring it down twenty decibels, please."

James approached and gave Eileen a hug. "How have you been? I haven't seen you since your first day back when you resembled a creature from the *Night of the Living Dead*."

Julia drilled an elbow into his gut.

"What was that for?" He rubbed his protruding stomach. "I just meant she was exhausted from flying."

"Eileen, dear. We haven't had a chance to talk." Her mom hooked her arm through Eileen's right one, using a bit of force to get the stiff arm to relent. "Now, who were you going to introduce me to when... I can't remember what distracted me? It's been one thing after another. Moments ago, the bar staff had an emergency."

"The mayor had just arrived," Eileen said and grit her teeth.

Naomi, as if in tune with Eileen's annoyance, steered her mother over to Trudy and her daughters.

Her mom separated herself from Eileen. "Is this Naomi?" she asked. "Why, I haven't seen you since you were yea high." She held her hand to hip height.

"Mrs. Callahan." Naomi dipped her head.

"It hasn't been that long, Trudy, since you've seen her. You came to Naomi's graduation party for high school and college." Sophia turned to Naomi. "You're still my baby, though, even if you're all grown up."

Naomi rested her head on her mom's shoulder.

Eileen, struck by the image, gazed at her own mom, not feeling a modicum of a connection.

Her mom glanced at Eileen's bad arm and then spoke to Naomi's mom. "Do you remember when Eileen fell off her horse when she was six or seven and broke her arm? She was determined to get back on that horse the very next day. Nothing ever stopped my Eileen. I wanted her to be a surgeon. Go on darling, show them your steady hands."

Right then, Maggie whispered into her mom's ear.

"Would you excuse me? I need to attend to something in the kitchen." Her mom and Maggie walked away briskly.

Julia shook her head, placing a comforting hand on Eileen's shoulder. In her sisterly way, she seemed to understand Eileen needed some space, and Julia whisked Sophia away on the pretense of showing her the Christmas tree in the library.

Naomi, with a supportive smile, asked, "Why don't you show me your bedroom?"

Upstairs, in her childhood room, Eileen leaned against the window sill. "It's changed drastically since I lived here."

Naomi's eyes swept over the austere room. A threadbare oriental rug was situated in the center. A wrought iron bed frame with a saggy mattress sat against the wall, a slate embossed quilt covering it. "It's surprising, really. Given the grandeur downstairs."

"Guests are never allowed upstairs."

"Are we breaking the rules?" Naomi's crooked smile enchanted Eileen.

"Most assuredly."

Naomi approached Eileen, threading her arms around Eileen's neck. "How come Phil doesn't know about your stroke?"

Eileen turned her head to the open door. "Did you hear that? I think it's time to sit down for dinner."

"Are you sure it is? Or you're avoiding the subject?"

"I would never." Eileen motioned they should go back downstairs.

CHAPTER EIGHTEEN

As they sat at the dinner table, Naomi was still digesting that Eileen was a Callahan. And that her own mother was here, at this very party, sitting right across from her and Eileen.

"It's so unlike my mother to not have assigned seats at a dinner like this," Eileen said nervously. "I wonder what caused this softening effect on her controlling ways?"

"Maybe she's just happy you're in town," Naomi's mother said. "Personally, I wouldn't know what to do with myself if Naomi left."

Naomi cringed. Not only because of her mother's overt adoration, but even more so because she didn't really know what to do about this situation.

Should she inform her mother that she and Eileen were seeing each other? If she'd known they were going to run into her here, Naomi wouldn't have hesitated for a second to tell her mom beforehand. Because now, surely, her mother was putting two and two together quickly—Naomi could practically read it on her face. Or maybe she was just being paranoid.

"I can certainly understand that," Eileen said.

Goodness. Was Eileen going to continue to give away hints like that as well? Naomi needed to get her mother away from the dining table as soon as possible. But they'd only just sat down. The dining room was buzzing with hushed voices and the scraping of chairs as the last couple of people found a seat.

"Do you remember babysitting Joey?" her mother asked Eileen, her eyes growing dark at the mention of his name.

"Yes." Eileen paused for a moment. "I think I do, actually."

"Joey dying so young really made Naomi our miracle baby." Her mother straightened her spine. "I'm not sure I would have coped if Naomi hadn't come along." She gave Naomi a warm look.

Naomi wanted to respond, but this whole conversation was making her unease grow a mile a minute. Finding out that Eileen had babysat her brother wasn't exactly helping. How was she going to break the news to her mother now? If she couldn't get her mother away from the table any time soon, Naomi could only resort to changing the topic of conversation.

"Did you know Eileen has won a Pulitzer, Mom?" she asked.

"Oh, I thought you were a photographer." She looked at Eileen.

"I am," Eileen confirmed.

"The prize isn't just for writers," Naomi said.

Her mother scrunched her lips together before saying, "Who would have thought."

"Photographers," Naomi muttered under her breath. Under the table, she felt a hand on her knee. Eileen must really be making an effort—and wanting Naomi on her best behavior—because she was sitting to Naomi's left and moving her right hand must be extremely difficult for her. Naomi knew that much.

Naomi looked away from the table for an instant, straight into Trudy Callahan's face. Surely Trudy was smart enough to put two and two together as well. Naomi needed to speak to her mother before anyone else said anything about what they suspected about her and Eileen. She didn't want her mom to find out that way.

She pushed her chair back. "Mom, can I talk to you in private for a minute?"

"Now?" Her mom eyed her quizzically. "The starters are about to be served."

"It'll only take a minute," Naomi insisted, and stood up. She avoided Eileen's gaze, afraid Eileen would try to interfere with Naomi's desire to confess. But it was Eileen who had brought her here, so she'd need to find a way to understand. She might not be close to her own mother, but Naomi was to hers, and she couldn't bear this secrecy any longer.

"Okay, darling." Her mother followed Naomi into the hallway. "What's going on?" she asked.

"Aren't you wondering how I ended up at the Callahan pre-Christmas party?"

"You and Eileen are friends," her mother said. "That much is obvious."

Naomi examined her mother's face, trying to figure out if she was playing dumb—being friends with the Callahans probably meant being very good at keeping the peace at all times.

"We're more than friends, Mom." There, Naomi had said it. She wished she could have broached the subject in a more delicate manner, and in the warmth of her mom's house instead of this cold corridor in the Callahan mansion, but the circumstances had given her no choice.

"W-what do you mean, darling? Eileen used to babysit your brother. She's old enough to be..." She paused and shook her head. "Surely it's not very serious." She took a deep breath. "I'm sorry, Naomi. I'm a bit shocked. I just never thought that you and Eileen were a possibility."

In her state of shock, her mother had, perhaps, found the

exact word for what Naomi and Eileen were. A *possibility*. Not one with many options, but a possibility nonetheless.

"I realize it must come as a bit of a shock. Especially having to find out here." Naomi glanced around the hallway. From the dining room she could hear the clatter of silverware. Dinner was being served. Naomi wasn't very hungry.

"Trudy doesn't know yet, I assume?" Her mother inched a little closer.

Naomi shook her head. "Nobody knows. Eileen didn't know I was your daughter and I certainly didn't know she was a Callahan."

"Oh, darling." Her mother wrapped an arm around her shoulder. She cleared her throat. "Are you, um, in love with her?"

Naomi huffed out a breath. "I don't know. How could I even be in love with someone who's only here for the holidays?"

Her mother held her a little closer. "The other day at lunch. That's what I was seeing. You'd met someone." Naomi felt her nod. "My motherly intuition is still very much in working order."

"At least she's not Jane," Naomi offered.

Her mother came to stand in front of her, and put both her hands on Naomi's shoulders. "Darling, whatever this is, or whatever it turns out to be, just enjoy it. I'm not going to be the one to judge you. I know that life is much too precious for that." She leaned in and kissed Naomi on the forehead. "Shall we go back in there?"

Naomi nodded and followed her mother back inside. Now she needed to find a way to discreetly let Eileen know that she'd told her mother. So much for this being just a fling, then. Maybe it was easy for Eileen to keep something like this from her family—they barely played a part in her life—but for Naomi, things were very different.

"Good thing the starter's a cold dish," Eileen said. "I was about to send out a search party for the two of you."

Naomi shot Eileen a sheepish grin. Before she could say anything, an immaculately dressed waiter asked if she wanted white wine.

"I'm driving," Naomi said, and held her hand above her empty wineglass.

Eileen leaned over and, with her left hand, scooted Naomi's hand away. "I'll call us a taxi. You look like you could do with another drink." Her soft gaze landed on Naomi's.

"Okay." Naomi allowed her wineglass to be filled.

When she looked across the table at her mother, she saw her glancing intently at Eileen's right arm.

"If I may be so indiscreet to ask, Eileen," she said. "What happened to your arm?"

"Oh, just a silly accident with some annoying long-term consequences," Eileen said quickly. She'd obviously come to this party with some rehearsed lines. Naomi wasn't going to contradict her in front of her mother, but she made a mental note to ask Eileen why it was so hard for her to tell the truth about her stroke. It wasn't something she'd brought on herself. It was something she'd suffered—and maybe that was the problem.

"Eileen has physical therapy at the hospital," Naomi said. "That's where we met."

Her mother nodded. "That looks quite serious to me. You'd best take good care of yourself."

"I will, Mrs. Weaver. I promise."

To Naomi's ears, it had sounded as though her mother had asked Eileen to take good care of her daughter—as in not breaking her precious little heart.

149

After dinner, Naomi dragged Eileen up to her old bedroom again.

"I hadn't expected a Callahan dinner to have such an effect on you," Eileen joked, although Naomi could sense some tension in her tone.

As soon as Eileen closed the bedroom door behind them, Naomi said, "I had to tell my mom. I couldn't possibly sit across from her for an entire evening, with you next to me, without her knowing. That's not how things go in my family."

Eileen nodded as though she had already sussed that out. "What did she say?"

"She was a bit shocked, as you can imagine. I mean, this entire evening has been one big shock for all of us."

"I know." Eileen gathered her in her arms. "I should have given you my full name. I just didn't think it was very important."

"It's been a bit of a whirlwind thing between us." Naomi rested her head on Eileen's good shoulder.

"Hey, I'm happy you can talk to your mom about this. She obviously loves you very much." Eileen held Naomi closer.

"She regrouped quite quickly. She said life's too precious to judge me."

"How about we spend Christmas with your family," Eileen said, her words flowing above Naomi's head. "They sound so much nicer than mine."

Naomi pushed herself away from Eileen's chest, eager to see her face. "Your mother gave me quite the look earlier. I think she knows you're keeping secrets."

"My relationship with my mom is built on keeping secrets. That and crushing guilt and disappointment, of course." Eileen gave a weak smile.

"I take it you won't be telling her any time soon that you're dating her friend's daughter then," Naomi said.

"We'll see." Eileen expelled a heavy sigh. "We'd best get back before more people start missing us—and start putting the pieces of the puzzle together. We don't want this to turn into our big coming out party."

Coming out as what? Naomi thought, and considered her mother's question from before.

Was she in love with Eileen? As she stood there looking at her, it sure felt like she was.

CHAPTER NINETEEN

Back downstairs, Eileen did her best to blend in with all the guests spilling out of the dining room into the common area. Naomi tripped on the edge of an oriental rug, causing her to stumble.

Eileen steadied her, smiling. "Maybe I shouldn't have encouraged you to have more wine."

"It was my heel," Naomi defended, a sheepish grin on her flushed face.

"Uh huh. Let's say a combo of the two. We should step outside for some fresh air." Eileen scanned the groupings of people in the room. "It's a bit stuffy and not solely because a third of the attendees are wearing bow ties."

"That sounds lovely. I'll get our jackets."

Julia sidled up to Eileen. "I see Naomi is heading to the coat room. Are you two leaving me so early to fend for myself?"

"Don't fret, sister dear. We're just going for a stroll by the lake."

"Is that code for—"

"Jules the Mule who Drools! It's like my return has brought

out the juvenile teenage boy in you. Not everything is about…
that." Eileen whispered the last word.

"Yes, it is and that's a yes, Smelly Ellie."

Eileen gnashed her teeth at her sister, not wasting a breath
arguing with Julia who clearly had imbibed enough wine to
loosen her tongue to Code Red level.

Naomi, with her coat draped over her shoulders, placed
Eileen's in the same fashion.

"You two have a *lovely* walk," Julia said, her emphasis
causing a muscle in Eileen's jaw to tense.

Naomi responded, "Would you like to join us?"

Julia's brazen smile spurred Eileen to say, "James is beckoning you, Jules." She shooed her away with a flick of her
fingers.

Leading the way out the front door, Eileen quickened her
pace on the off-chance Julia would take Naomi up on her offer.
An overly inebriated Julia was proving to be a loose cannon and
the evening had already dealt Eileen enough shock to process.

Outside, Eileen steered them to the dirt path along the side
of the house, leading to the water's edge.

"Will you be okay in your heels?" Eileen asked.

"Yes, as long as we don't go too far." Naomi wrapped her
black wool coat tighter around her torso.

They walked shoulder to shoulder, not speaking. Faint
moonlight shimmered on the dark surface of the lake, and the
water lapped the shoreline.

Naomi bumped Eileen's left side. "Earlier, when I pulled up
in my car, what were you really laughing about?"

"This is the downside of dating a woman so much younger
than me. Your ability to remember tiny details such as that."

"This is the downside of dating a woman who attempts to
change the subject every chance she gets." Naomi pecked her
cheek, threading her arm through Eileen's, holding on tight.

Eileen glanced at her profile. "You've noticed, eh."

"Hard not to. Remember, I'm young enough to remember everything."

"What's that like? I can't remember."

Naomi laughed. "Oh, you're good."

Eileen nuzzled her nose into the warmth behind Naomi's earlobe. "I hope so, even with…" She didn't feel the necessity to mention her arm.

Naomi rested her head on Eileen's shoulder. "Never worry about that, *Ellie*."

Eileen smiled over the use of her nickname. "Why's that? Because I'm okay or you're too kind to hold my restrictions against me?"

Naomi stopped in her tracks and stood right in front of Eileen. "First, you're way better than okay. Second, your arms, both of them, are part of you. Newsflash: I like all of you, Eileen Makenna Callahan." She shook her head. "It's still hard for me to wrap my head around the fact that you're a Callahan. Your family has lorded over Derby for generations." Naomi placed one hand on each of Eileen's shoulders. "I feel foolish, really, not making the connection between Eileen Makenna and Eileen Callahan. There aren't too many Eileens from these parts."

"It isn't the most popular of names, no. I've always been the only Eileen in school and at the office. So many girls my age were named Amy or Jenny."

"I'm trying to think of a famous Eileen—besides you, obviously."

Eileen laughed. "I'm not that famous. Even your mom didn't know I'd won a Pulitzer. And, the fact you can't think of the famous Eileen I'm thinking of only highlights our age difference."

Naomi scrunched her brow. "Who?"

"Eileen Brennan. She was an actress. Ever see *The Last Picture Show?*"

Naomi shook her head, chewing her bottom lip, her eyes large and alluring in the moonlight.

Eileen moved her head closer to Naomi's. "Had a feeling. What about *Private Benjamin?*"

"That sounds familiar. Who else is in that?"

"Goldie Hawn."

"I loved her in *The First Wives Club*. That's an oldie, but goodie."

Eileen burst into laughter. "An oldie. Oh, wow!" She mulled this over. "You were probably a wee one when that came out."

Naomi brushed her lips against Eileen's. "Stop that. It doesn't matter."

Eileen's breath hitched. "What does matter?"

"What you were laughing about earlier this evening? Clearly."

"I didn't distract you enough, huh." Eileen wore an *aw-shucks* expression.

"While I applaud your efforts, no, nothing gets past me."

Eileen jerked her head to the moon overhead.

Naomi studied the night sky. "I'm going to need more."

"The moon. I was laughing at the moon. Well, not at it." Eileen wrapped her arm around Naomi's waist, pulling her closer, eliminating the space between them. "I was struck by it. How it seemed romantic, which isn't how I usually view the moon or most things, really. I've always been a bit serious. I think part of it comes from being the eldest child. And the expectations placed on me being a Callahan." She sucked her lips into her mouth, not wanting to broach the part of her life that haunted her—the one her mom never let Eileen forget. "My job—it can be difficult to stay upbeat and not dwell on the worst sides of humanity." She looked at the moon. "Before you picked me up, for the first time in years, when I stared at it, I didn't associate it with a negative memory, but with romance. I naturally attributed this change to you. Being around someone so young. Full of life. It's... it's almost as if the universe knew you were the one thing I needed most in my life right now. To confront... the thing I can't even tell my relatives about. Not even Phil. We basically grew up together and he'd do anything for me, but the thought of him knowing, or anyone—it kills me." Eileen rested her forehead against Naomi's.

Naomi's lips landed on Eileen's. The forcefulness of the kiss took Eileen momentarily by surprise, before Eileen met her passion and kicked it up several notches.

"That was... so very honest." Naomi's hand cradled the back of Eileen's head. "Truth be told, I'm completely taken aback by your words."

"In a good or bad way?" Eileen peered into Naomi's dark eyes, searching for a sign, even the smallest, that excited and terrified Eileen.

"I never would have guessed this side of you."

Confused, Eileen asked. "Which side is that?"

"Your vulnerable side."

Eileen playfully groaned. "Julia told me chicks dig it when a woman shows that side."

"Are you following her advice?" Naomi's voice was soft.

Eileen slowly turned her head to the left and then right. "It's you. I want you to know me. And it scares the crap out of me."

"Because?"

"Because I don't know if I want you to know things about me as a way of pushing you away or to be closer to you."

"Knowing you, perhaps it's both. But you aren't the only stubborn person involved." Her pupils nearly tripled in size. "You can try pushing me away, but I know right now, I want to be with you." Naomi pulled Eileen against her. "I need to be close to you. Inside you."

Eileen took Naomi's hand. "Follow me."

On the far side of the house, about twenty yards away, was a small outbuilding. "My grandfather built this so he could have privacy from his wife and seven children. Unfortunately, my dad keeps it locked, but on this side, we're out of sight from all prying eyes."

"Do you think he and your grandm—"

Eileen placed a finger over Naomi's lips. "Please, it's weird enough with everyone inside." She jerked a thumb over her shoulder.

"We don't have to—"

Eileen pressed her mouth to Naomi's, kissing her hard.

Naomi clutched each side of Eileen's face, pulling her more into the moment, their tongues hungry for each other.

The passion between the two rapidly increased, Naomi's hands reaching under Eileen's clothing, her fingers digging into the flesh.

Eileen, with one swift movement of her shoulder, jerked her coat off, no longer needing protection from the chill in the air.

Naomi's hand was on Eileen's belt.

"Here, let me help," Eileen placed her left hand onto Naomi's.

"I've got it. You don't have to hide anything from me. Not ever."

"I'm not useless, either."

"Never said you were and I've never thought that." Naomi pinned Eileen with a sensual look. "Sometimes it's okay to let me take the wheel, so to speak." Naomi unzipped Eileen's dress slacks before slipping her hand into Eileen's panties.

Eileen let out a gasp when Naomi slipped a finger inside.

"I love how wet I make you," Naomi whispered into Eileen's ear.

"Oh, I'm sure you love it—"

Naomi plunged in deeper, causing Eileen to toss her head

back against the siding of the building, snapping her eyes shut. Another finger had been added inside her. A whip of cold alerted Eileen her slacks and panties had been shoved down around her ankles. "What are you...?"

Naomi was on her knees, using their coats as a cushion of sorts, her tongue teasing Eileen's clit, stifling her question.

The intensity of Naomi's fingers and tongue was matched only by Eileen's ragged breathing.

"Oh, Jesus," Eileen said, when Naomi pushed in deep, thrusting as she circled Eileen's clit with her tongue. "Je-sus!"

Naomi didn't let up.

Eileen looked down at the gorgeous woman on her knees, fucking her. She hadn't been the type for sex out in the open, thinking it dirty, somehow. But seeing Naomi here, feeling the incredible sensation of the orgasm bubbling inside, the moon overhead, the crisp winter air, and the smell of wood fireplaces —nothing about this was dirty. It was beautiful, under the stars, just the two of them in the moment. She'd never experienced anything like this with anyone.

And then it hit her.

Eileen's body spasmed and she reached for the back of Naomi's head. "Oh, God, don't stop," she whispered, pinching her eyes shut.

Naomi didn't.

The spasms intensified, Naomi going in as deep as she could, holding it there until Eileen was spent.

When Eileen's legs faltered some, Naomi rose, propping up Eileen as the final gasp of orgasm worked its way through her body.

"That was amazing," Eileen breathed heavily.

Naomi circled her arms around Eileen's neck. "It was. Are you cold?"

Eileen shook her head. "Not yet. Don't move."

A rustling sound around the corner ruined the moment and

Naomi hastily yanked up Eileen's panties and slacks. When Eileen was decent, they stared into each other's eyes, silently laughing.

There was a click of a lighter.

The two of them skirted the corner of the building looking as if they were simply returning from a casual stroll.

"Smelly Ellie, what are you doing out here?" Phil puffed on a pipe, releasing a plume of smoke.

"Cooling off," Eileen said with honesty.

Naomi chomped down on her bottom lip.

"It was getting toasty inside." Phil tugged on one side of his tartan bow tie, undoing it.

"Are you coming back in before you leave?" Eileen asked Phil.

"In a bit." He held his pipe aloft. "I'll be sure to say goodbye before I head out. Who knows when I'll see you again."

"Christmas, I'm assuming. But, please do say goodbye."

Eileen and Naomi, once again walking shoulder to shoulder, headed back to the house, taking the longer route around back, giving them more privacy.

CHAPTER TWENTY

Naomi glanced at Eileen from the corner of her eye. To call today intense would be an understatement, and it was all down to the woman who was holding her hand. It was strange enough that she was walking underneath the moon-light on the Callahan estate, but what she'd just done to Eileen behind that outbuilding took the prize. Some of the tension really needed to be relieved. Naomi squeezed Eileen's hand, who turned to smile at her.

"Just so you know, what we just did is not something I've ever done before."

"Hm," Eileen hummed. "Not according to my recollection." She squeezed Naomi's hand back.

"You know what I mean."

"And here I was thinking you went down on women in the great outdoors all the time," Eileen joked.

"I wouldn't exactly call your parents' back yard the great outdoors." Naomi pressed herself a little closer to Eileen. It was cold and the heat they'd generated between them earlier was starting to wear off.

Eileen chuckled and stopped in her tracks. She turned

around. "If you stand with your back to the house, and pretend it's not there, this view is pretty impressive."

"Well, I guess this is your inheritance we're talking about," Naomi said.

"It's really hard to get a serious word out of you, isn't it?"

Naomi curved her arm around Eileen's waist and nestled herself quickly in Eileen's embrace.

"I just really prefer to look on the bright side of life. But I'm not deflecting, if that's what you're thinking. And yes, it is beautiful here. It was a privilege to, you know, do what I did just then, out here."

"You're so full of life," Eileen said. "One of the reasons I can't stay away from you. It's almost contagious."

"Almost?" Naomi asked, but Eileen didn't say anything. Silence grew between them and they stared ahead, Naomi's gaze fixed on the lake.

"I had completely forgotten that I used to babysit your brother," Eileen said. "It must have been hard that you never knew him, yet his death must have impacted your life a great deal."

Naomi shrugged. "I guess." She inhaled deeply. "For as long as I can remember my mom has been calling me her miracle baby."

"That's a lot to live up to."

"It comes pretty naturally to me to always want to paint a smile on Mom's face, although it isn't always easy to do. Losing a child is not something she will ever get over, I realized that pretty quickly, but she has always been a great mother to me."

"Is that why you volunteer at the hospital on top of working there full-time?" Eileen asked.

Naomi nodded, although they were both staring ahead. "If I can give one kid a single spark of joy, it's worth spending my time with them."

"There aren't many people like you, you know. With such

zest for life," Eileen said. "I think I'm becoming addicted to being around your infectious energy."

A smile grew on Naomi's lips. "My infectious energy will always be here for you."

"Have you never thought about leaving Derby? Spreading some of your joy beyond this town's borders?"

Naomi shook her head. "No. I know in my heart that my place is here. I'm happy here."

"Because of your family? Your mother was pretty clear about how she'd feel if you left town."

"My family is a big part of that, but I've never believed in running away. This is my home. I have roots here. And now I even have an in with the Callahan clan." She pivoted to face Eileen.

"I've been all over the world, but I've never met anyone like you." Eileen smiled. "I had to come home to find you."

"Another perfect example of the great things Derby has to offer." Naomi scanned Eileen's face. "I remember you saying you didn't like the Mona Lisa because of her smile, and you may not like hearing this, but you have a real... Mona Lisa smile. I see happiness at first, but then it morphs into... indifference."

"Indifference?" Eileen said. "No way."

"What looks like indifference, but is actually a whole lot of life. And pain. And fear even."

Eileen laughed. "Is this how you sweet-talk all the ladies after having sex with them?"

"I don't have a set-in-stone formula." Naomi kept her gaze on Eileen. "And you accuse me of deflecting, while you are a true champion at it."

Eileen rubbed her hands together. "It's getting cold out here, don't you think? Shall we head back inside?"

"Sure." Naomi tipped forward and kissed Eileen on the lips. She'd been working toward a question—a burning question that hummed in the back of her mind at all times when she was with Eileen—but the right time to ask it never seemed to present itself. Maybe because the right time for it hadn't come yet.

As they headed back toward the house there was no doubt in Naomi's mind that she wanted Eileen to stay much longer than she had planned—and that she'd need to ask that particular question soon. Time, after all, was quickly running out on them.

"Your place or mine?" Eileen asked after they'd gotten into the taxi.

Naomi had offered to drive her own car because spending all that time outside had sobered her up considerably, but neither Eileen nor her mom would hear of it.

"Mine?" Naomi offered. "No offense, but your place doesn't really brim with Christmas spirit."

Eileen gave the taxi driver the address.

"I can only imagine your offense at my admission that I wasn't even going to put up a tree," Eileen said. She put her hand on Naomi's knee. "My place is only a short-term rental. Plus, it would be kind of hard to decorate with one arm."

"Well, erm, I happen to know someone who has a real knack for decorating Christmas trees." She covered Eileen's hand with hers.

"Let me guess…" Eileen pretended to think long and hard. "A fellow volunteer at the hospital?" She gave Naomi a big smirk.

"Honestly, it would be my pleasure to get you a tree," Naomi said.

"Why go through the hassle if I can just go over to yours

and enjoy your tree? Your apartment is a million times cozier than mine. I love spending time there."

Naomi only allowed herself to enjoy the flutter in her belly for a brief instant. She had an opening to inquire about Eileen's plans. "Until when have you rented your apartment?" she asked, unable to hide the nerves in her voice.

"Early January," Eileen said. "My boss is expecting me back in London after the new year."

"Will you be able to work then?"

"I fulfilled my assignment for *The Derby Gazette* to everyone's satisfaction, I believe," Eileen said.

"You did have assistance with that." Naomi didn't want to press the matter further. She was hoping Eileen would reach the real topic of conversation Naomi wanted to broach, on her own. Surely, the thought must have crossed her mind. How could it not have?

A silence fell in the cab. Naomi looked out of the window, at the empty streets of her town. Maybe what Eileen had asked her earlier, when they'd stood gazing over the lake, had been her way of instigating this very conversation. What if she'd really wanted to ask if Naomi would leave Derby for her?

"Hey." Eileen turned over her hand on Naomi's knee and laced their fingers together. "Please don't think that meeting you hasn't made me think about some things. It really has. I'm just not ready to discuss them yet. I think neither one of us is prepared to lay our cards on the table."

The car turned into Naomi's street, pre-empting her from saying something snarky about Eileen loving and leaving her. They paid for the taxi and hurried inside Naomi's building.

Once inside Naomi's apartment, Eileen immediately pulled her close. "I may take you up on your offer of getting me a tree. But first, I'll need to see yours." She glanced over Naomi's shoulder. "Where are you going to put it?"

"I'll have to shuffle some things around as this is nothing

like the Callahan mansion." If they weren't going to have a serious talk about their future—and now that Naomi put it in those terms, it did sound a bit silly—she might as well get swept up in the Christmas spirit.

"I'll be moving that plant into my bedroom so I have room for a tree."

"When were you planning on putting it up?"

"I would have done it this weekend, but I was a bit busy, not to mention completely and utterly distracted by some green-eyed beauty."

Eileen batted her lashes. "I plead guilty and… I'd very much like to distract you again." She kissed Naomi just underneath the earlobe.

At least Naomi wouldn't be spending Christmas without a plus-one. She'd been preparing for it, and had signed up for some extra volunteering shifts at the hospital—it was always hard to find the volunteers needed when Christmas came around.

This year, she and Eileen could volunteer *and* celebrate together. She remembered Jane's antics last year, when she'd accused Naomi of spending more time at the hospital than with her girlfriend. Somehow, she didn't think Eileen would even dream of saying something like that. They might not have talked about certain things yet, but Eileen already knew what was most important in Naomi's life.

"I'm losing focus already," Naomi whispered in Eileen's ear, as she succumbed to the onslaught of kisses Eileen peppered her with.

CHAPTER TWENTY-ONE

"It's not fair that I have to rush off this morning." Naomi wrapped her arms around Eileen's neck.

"Picking up an extra shift on a Sunday. That's dedication there. Are you sure you don't want me to call you a cab?" Eileen glanced at Naomi's running pants, red Nike long sleeve top, gloves, and headband. "I was the one who encouraged you to have wine during dinner."

"It'll do me some good to run. I'm still in training for the Boston marathon. Although, someone has been distracting me lately."

"Distractions can be dangerous," Eileen teased.

"Or wicked fun. If things aren't too crazy at work, I'll stop by for lunch. That is, if you'll be home."

"It happens I don't have anything planned, so please do stop by if you can." Eileen smiled.

"I'd better leave now or I won't leave at all." She kissed Eileen on the lips before heading toward the door.

"Have a good day." Eileen almost added sweetheart, much to her shock.

Eileen waited ten minutes before leaving Naomi's apartment to walk home, not wanting to risk calling for a cab. They'd already rolled the dice the previous night, but a handful of the other party attendees resorted to sharing rides or cabs to get home safely. Surely, they'd outwitted Derby's gossips. And if they hadn't, what did it matter? Naomi's mom knew. As did Julia. Eileen's dad wouldn't give a shit.

Trudy Callahan was the issue. At forty-nine, Eileen just couldn't give two hoots about gaining her mom's acceptance. No siree. She was not going to let her mom get to her. Not anymore.

Along the way, several homes had fires blazing, the smell of burning wood permeating the crisp December air. Eileen sucked in a deep breath, the cold awakening all of her senses. Even her arm didn't feel quite as heavy this morning. She joggled the shoulder up and down to further loosen the contracted muscles.

Eileen sensed she was grinning like a fool, but who could blame her. The evening could have been disastrous, after she'd learned that the woman she was sleeping with was the youngest sibling of Joey Weaver, a boy Eileen had babysat so many years ago. That fact shone a particular light on the age difference between them—and had brought back to Eileen's mind her secret crush on Mrs. Weaver at the time. But that was so many years ago. What did it matter now? The only thing that did was Eileen waking in Naomi's arms after a fantastic night of making love.

Eileen should be exhausted, but a surge of positive energy radiated within her. She truly enjoyed Naomi's zest, which was proving impossible to stay away from. Nothing was going to wreck Eileen's mood right then and there. She was feeling so alive. Once again, Eileen gulped in a mouthful of the fresh air, looking up, appraising the thickening clouds. Would they bring rain or snow? She hoped for snow. Much more Christmassy.

Dear God, was she becoming that woman? The type who

looked forward to the holidays? This was all Naomi's doing. Eileen's smile broadened and she then started to hum "Jingle Bells."

Eileen, following Mack's advice, taped the peanut butter jar to her right hand, with a straw on it so she could see how much improvement she was making since starting physical therapy a few weeks ago. The first time she had done this on her own, the straw had barely budged from the center.

This morning, sitting at the table in her kitchen, she rolled the jar back and forth, the straw sailing to one side and then the next, nearly touching the tabletop.

There was a knock on the front door. Julia always waltzed right in, so it couldn't be her. Naomi had mentioned she may pop by for lunch, but maybe she had decided to come earlier for a cup of coffee.

In her rush to get to the door, Eileen neglected to remove the jar. She swung the door wide open, grinning ear-to-ear.

Her grin fell when her mom came into view.

"Oh, hello," Eileen said, trying her best not to sound too disappointed, but knowing she had failed miserably.

"Hello, darling." Her mom put her arms out for a hug and Eileen started to reciprocate, but the jar taped to her hand stopped Eileen cold.

Eileen shook her arm with the assistance of her left hand, but the duct tape didn't budge.

"Why on earth do you have… that taped to your hand?"

"Uh…" Eileen didn't want to confess to her mom she'd been doing exercises so she could eventually grasp something with her right hand.

"And the straw. That's just bizarre." Her mom's puckered lips were enough proof as to why Eileen didn't share anything personal with her mom. "Is… s-she here? Is that why you have this… contraption on your hand… for that?"

There was so much to unpack from her mom's ramblings, Eileen struggled to zero in on what part to address first, resulting with Eileen remaining silent.

"Is she?" Her mom repeated.

"Is she what?" Eileen asked.

"Here?"

"Is who here?" Eileen's face morphed into a mask of confusion.

"You know who I mean." Her mom's eyes tapered nearly shut.

"Julia?" Eileen mentally kicked herself for trying to evade what was rapidly becoming crystal clear. Trudy knew all about Naomi and despite Eileen's earlier protestations that she didn't care if her mom found out, coming face to face with it now was proving much more difficult. Eileen hated this power her mom had over her.

All the color in her mom's face slipped off like water circling down a drain. "Don't be disgusting." She straightened. "Is Naomi Weaver here?"

On guard now, Eileen steadied her nerve before seeking another attempt at deflecting. "Why would Naomi be here? In my apartment?"

"Don't treat me like a fool. Really, you'd think you'd have the decency to remove that"—she pointed to the jar on Eileen's hand—"before answering the door. Is she tucked away in your bedroom? Does she also have one…?" Her mom pointed to Eileen's right hand.

A troubling thought entered Eileen's mind. Was her mom insinuating that Naomi and Eileen had been in bed when she arrived and that somehow, the peanut butter and straw were part of their bedroom activities? How did her mom factor in either? Okay, the peanut butter could be part of food play, but really, it would be time consuming and extremely messy. And the straw? Was that meant to be some type of breathing apparatus while... Eileen's mind couldn't go any further into the rabbit hole without irreparable harm.

"She's not here. No one is here. This...".—Eileen slowly raised her hand—"is one of my physical therapy exercises to regain the use of my hand." She hadn't wanted her mom to know the extent of the damage done by the stroke, but the thought of her mom thinking she was some type of peanut butter and straw freak in bed—that was simply too much for Eileen to leave alone. How was it possible in today's world that some still associated lesbian sex with kinky sex? And her own mom of all people? Who had been determined for Eileen to get back together with Melissa even though Eileen and Melissa had barely communicated for well over twenty years.

Her mom had clearly lost her marbles. There was no other explanation for any of this.

The unwelcome woman glanced around Eileen's apartment, her expression souring even more. "This is convenient."

It was an odd word to use for someone's living space. "Would you like to sit?"

Eileen motioned with her left hand to the charcoal sectional.

Instead of taking a seat, her mom pressed on. "I know about you and Naomi."

"What are you talking about?"

"Please. Showing up at the party together—"

"She gave me a lift since I can't drive." Eileen pointed to her hand with the goddamn jar still taped to it, vividly recalling a silly Father's Day card she'd once sent her dad. The image on the card implied that if her dad had been on the Titanic, it wouldn't have sunk because her father, who attempted to fix everything with duct tape, would have had an endless supply, thus reversing maritime history.

Her mom clutched her purse, slung over her shoulder and tucked against her breast. "Don't bother. I have it on good authority you're more than just casual acquaintances."

"Ah, yes, the Derby grapevine. They also think the Vaughan's dog is possessed by demons."

"I saw you two!"

Eileen backpedaled, but quickly said, "At your house. Yes, I was there with Naomi as a friend." Eileen wondered if Julia or Sophia had clued her mom in about her relationship with Naomi. Her instinct was to admit nothing unless absolutely necessary. Her mom wasn't accepting of Eileen as it was, and given the age difference, Eileen would rather not hear what her mom had to say about that.

"Much more than friends. I spied you two outside. The two of you canoodling out in the open."

Had her mom seen Naomi on her knees? Eileen found herself unable to utter a word at the thought.

No, not possible.

Oh, for all that was holy...

"The two of you sneaking in the back of the house... H-holding hands," she spat out.

A whoosh of relief flooded Eileen's system.

"You need to end things now with Naomi."

Eileen furrowed her brow. "And who gives you the authority to tell me who I can and can't hold hands with?"

"You admit, then, that you're seeing Naomi?"

It seemed fruitless to deny at this point—not that she'd done a stellar job before—so Eileen nodded.

"No!" Her mom slapped the couch cushion. "That can't be."

"It can, actually."

"It's unnatural." She groaned. "What will everyone think? She was a baby when you started dating Melissa."

The timing didn't quite match up, not that Eileen felt the need to correct her mom.

"You'll ruin her, just like you did Melissa. Not to mention the mess you made of my life."

Eileen sucked in a breath as if her mom had sucker punched her smack dab in the gut.

Her mom continued, "The way you left. Without saying goodbye to any of us, especially Melissa. Have you never wondered how that affected... her? Your selfishness. And, now you're back in town doing the same thing all over again. Whisking Naomi off her feet and then you'll do another runner. That's what you do. You have no intention of staying in Derby, but I'll have to deal with the consequences of your actions, pick up the pieces. Everyone will talk about how you broke Naomi's heart."

"I have zero intention of hurting Naomi!"

"Mark my words, Naomi will end up like Melissa."

"Melissa's fine. She married—"

"Her wife died."

Eileen smothered her heart with her good hand. "And that's somehow my fault?"

"If you hadn't left, she wouldn't have met Susan and experienced the heartache of losing a wife."

"The three of us went to school together!"

Her mom locked her eyes on Eileen. "You know what I mean. Melissa has never been the same. Not since you abandoned her. I can't stand by and watch you repeat the same thing with Naomi. She's such a sweetheart." She spoke the last words with feigned sweetness.

"Give it a rest, Mom. You didn't even remember attending Naomi's high school or college graduation parties. You aren't here for Naomi's sake. Why don't you tell me what's really bothering you?"

"I most certainly am here for Naomi. And for Sophia Weaver. My dear friend." She shook her head sadly.

Eileen let out a bark of laughter. "Please. You aren't close

173

friends with Mrs. Weaver. You aren't close with anyone. You're too proud to let down your barriers and you act as if you rule this town, throwing parties for all the who's who. None of it's real. Nothing is."

"Don't think just because you don't use the name Callahan that you can forget what it means to be part of the family. What it means to be my daughter. I gave up everything for you. If you stay in Derby, everything I've sacrificed will all be for nothing. You owe me."

"You have no idea what you're talking about. I don't owe you a thing." Eileen's voice had lost its confidence and the words came out no more than a whisper. How could her mom make her feel like an unloved little girl all over again?

Trudy closed the gap between them, with a finger in the air. "You're my daughter. Julia is weak like your father, always bending to everyone else's will. But you know deep down you're just like me. Only, I've showered you with opportunities to be everything I couldn't be. I didn't raise you to be a quitter. I don't even recognize the woman standing before me. It makes me sick to think of everything I gave up for you only for you to come running home with your tail between your legs."

Eileen was unable to mount a defense, standing before her mom who only seemed to grow in size as Eileen wilted.

"And I most certainly didn't give up everything for you to fall in love with a Weaver. Melissa was your high school sweetheart. She's the only suitable woman for you. Do you know she's been offered a job in London? You can go home. Leave Derby and leave Naomi. You never belonged here. And do you really believe that after the shine wears off, she'll love the likes of you? Jesus, you can't even get a peanut butter jar off your own hand. You've been a burden since before you were born!"

Eileen controlled the urge to call her mom an irrational meddling bitch, but couldn't stop herself from shouting, "Get out!" She took a deep breath and added in a weaker tone, "Please. Just leave me be."

Her mom stayed where she was, her chest heaving up and down.

"Don't make me ask again." Eileen motioned to the door.

"Well, I've never!" She marched past her daughter. Before leaving, she said, "Mark my words, Naomi will grow to resent you."

The door slammed shut.

Eileen attempted to scream, but the fury lodged in her chest, causing a burning sensation she'd never experienced before.

CHAPTER TWENTY-TWO

Naomi knocked on Eileen's door, butterflies tumbling all over each other in her belly. She wished she'd already finished her shift so she and Eileen could enjoy the rest of the day in each other's company—or better yet, go out and buy ornaments for the Christmas tree Naomi was going to put up for Eileen. Naomi would focus on her own tree later. Eileen's came first. But that was for later. Just having lunch with Eileen would have to do for now.

It took a while before Eileen answered the door. Maybe she'd been in the middle of one of her physical therapy exercises.

When Eileen did finally open the door, Naomi burst out laughing. Eileen had told her about taping the jar of peanut butter to her hand, but Naomi hadn't actually seen the whole thing with her own eyes.

When she glanced up at Eileen's face, however, any inclination toward more laughter soon left her.

"Hey." Naomi kissed Eileen on the cheek. "Do you need some help getting that off your hand?"

"That would be really nice." Eileen didn't sound very

grateful for Naomi's help. "This bloody thing." Eileen looked as though, if she'd had the power in her arm to do so, she would smash the jar to smithereens against the wall.

"What's going on?" Naomi took Eileen's hand in hers and gently peeled off the tape. In no time the jar and straw were disposed of.

"My mom came by for an unexpected visit." Eileen paced to the window and back. "She knows about us." Her voice shot up.

"Can we sit for a minute?" Naomi sat on the couch, hoping Eileen would follow her example. Her angry energy was increasing and Naomi needed to calm her down.

Eileen glared at her, then acquiesced.

"So, your mother knows," Naomi said. "Can't that be seen as a good thing? As in no more secrets?"

"My mother is not your mother, Naomi." The anger Eileen couldn't express by pacing around now shone in her eyes. "Why do you think I haven't been back to Derby for so long?"

"What did she say?" Naomi asked.

"She said that I should break things off with you immediately because I would only end up hurting you, like I hurt Melissa." The words rolled quickly off of Eileen's tongue, as though she needed to get them out as soon as possible.

"Why would you hurt me? Why would your mother even think that?" Naomi was confused by Trudy's concern for her well-being over her own daughter's.

"Because that's how my mom thinks of me. Perhaps I haven't given her enough reason not to believe that about me. I did hurt Melissa when I left Derby."

"But that was almost thirty years ago." Naomi held back from scooting closer to Eileen. She didn't think this was the kind of thing that would blow over just by taking Eileen into her arms and telling her everything would be all right.

"My thoughts exactly." Eileen's voice had dropped to a whisper.

"Could it be that she was a bit shocked because of the age difference between us? My mother was taken aback by that too and most people take more time to adjust to something like that than my mom."

"I'm not my mom's miracle baby, Naomi. I'm the eldest and I've always had a shitload of expectations heaped upon me. None of which I ever met, for the record." Eileen stared down at her arm. "Look at me now. I can't even move my right arm anymore. I've become even more of a failure. Even my own body is letting me down."

"You had a stroke." Naomi tried to keep her voice as level as possible, but it was hard. This wasn't one of the children at the hospital she was talking to—this was the woman she was falling in love with who was falling to pieces right in front of her eyes.

"How's having a stroke not my body failing?" Eileen looked her straight in the eye now, her glance defiant, as though she wanted to challenge Naomi to talk her way out of that extremely logical conclusion.

"Something went wrong in your body, yes. But that's not your fault, Eileen. The thing that happened to you happens to millions of people every day. It's not a failure at all. You fell ill. You can't possibly blame yourself for that."

"I'm not blaming myself. My mom's blaming me. Just like she's always blamed me for everything!" Eileen sounded like a petulant child now.

"I don't think that's true. Although you're clearly embarrassed about having had a stroke."

"Of course I am." Eileen's voice shot up. "It makes me feel like I'm ninety years old instead of not even fifty."

"You could see it as a challenge instead of an embarrassment or a failure or however you want to call it." Eileen was a stubborn woman, Naomi already knew that—she'd seen it in her glance that first day at the coffee shop. She wasn't a child who could be talked off the ledge of desperation with some well-intentioned words.

"I don't expect you to understand," Eileen said, turning away from Naomi.

"I won't pretend to fully understand what you're going through, but things don't have to be as black and white as you make them. Eileen," Naomi pleaded. "Will you look at me?"

Eileen snapped her head back into Naomi's direction. "What do you know about anything, really? You've barely crossed the borders of this town. You don't live in the real world, where I've been spending all my time. You know, with the *adults*."

Naomi took a deep breath. She knew Eileen was speaking from a place of deep pain and she tried to take that into consideration. "Derby *is* the real world. At least it is to me. I may always try to see the good in people and in a certain situation, but at least I'm not always pushing everyone away to prove some silly point. Like that I'm too strong to need love."

"Love?" Eileen spat out the word, then she rolled her eyes.

Naomi tried to look into Eileen's eyes, to catch a glimpse of something other than all this unbridled rage, but Eileen couldn't hold her gaze. She had to look away. Maybe Naomi shouldn't have said the word love. Maybe she shouldn't say anything at all anymore. Maybe the next move should come from Eileen.

Eileen rose and towered over Naomi. "You know what? My mom was right. Come January, I'll be out of here. I'll be leaving your precious Derby. So it's probably for the best to end this now."

A knot grew in Naomi's belly—in the same spot where a few minutes earlier butterflies had been frolicking at the mere prospect of spending an hour with Eileen. Naomi barely recognized the woman she'd had such a lovely time with over the past few weeks.

She stood up, rising to Eileen's height.

"You're breaking up with me?" Naomi had trouble pushing the words past the lump in her throat.

Eileen gave a one-shouldered shrug. "What's there to break up from even? This was never going to be anything more than a roll in the hay. We don't see eye to eye on most things. It's not only the difference in age, although that plays a big part in it as well. We're simply too different, you and me."

Tears stung behind Naomi's eyes. "Are you serious?" She well and truly raised her voice now. "After all the things you said to me this weekend? Suddenly, none of that's true anymore?"

"It doesn't matter." Eileen deflated in front of her. "None of it matters. I'm not right for you. And I'll leave town again and hurt you, just like I did with Melissa…"

"I'm not Melissa and history doesn't always have to repeat itself."

"It does. Because did you really think I was going to stay in this one-horse town for you?" Eileen shook her head. "I'd go mad here. This may be your real world, but it isn't mine."

Eileen's words felt like a blow to the stomach. Naomi couldn't keep the tears from spilling any longer. She didn't care that Eileen saw her cry, even though she'd probably consider that just another sign of weakness.

Naomi couldn't think of anything else to say. If Eileen really wanted to end things between them, she had found the right words to do it with. She wasn't going to stay. Naomi wasn't important enough to make her even consider that possibility.

She cast one last glance at Eileen, whose shoulders had started to slump, turned around, and fled the apartment.

Once she'd banged the door shut behind her, she leaned against it for a few minutes, panting. She could barely wrap her mind around what had just happened. Tears fell freely down her cheeks and Naomi tried, in vain, to catch them with the sleeve of her coat. At least Eileen had told her how she truly felt about their future—making Naomi feel even more foolish for having even used that word for the flimsy thing they'd had between them.

How could she not have seen Eileen's true colors? She was a Callahan after all. Someone to steer clear of. Naomi would do just that. But first, she needed to come up with a way to deal with that sinking feeling in her gut.

She straightened her spine and, for a split second, considered listening at the door. Maybe seeing her leave had made Eileen change her mind. Maybe she'd throw open the door and apologize for her unfounded anger. But Naomi didn't hear anything. No sniffling and no footsteps. Everything was deadly silent on the other side of the door. So she slunk off, hurt and defeated, with no more room for Christmas cheer in her heart.

CHAPTER TWENTY-THREE

On a chilly December day, Eileen entered the Boston newsroom and looked around. When she'd started working for the company in the US, in what seemed like a different lifetime, this office had hummed with people clacking away on computer keyboards, and chatting about stories they were working on. There'd been only a handful of televisions.

Now, the space had been renovated and transformed into wall-to-wall TV news hell. Yes, that was the word for it.

Mounted overhead were many screens showcasing various American politicians fielding questions from pundits and newscasters. A live shot of the empty James S. Brady Press Briefing Room. Stock market updates. Replays of all the past weekend's sporting events. An illuminated map of the world with clocks indicating the current time in all the zones. And several screens filled with European news broadcasts.

Each employee had at least two computer screens on their desk.

"Whoa, information overload," she muttered under her breath.

"Is that Eileen Makenna?"

Eileen wheeled about. "Seth Quigley!" Squinting, she asked, "Is it really you?"

The lanky man crossed the room in five long strides, and wrapped Eileen in a bear hug, lifting her briefly off the floor. "I didn't know I'd see you today." He broke off the hug, but kept his massive hands on each of her shoulders. "I thought you were stationed in London these days."

"I'm stateside for a bit for the holidays."

"Christ, it's good to see you. How long has it been?"

Eileen took a second to recall. "Iraq, I think. Back in 2004."

He grinned, displaying his yellowed smoker's teeth. "That's right. Do you remember those cots and scratchy blankets provided by the Marines?" He shivered. "And all the action. There's nothing like covering a war to make you feel alive." He beat his chest with a fist, three times. "I still have nightmares about it." The twinkle in his eyes was difficult to reconcile with the sentiment of the statement.

Except Eileen understood completely. Only those who'd undergone what they'd experienced together could comprehend.

"Getting the truth to the world, though, is worth it." Seth squeezed her left shoulder as if he needed her support to find the right words, seeming to fail nonetheless. His eyes clouded over. "Now, it seems the frontlines are here. The battle against the fake news smear." He shook his head, a smile sliding back into place. "God, it's good to see you."

"Are you staying in the US, then?" Eileen asked.

He shook his head. "Thankfully, no. Heading to Syria."

Eileen whistled. "Stay safe."

He belly laughed. "That's the goal, but when heading into hell, you never know what's going to happen. Any chance I can convince you to come with me? You're one of the best. Think of the prizes we'd nab if we joined forces again."

"Wish I could… it's just not in the cards right now." Eileen pivoted her body to hide her right flank.

"That's right. I heard you were on leave." Someone across the newsroom waved both arms overhead to get his attention. "Gotta run, Ellie. If you change your mind, you can find me wherever all hell is breaking loose."

Eileen called out, "Remember, Quigley. You're supposed to report on the news, not cause it."

He waved *yeah yeah* over his shoulder.

Kris, who must be in her fifties now and was wearing her age well, sidled up to Eileen. "He'll never change."

Eileen agreed. "The world needs a hundred more like him. How are you, Kris?"

Kris, in black slacks, crimson cardigan, and white blouse— her typical office attire—said, "Better now that you're here."

"Such a sweet-talker, you."

"Have you outgrown it?" Kris stepped closer to Eileen, pressing her shoulder into Eileen's. "I seem to remember you liking it a lot in the past."

Eileen fought the urge to break away, the thought of Naomi entering her mind. She wanted to speak to her, but was pretty sure Naomi wouldn't welcome any contact after all the hurtful things Eileen had tossed at her. "Is this appropriate now? In the workplace? Seems to be a lot of hoopla about it in the news."

"How would you know? You've been hiding in… what's the name of that one-horse-town you're from? Besides, *we* happened when we worked for competitors."

The one-horse phrase ripped through Eileen, reminding her of saying those exact words to Naomi, when she ruthlessly pushed the young woman away. Eileen regretted letting her mom get into her head like she was a scared child, but she had never been good at saying sorry and owning up. "Funnily enough, it's actually called One-Horse-Town."

"That is funny. You haven't changed one bit. There's hope for the future yet."

"Because I haven't changed?"

"You're one of the good ones, so yes, it's good to know you still have fighting spirit. How are you doing? Really?" Kris stared intently at Eileen's arm, making it clear she wanted the truth.

"It's... getting better."

Kris folded her arms, slitting her eyes. "Don't bullshit a bull-shitter. I was in London when it... happened. I visited you in the hospital, for crying out loud. So, how is it?"

Eileen sighed. "Slowly. It's getting better, slowly."

"The big man is in Beantown and wants to speak with you."

"That's why you summoned me? I had wished he'd be in London or any of the other fifty cities checking on his minions?" Eileen glanced around the newsroom, in search of the distinctive white hair of Ray Steffens.

Kris shook her head. "You aren't the only one thinking the worse, given all the recent layoffs in the business. But it's actually good news, for once. He's here to hire eight more journalists and an editor to cover the 2020 elections, which should be ramping up soon. The American political circus is turning out to be a boon for the media business. Go figure."

Eileen had never cared for domestic news, let alone in the political sphere. "What about you? Are you staying in Boston for long? Or heading back to the London office?"

"Boston for the next year or so. But who knows. In this business, when news happens, we all drop everything and converge on the next hot spot. It's tiring. I'm not young like you." She waggled her brows over her nerdy black-framed glasses.

Eileen chuckled. "Yes, I'm still in my forties for another few months."

"Forty is the new thirty. And fifty is the new forty. Haven't you heard?"

Eileen swallowed a nasty comment about how her thirty-year-old body hadn't failed her.

Kris straightened. "You might as well get it over with. Mr. Steffens is heading right for you."

"How much have you told him?" Eileen whispered.

"I haven't said a thing. You'll need to put on your big girl pants and handle it. Today." She gave Eileen her no-nonsense stare.

Eileen shot Kris a steely-eyed look.

Kris dished it back.

"Ellie Bean! I'm so glad you came in today. Let's go to my office. And, Kris Cross, can you come up when I'm done with Ellie?" Their boss never broke his stride, expecting Eileen to fall in line, tailing him to his office at the top of the stairs.

"Yes, sir," Kris, rolled her eyes over the use of her nickname, as she spoke to his retreating back. She gave Eileen a supportive *you can do it* smile.

Eileen sensed all eyes watching their retreat as Mr. Steffens, a man more than two decades older than her, charged up, taking two steps at a time. Eileen did her best to keep up, but the man had six inches on her, not to mention she was willing to wager he'd never suffered from a cold, let alone a stroke.

Inside his office, which was almost as large as Naomi's apartment in Derby, Mr. Steffens motioned for Eileen to take a seat on a burgundy couch. "Would you like something to drink?"

"No, thank you."

"I'm still on London time, so if you don't object, I'm going to have a nip of brandy."

Mr. Steffens was constantly flying all over the world checking in on all his media outlets. His plane logged more miles than most commercial crafts.

After pouring a dram of brandy into a snifter, Mr. Steffens took a seat on the couch facing Eileen. He unbuttoned his dark gray suit vest and loosened his powdered-blue tie. "So, you ready to get back to work?"

"Very soon, yes."

"Define soon." He inhaled the scent from the brandy, but didn't take a sip yet, as if he'd enjoyed the process of pouring and holding the drink more than imbibing.

She met his eyes. "I'm still hoping to be back in January."

He held her gaze. "Can you hand me today's newspaper edition? It's on the table right behind you."

Eileen reached for it with her left hand and extended her arm over the coffee table to hand it to him.

"Hold this for me?" Mr. Steffens attempted to hand off the snifter.

Eileen momentarily froze, then opted to drop the newspaper onto the seat next to him and grabbed the glass with her good hand.

"That's what I thought. I'd heard rumors, you see." He motioned for Eileen to relinquish his glass, which she did. He took a thoughtful sip. "Can you even hold a pencil with that one?" Mr. Steffens gestured to her arm.

"I—"

"Listen. I get why you didn't want to come forward completely. This is a cutthroat business. But not disclosing the true nature of your injury—I thought we knew each other better than this." His eyes softened. "I understand, though, really I do. My mom had a stroke and dammit if she didn't want to tell a soul, either."

"I'm sorry to hear about your mother. I didn't know."

"If you had, would you have come to me sooner?" His striking sapphire eyes nearly burned a hole into her forehead as if he were using mind powers to rip the truth out of her.

"I—"

"Probably not. If it makes you feel better, my mother is still just as stubborn as you are and she's nearing one hundred."

Did Mr. Steffens just compare Eileen to a woman almost in the triple digits? "That's wonderful."

He plowed on, not picking up on Eileen's stiffening posture. "We can't put you into the field with that." Mr. Steffens waved to her arm. "A shame. You'd be a great addition to Jiggly Quigley's team." Taking another sip, he stared over Eileen's head. "However, I'm here to beef up our coverage of the upcoming election."

Eileen braced herself for the one assignment she'd never wanted. Taking puff photos of preening politicians.

"We need more op-ed pieces, as well." He stroked the two-day stubble on his chin. "With your experiences from all over the world, you truly understand the plights of migrants and immigrants. And, I think you should pen your memoirs." He got up strolled to his desk, and rifled through the desk drawers. "Here. Take this."

He tossed her a small recording device, which she caught with her good hand. "I know many use their phones these days, but I used that when I was working on my memoir last year. Maybe it'll bring you luck or inspiration. Both perhaps. And, it'll be a hell of a lot faster than typing with one hand." He retook his seat, picking up the snifter again. "What else can we do to help you with your recovery?"

"Uh...?" It wasn't unusual for Mr. Steffens to jump from one subject to the next, making decisions as he went along. Still, Eileen wasn't sure if this was really happening. Op-eds. She'd occasionally written pieces when the company was in a bind, but never as a full-time gig. Truth be told, she'd enjoyed writing, but never considered it as a logical next step in her professional life. Could it be? If need be. She'd miss traveling. Or could she still travel in this new position? Perhaps that was something to bring up later.

His eyes softened. "Ellie, you've been with us since leaving college and I damn well know you had offers from competitors." He put his hand up to stop her from interrupting, although she was not inclined to do so. "You stuck with me through thick and thin. You've won awards. You volunteered for the shittiest assignments, not to mention the most dangerous. This is when you ask *me* to help *you*. Besides, my mom would box my ears if I didn't." He laughed, his kind eyes showing he meant every word.

Eileen held the recorder up with her good hand. "This is enough. Truly. I thought you'd fire or force me out when you found out the whole truth. Not give me a new assignment."

"Glad to see my reputation for being an asshole is still going strong. Do me a favor. Don't tell anyone I'm actually a softie. Let them"—he motioned to the team on the newsroom one floor below—"think I gave you hell."

"Will do." She rose.

"I expect your first piece in one week. You can work from Derby. Family. If they're anything like mine they're driving you batty, but… they hopefully mean well."

Eileen's mind flittered to Naomi.

"By the way, the photos in *The Derby Gazette* were good, considering. You're still a photographer. Always will be. And, you're a stubborn shit. I wouldn't put it past you to beat this so you can charge back into war zones with your camera."

Eileen's brain tried to process everything. He hadn't fired her, but instead he'd offered her a desk job. How would she adjust? Although, what was the other option? Quit and do nothing? He'd left the possibility open for her to return to photography while keeping her employed, giving her body the time it needed to recover.

"Can you send up Kris Cross?" He marched to his desk, picking up the phone receiver.

On the other side of the closed door, Eileen wondered how

in the hell Mr. Steffens knew about her photos in the tiny newspaper. Did he ever sleep?

Kris approached. "How'd it go?" she asked.

"I'm an op-ed contributor now."

"Ohh… look at you, Miss Fancy Pants." Her teasing smile faded. With a hand on the doorknob, she proclaimed, "My turn."

As Eileen descended the staircase, she wished she could call Naomi to celebrate, but after she'd acted like such an ass the other day, she doubted the one person she really wanted to tell would bother taking her call.

CHAPTER TWENTY-FOUR

Naomi wrapped her fingers around her coffee cup. Her mom had added a dash of cinnamon, just the way she liked it.

Sophia wasn't the type of woman to flat-out ask Naomi to talk to her about whatever was bugging her, but Naomi could tell from the look on her face that she was more than ready to have a much-needed conversation with her youngest daughter.

Naomi cleared her throat. Her mother stowed away the last of the ingredients she'd used to bake Naomi's favorite apple pie. The pie was in the oven and the kitchen was already starting to fill with the irresistible smell of what was to come.

Sophia took the chair opposite her and offered a smile.

"I won't be bringing Eileen to your Christmas party," Naomi said, her throat tightening as she spoke.

"Oh, darling." Her mother put a hand on her arm. "I knew something was up. What happened?"

"She made it very clear she doesn't want to be with me anymore." Naomi shook her head. "Some people are just too stubborn to be in a relationship, I guess."

"Maybe." Her mother tilted her head. "Probably even more

193

so when you're a Callahan. She must take after her mother in that way."

"Yet Trudy has been married for a very long time."

"That might be so but take it from me, darling, that's not a relationship you want to emulate."

Naomi sighed. "My biggest problem is that I can't stop thinking about her. There's no one like Eileen in this town." She looked into her coffee cup, where only some wet cinnamon dust remained. "Anyway, she'll be leaving soon, so it's probably for the best."

"It's never for the best when someone hurts you. You're clearly very fond of her." Her mother gave Naomi's arm a light squeeze. "Are you sure you don't want to try and patch things up? To not have her leave town with these unresolved feelings between the two of you?"

"What does it matter if we never even speak again?" Naomi realized she was sounding as defeated as Eileen on the day she'd broken up with her.

"You can at least get some closure. Put the whole thing behind you so you can move on." Her mother leaned over the table a little. "I don't mean to pry, darling, but was it the age difference?"

Naomi gave a curt shake of the head. "No. At least I don't think so." She knew her mother probably had a point—Naomi was someone who liked to close a chapter before starting a new one. But chances of her running into Eileen in this town— she recalled the vicious tone in Eileen's voice when she'd called Derby a one-horse town—were pretty high. She should just leave it up to destiny. Or to Eileen, who had said some pretty hurtful things. "Eileen believes she's somehow unlovable, even more so now she's had a stroke."

"That's a lot for you to take on, Naomi."

"It's not." Naomi looked her mom in the eye—she didn't need anyone to tell her what she could or couldn't bear. "If only she wasn't such a bloody stubborn Callahan. Because that's what upsets me most. We were doing fine, but Trudy must have gotten to her and said some things that made Eileen dump me."

"It shouldn't be that way. Imagine if I had tried to talk you out of seeing Eileen—"

Naomi held up her hand. "No, it wasn't like that, Mom. From what I understood, Trudy advised Eileen to break up with me to spare *my* feelings." Naomi huffed out some air. "Since when do I need Trudy Callahan to look out for my feelings?" Naomi had rehashed Eileen's words over and over again in her head. It didn't make sense that Trudy Callahan would look out for Naomi more than for her own daughter. She guessed what Trudy was really so afraid of was Eileen leaving town again and not returning to Derby for another five years.

"I know Trudy's a tough cookie, but she means well." Her mom tapped her thumb on Naomi's underarm. "Imagine how that must have made Eileen feel, though. Her own mother coming down on her like that." She pursed her lips. "She has always been so hard on her children, especially on Eileen." She paused. "Have you considered that what Eileen needs most is some time to process the things Trudy said to her? And to make her realize that Trudy's outburst wasn't so much about her as about Trudy herself and the impossible pressure she has always put on Eileen?"

"Time?" Naomi couldn't believe it. She and Eileen had been running out of time since the day they'd met. Surely Eileen would prefer Naomi's company—and help—over time to mull over her mother's words. And shouldn't Naomi's words count more under the circumstances? "She's leaving town in a few weeks." There was that heaviness in her chest again, although Naomi couldn't really fathom Eileen leaving so soon. She could move her arm a little bit more than when they'd first met, but she had hardly made miraculous strides in her recovery. How could Eileen possibly return to work so quickly? Her job wasn't one that could be performed on willpower alone.

"Yeah," was all her mother said next. Maybe there wasn't anything left to say. "You can't save them all, darling," her mother said after a while.

"I wasn't trying to save her." Naomi's voice sounded small and wounded. "Eileen's not a turtle."

"Of course not, darling." Her mother offered a smile.

"I was falling in love with her," Naomi said on a sigh. There. She'd said it. Not that it made the slightest bit of difference, but it felt good to admit it.

At least Naomi had a mother she could talk to—Eileen had been right about that. She couldn't picture Eileen having a heart-to-heart with Trudy right now—on the contrary. She wondered what Eileen was doing to distract herself. As far as Naomi knew, she kept herself to herself, and apart from her physical therapy appointments, Eileen didn't venture out much. Or maybe she was confiding in Julia. Naomi had liked her at the Callahan Christmas party.

"I know this isn't what you want to hear, but you're still so young," Naomi's mother said. "You have so much to offer another person. If they can't see that, it's their own fault. I also know it hurts right now, but the pain will become less and less, and you will fall in love again, Naomi. I can't say many things for sure, but I'm certain of that."

"You're right." Naomi withdrew her hand. "That's absolutely not what I want to hear."

"I know that very well." Her mother smirked. "But I had to say it."

"I don't know what to do." Naomi rubbed her eyes with the heels of her hands. "It didn't feel like this when Jane and I broke up, even though we'd been together for nearly three years. I didn't feel this massive gaping hole inside of me."

"Oh, darling." Her mother rose and Naomi, still keeping her

hands in front of her eyes, heard her walk toward her. She put her arm around Naomi's shoulders. "I wish I could do something to help. Especially because Christmas is fast approaching and I've never met anyone in my life who's as crazy about the whole ordeal as you." She planted a kiss on the top of Naomi's head. "Whether you like it or not, I'm starting Operation Get-Naomi-Into-The-Christmas-Spirit right now." She squeezed her shoulders. "You haven't even put up your tree. So, come on. Wipe those tears. You and I are going Christmas tree shopping right now."

Naomi's shoulders slumped. "That's the last thing I feel like doing."

"Well, sometimes you have to fake it until you make it."

"You have a pie in the oven," Naomi protested. Even though it would only be a short drive to the garden center, she couldn't face the business of picking out the best tree for herself. She was used to making a real spectacle out of it and Pauline, the woman who ran the garden center, always made sure to play along with Naomi's antics. Picking out her Christmas tree was such a big part of Naomi's festive season, and it always made her feel so warm and fuzzy inside, she couldn't face doing it in the sulky mood she was in today.

"It'll be ready in fifteen minutes. The time it takes for you to turn that frown upside down," her mother said.

"How about I watch the pie and you get the tree?" Naomi asked.

Her mother rose to her full height and folded her arms across her chest, indicating she wouldn't be taking no for an answer much longer. "Naomi Weaver. For twenty-seven years I've allowed you to knock me over the head with your endless Christmas enthusiasm, even when I really wasn't in the mood for it. Today, I'm returning the favor." The expression on her face softened. "I promise it'll make you feel better. It'll be so much nicer to come home to an apartment with a lovely tree in it. Remember those new decorations you got in the summer sale? You've been dying to hang those up since July."

"Oh, all right then." Naomi got up because she realized she had no other option. She had to fake it. She wasn't going to let Eileen Callahan ruin her Christmas as well. Because Eileen might have broken her heart, but Christmas came around every year—and Naomi would be celebrating its wonders long after she'd forgotten all about Eileen.

"I've been expecting you." Pauline rubbed her hands together. "In fact, I saved you a beauty. Come around the back."

Even though Naomi wasn't a frequent visitor to the garden center—her apartment didn't come with any outside space and she already had all the indoor plants she had room for—Pauline always treated her like a VIP customer. Maybe because Naomi was the most enthusiastic Christmas tree shopper on the east coast.

"I put it aside because, truth be told, the best-looking trees have sold already." Pauline guided Naomi and her mother to a warehouse behind the shop. "But I knew you'd make it eventually. Been busy, have we?"

"Yeah." Naomi wasn't going to pour her heart out to Pauline.

"Look at this gorgeous specimen." Pauline pointed at a large conifer that, at first glance, looked way too big to even fit in Naomi's car—let alone that she could find a spot for it in her apartment.

"It's a bit bigger than what I'm used to," Naomi said, knowing, as she inspected the tree, where it *would* fit. In Eileen's living room, which desperately needed a Christmas tree like this. But she knew Eileen wouldn't bother putting it up herself, and she had been officially dismissed from the task.

"I'm sure we can make it work," Naomi's mother prodded the tree. "Let's be honest, we say it's going to be too big every year, yet we always make it work."

Naomi nodded. If anything, trying to fit that tree into the apartment she had shared with Jane for almost three years, and had then made some wonderful memories with Eileen in, would take her mind off all of that. And it would give the place a brand-new focal point, even if only temporarily.

"I'll take it," she said, and, despite herself, her heart swelled a little.

CHAPTER TWENTY-FIVE

Not wanting to face sitting in her apartment alone after her physical therapy appointment, Eileen popped into the café next to the hospital. It wasn't the typical type of establishment she frequented back in London, but none of the American chains had invaded Derby, leaving Eileen's options limited.

Sitting at the table, nursing a gingerbread latte, Eileen's eyes studied one of the paintings on the wall. The artist, who Eileen was willing to bet was a local, had painted a striking blue background, a black bridge spanning a chasm, and one lone red vehicle crossing the bridge. There were a few black birds flying in the same direction as the vehicle. Were they vultures? Migrating? Up to the viewer's interpretation?

Try as she might, Eileen couldn't stop staring at the image, feeling a connection to whoever was in the red VW bus. The sense of escape. Adventure. Crushing loneliness.

Forcing the last thought out of her mind, Eileen pulled out her leather-bound notebook and pen. One of the good things about being an adventurer was learning to adapt when you broke an arm, wrist, or finger on your dominant hand. Which

Eileen had done a handful of times, forcing her to learn to write with her left. The stroke was the first time Eileen had to contend with not being able to use her right arm at all. Even when she'd fractured her wrist or arm, she still had use of her fingers.

Once again, Eileen shut down her mind. Biting on the cap of the pen, she removed it to get to work on her first op-ed piece.

"Look who it is."

Eileen slowly tore her eyes from the paper to peer into Melissa's soft brown eyes, orbs that seemed years younger than the rest of her. She had rounded out with age and her hair had turned a soft gray, but she still wore it pulled back in a ponytail.

"I saw you through the window and decided to pounce. Otherwise I'd never get a chance to talk to you alone."

"You've always been honest. I give you that. Can I buy you a drink?" Eileen started to rise.

"I've got it." She placed a hand on Eileen's shoulder. "I'm going to the counter to order a black coffee. The transaction should only take a couple of minutes. I expect you to be here when I get back. Or there'll be consequences." Her fingers dug into Eileen's shoulder.

Eileen smiled. "I've missed your threats. What type of consequences are we talking about?"

"The severest kind." Melissa drilled her gaze into Eileen's.

"I'm almost tempted to leave just to find out." Eileen grinned.

Melissa's grip relaxed and she laughed. "That's one question answered. You haven't changed one bit. Stubborn as hell. Be right back."

Eileen shoved the Monopoly box that'd been sitting on the table when she arrived to the far side to make room for Melissa, thinking she might as well get another tongue-lashing out of the way. Oh, the joys of coming home for the holidays after such a long absence.

Leaning back into the upholstered chair, Eileen gripped the mug with her left hand, forcing the fingers on her right to wrap around the warmth. She could practically hear Mack's words: create new pathways.

Without much fanfare, Melissa plopped into the only other armchair at the table, not sitting prim and proper. Not that she ever had. "Besides the obvious, how have you been?"

"What's the obvious?"

Melissa blew into her mug. "I see you've chosen the hard way to do this. Shouldn't have expected differently."

Eileen bristled. "Everyone seems to have formed their opinions about me no matter what I say or do."

"Is that why you never come home to visit friends or family? To avoid all the judgy people in your hometown? And not allow yourself to reconnect with where you came from to stay grounded?" She fixed her gaze upon Eileen.

"Maybe I stay grounded by not coming home." Eileen sighed. "Why in the hell is everyone in Derby so touchy feely these days?"

Melissa sat up in her seat. "That's an interesting observation. I know you aren't talking about your family. Your mom is cold and demanding and your father is—I don't know how to describe him—beaten down perhaps. Julia's too busy trying to keep the family going to allow much time for anything beyond surviving." She rapped her fingers on the table. "So, who are you referring to?"

"Besides the person I'm currently conversing with, no one," Eileen dodged.

"Now you listen to me, Eileen Makenna Callahan, I'm not buying your act." Melissa waggled a finger in the air, which had always been one of her favorite ways of reprimanding Eileen.

Eileen stared at the vehicle in the painting. "No one calls

me that anymore. I can't…" She was about to say she couldn't remember the last time she'd heard her full name spoken aloud, but then Naomi's distinct voice saying it played in her head. And, she'd loved it when Naomi said it. Not that Naomi ever would again. No, she'd only hear Naomi say her name in her imagination from here on out. According to her mom, that was for the best. Eileen should stay away or one day Naomi would be sitting where Melissa sat, giving her the third degree.

"You used to love your full name and were the only one in elementary school who'd turn in assignments with all three. You wouldn't even answer when called upon unless a teacher said them. What's changed?"

"Ah, that was before I learned what it really meant to be a Callahan. The expectations. Pressure…" Eileen motioned the list was endless, not even mentioning the most burdensome of all: the crushing disappointment she'd been to her mom since she had to drop out of college to have her.

Melissa examined Eileen's face before responding. "You know, Ellie. All the pressure you feel isn't because you're a Callahan. It's you who puts this pressure on yourself. It's as if you have to live up to the mythical name, when in reality, no one else thinks that way."

"My mom most certainly does."

"Ah, there's that." Melissa sipped her coffee. "That was one of your favorite excuses to fall back on when pushing yourself too hard." Melissa set her mug down and rested her forearms on the table. "It's funny. You expect so much from yourself, but when it comes to others, you're much kinder and forgiving. I remember many a time when you calmed me down if I did poorly in school, had a fight with my parents, or anything. You always knew exactly what to say or do to cheer me up."

"I think you're wearing rose-tinted glasses when remembering the past… with me." Eileen continued to give her attention to the painting, purposefully avoiding Melissa's knowing gaze.

Melissa sat back in her chair, letting out a whoosh of breath. "Mack tells me you're planning on being back to work by early January."

Eileen snapped her neck to the left to see her. "Is it legal for Mack to discuss my sessions with you?"

Melissa arched one eyebrow. "Are you going to sue my baby brother?"

"What? No... I was only asking."

"What am I going to do with you, Ellie?" Melissa shook her head.

Eileen cocked her head to the side, as if changing the view slightly would provide her with a clue about Melissa's question. Not finding one in Melissa's expression, she asked, "What do you mean?"

"After all these years, you still haven't forgiven yourself for leaving."

Eileen shifted in her chair. "I don't know what you're talking about."

"You most certainly do. Recently, I had lunch with your mom and she went on and on about how you regretted your decision—"

"I never said that!"

Melissa laughed. "I know. But if she's saying that, she's probably insinuating things to you that just aren't true. Like how I've been pining for you all the while hating you for leaving."

"Do you? Hate me, I mean?" Eileen's voice was barely audible.

"No. Not even when you left without saying goodbye. Sure, it hurt. But deep down I always knew why you left. And, I understood why you did it the way you did. If you'd told your mother you weren't going to med school, but instead intended to pursue photography, she would have said things. Hurtful things and you, in all probability, wouldn't have chased your dreams. And if you'd told me... I was young enough not to understand completely and I may have done the same. If that had happened, I'd regret everything to this day."

Eileen started to speak, but stopped, unable to find the words to express the relief she felt about Melissa's understanding and the shame for not seeing through her mom's meddling.

"I've followed your career from the beginning. The stories you've told through your photos. Making the atrocities that take place in tiny corners of the world real to the rest of us. You've always wanted to do your part in saving the world and you've succeeded."

"Yeah, right." Eileen snorted. "No matter how many photos I take, these things keep happening."

"That's because people are terrible."

"Exactly." Eileen reached for the pen, needing to occupy her left hand. "Sometimes I wonder what's the point."

"You may not be able to stop all the people on the planet from hurting others, but you can shine a spotlight on those who do, so people like me, who stay in cozy homes in safe towns, know what's going on. It's not just me, either, who appreciates what you do. Your photos are everywhere. Online, in newspapers all over the world—it matters. Your work matters."

"It did until..." Eileen glanced down at her arm, trying to block out her mom's taunting about the jar.

"I know you better than most, even if I haven't seen you in far too long. You're probably already working on another way of bringing the truth to people." Melissa placed her hand on Eileen's open notebook. "You've always been a fighter."

"Are you sure I was the one who knew how to cheer you up

and not the other way around?" There was a faint smile on Eileen's lips.

"I learned from the best." Melissa squeezed Eileen's hand. "Can you do me a favor?"

"What?"

Melissa leveled her gaze onto Eileen's pinched face. "Promise me first."

"You're cheating. You've always cheated this way." There was a hint of nostalgia in Eileen's voice.

"And have I ever given you reason not to trust me."

"You're still cheating."

"You're still not giving me your word."

"Fine," Eileen said through gritted teeth. "I promise."

"Forgive yourself, Eileen Makenna Callahan."

"For?" Eileen placed the pen back on the paper.

"Leaving. You did what you had to do or you would have been miserable. No one should feel guilty for being who they are."

Eileen rested her chin on her hand, plucking up the courage to say the words she'd always wanted to say. "I should have said goodbye, though. I'm sorry for that."

"Maybe. Maybe not. It was so very you back then." Melissa shrugged.

Eileen tapped her fingers against her cheek. "Meaning I was an asshole."

"I never said that. And no, you weren't." Melissa's expression darkened with worry. "Tell me, Ellie, who has you this worked up?"

"Who else?"

"Your mother." She said without having to put too much thought into it. "Why do you let her get to you? Julia has learned how to handle her."

"She's had more practice." And their mom didn't resent Julia's very existence.

"There's that, but Julia also decided not to give a crap about the stuff your mom says. Be like a duck."

"And let it roll off my back." Eileen groaned. "I'm one hundred percent positive I never said anything like that to you when I was supposedly acting like Oprah or Dr. Phil."

"No, you probably said something like, *suck it up, buttercup.*" Melissa grinned.

Wide-eyed, Eileen asked, "And you found that helpful?"

"Coming from you, yes. Because it'd make me laugh, instantly perking me up. That was the one thing you could always do. Make me laugh."

Eileen sighed. "I don't know if I have that power anymore."

"I'm sure you do still somewhere inside."

Why bother trying to uncover that ability if she wouldn't have the chance to make Naomi laugh again? "I hear you're moving to London."

Melissa smiled. "Did I hit too close to home, prompting you to switch topics? I was considering the move, but have opted against it."

Eileen nearly burst into laughter. All of her mom's scheming to get Eileen back together with Melissa would have been for naught.

"Is it just your mom that has you worked up? And not a certain person I've been hearing rumors about?"

Eileen massaged her eyes, taking in a deep breath. "Not you too. This town is ripe with gossip."

"If you ask me, I think she's a good fit for you."

"She's so much younger and idealistic."

"Says the woman who ran off to save the world one picture at a time." Melissa gulped her drink. "Don't write off someone for such silly reasons. If you like her, you like her. It's as simple as that."

CHAPTER TWENTY-SIX

Naomi sat across from her best friend, who still didn't know she'd gone through the entire process of having the hots for someone, sleeping with her, and breaking up. On top of how lousy she felt about the break-up, it made Naomi feel like the worst best friend in the world.

"I'm all ears, Nomes," Kelly said.

Naomi studied her face. Had she figured it out without Naomi having to spill the beans?

"For?" Naomi asked.

"Christmas is one week away. You must be full of plans for the kids. What extravaganza are you cooking up this year?" Kelly knitted her eyebrows together. "Although, I have to say, you don't seem as possessed with the Christmas spirit as you've been in all the years I've known you."

"Remember that woman..." Naomi started. Because she really needed to confide in her friend. She needed to get some things off her chest that she couldn't share with her mother. "The one who came in here one day and dropped a bunch of coins on the floor?"

Naomi gazed at the spot where she and Eileen had first

exchanged a few words. Eileen's attitude had been frosty then, and had only thawed after some insistence from Naomi—only to turn cold and dismissive again a few weeks later.

"Yeah. Eileen Callahan," Kelly said.

"You know Eileen?"

"I don't know her personally, but I've heard of her," Kelly said. "Tyson, for one, can't stop talking about her. And I also happen to know she's of your persuasion…" The penny seemed to drop. "Oh. Did you…"

"We had a thing. If you can even call it that," Naomi said, sadness dropping like a heavy stone in her stomach once again.

Kelly's eyes grew to the size of saucers. "No way." She shook her head. "My best friend had a 'thing' and she didn't breathe a word about it to me? I don't think that's possible."

"We kept it on the down-low. Obviously, that was for the best because it had barely even started when it ended." Naomi heaved a sigh. "Believe me, I wanted to tell you, but I didn't know where to begin."

"I can imagine. Tyson did refer to her as that sweet, 'middle-aged' lady." She gave a chuckle.

"All kids think anyone above thirty is old," Naomi rebuffed. Speaking of Tyson made her think about the small farewell gathering she had put together for him later. Tomorrow, he would finally be allowed to leave the hospital. She'd seriously considered putting her own feelings aside and asking Eileen to stop by, but she hadn't been able to do it. Not yet. Not even for the sake of one of the kids in the ward.

"How old is she?" Kelly drummed her fingertips on the table.

"Forty-nine. Way too old for me," Naomi said, even though she didn't mean a word of it.

"What happened?" Kelly had lowered her voice.

"She flew off the handle one day and just ended it."

"Can you be just a tiny bit more specific, pretty please?" Kelly smiled at her.

"She has a bunch of issues, such as not being able to accept that she had a stroke. Some family drama. She and her mom don't get along very well so that stressed her out also. Plus, she has no definite plans to stay in Derby, so there's that minor detail as well."

"So, it was like a holiday fling for her?"

"Maybe." Naomi nodded. "Maybe I was just a welcome distraction from all her problems."

"What was she to you, though?" Kelly drained the last of her tea.

"It's hard to say." There was that lump in her throat again. Deep down, Naomi knew very well what Eileen had been to her. She just found it very hard to translate that feeling into words. "I fell for her, I guess. Maybe, to me, she was just a rebound person after Jane."

"Maybe... or maybe not," Kelly said.

"It doesn't matter anymore now, anyway. The stubbornness of that woman." Naomi shook her head. "I deal with people who are in difficult situations every day, and I can so clearly see how certain things are very hard to accept, but Eileen really takes the cake." Naomi wasn't sure where those words were coming from all of a sudden. "It's not so much self-pity. If it was, I would have run a mile." She paused to think for a few seconds. "It's this deep-rooted belief that she's somehow a failure. And for that reason, undeserving of love."

"Wow." Kelly leaned back in her chair. "Her age aside, that doesn't sound very much like someone who's ideal relationship material."

Naomi shrugged. "You know I like a challenge."

"Maybe you like a challenge a little bit too much." Kelly gave a warm smile. "Trust me when I tell you that I mean that in the nicest possible way."

"You sound just like my mom right now." Naomi found it hard to resist Kelly's smile.

"What did she have to say about it? She wasn't too freaked out by the age difference?"

"She was at first, but after that she was surprisingly mellow about it. Probably because Eileen broke up with me only a day after I told her."

"I'm sure that's not true. Your mom has only ever wanted you to be happy."

"Yeah, well, fat chance of that now."

"Oh, no, no. I'm not going to have you wallow in self-pity a week before Christmas." Kelly squared her shoulders. "Let's start making some plans right here, right now."

Naomi tried to mimic her friend's posture—and Christmas spirit. Why was it so hard to forget about Eileen, anyway? It wasn't as if they'd ever stood a real chance. Maybe this wound that had opened up inside her was more due to Naomi having allowed herself to be so swept up in the whole thing, without considering the consequences. But that was how she was. She got swept up in things, in their magic and wonder, and sometimes, she had to pay the price.

"Let's start planning," she said, painting on a smile.

"Okay, big man," Naomi said. "Enjoy this view one last time, because this will be the last you'll see of me." She shot Tyson a big grin.

"I'll see you in a few months when I come in for my check-up," he said, sounding very much like a tiny wise-ass.

"Is your friend not coming?" Deborah, Tyson's mother, asked. "We would love to thank her for getting Tyson so excited about photography."

"Guess what I asked Santa to bring me?" Tyson had a big smile plastered across his face.

"Aren't you a little old to be asking Santa for presents?" Naomi asked, avoiding Deborah's question.

"W-what do you mean, Naomi?" Tyson said in a pretend-shaky voice.

"Are you sure you want to take him home?" Naomi winked at Deborah, hoping she wouldn't bring up Eileen anymore.

"You'd better take him home," one of the nurses, said. "We've had enough of his wise-cracks on this ward. She shot Tyson a toothy grin.

Naomi looked at Tyson as his face broke into the widest smile. She thought it a perfectly normal smile for someone who had been receiving invasive cancer treatment for far too long and was finally declared well enough to go home. Until she noticed how Tyson turned his head toward the door and Naomi found out who that warm smile was actually meant for.

"Sorry I'm late," Eileen bounded into the room. "Thank goodness you're still here." She was carrying a plastic bag.

"I only get to leave tomorrow," Tyson said.

Eileen briefly nodded at Naomi, then focused all her attention on Tyson. "Just in time to deliver this then." She put the plastic bag on Tyson's bed.

"Is—is that for me?" he asked.

"Yup, but don't get too excited." Eileen contradicted her words with the sparkle in her eyes. She appeared extremely excited herself about giving Tyson this present.

Tyson dug into the bag and unearthed what looked like a very old camera.

"This was made decades before you were born," Eileen said. "I found it in my old bedroom. It's the very first camera I ever owned. The one that started everything."

"That's way too much," Deborah said. "That must have such sentimental value to you."

Eileen turned away from Tyson, who was inspecting the camera with a furrowed brow, touching a finger to all its buttons. "Honestly, I forgot I still had it and it will make Tyson so much happier than it does me. I've had my use of it," she muttered under her breath.

"What do you say, champ?" she asked Tyson. "Will I see your name on the Pulitzer winner list in a decade or so?"

Naomi was awestruck by Eileen's gift-giving ability. Because not only had she given Tyson something he really liked, but by doing so, had taught him to look far into his future—a future that had hung precariously in the balance for the past couple of months of his young life.

"How does this thing work?" Tyson asked. "It's not the same as the disposable camera you gave me." He kept fiddling with a button that didn't move.

"How about we meet up in the new year and I give you some lessons?"

In the new year? What was Eileen talking about? Wasn't she meant to go back to London and start work again?

"Awesome," Tyson said.

Eileen addressed Deborah and Tyson's dad. "I've been looking into setting up some photography classes for kids in town. It may take a while, but I'm hoping to get it off the ground sometime next year.

Naomi couldn't believe what she was hearing. Did this mean that Eileen was staying? But if she was, why wouldn't she have told Naomi?

There was only one plausible conclusion: her decision to stay had nothing to do with Naomi.

All the harsh words Eileen had spoken to her flitted through Naomi's mind again. Eileen staying didn't change anything for the two of them.

She tuned out the conversation the others were having and looked away from Eileen. She took a deep breath. A part of her hoped Eileen wouldn't show up during her volunteering shifts too frequently, but, of course, the bigger part of her was happy that the kids would have someone like Eileen to spend time with and look up to.

Then, as she looked at the smile on Tyson's face again, and Eileen's body language, which was the complete opposite of when Naomi had last seen her, she was overcome by the need to get out of the room.

"I have to go, Tyson," Naomi said. She walked toward him and opened her arms to him. He accepted her hug as graciously as a thirteen-year-old could.

"Naomi," Eileen said. "Can we t—"

Naomi just shook her head. She just wanted to get out of there and try to forget all about Eileen—again. "I'm late for something," she lied, and hurried out.

CHAPTER TWENTY-SEVEN

Eileen brushed off snow from her jacket before entering The Irish Store, which was owned by a granddaughter of immigrants and had been handed down from generation to generation. In addition to genuine Irish imports, the store was a treasure trove of kitsch of the type that appealed to Americans with Irish heritage, who couldn't seem to get enough of wall plaques emblazoned with Celtic knots or aprons that proclaimed "The best cooks are Irish."

Michael Bublé's "It's Beginning to Look a Lot Like Christmas" assaulted her ears. She'd never been gung-ho about the holidays and, after Naomi had dashed away from her at the hospital, Eileen had zipped past Grinch level to something that was nearly impossible to quantify. Was there a Grim Reaper equivalent for Christmas?

Melissa had been wrong when she'd said the only thing that mattered was Eileen liking Naomi.

Liking Naomi wouldn't get her very far if the mere sight of Eileen sent Naomi running for the hills. One-way liking was torture. Probably what she deserved, though.

Eileen's mind wavered. Should she leave Derby and head to

Boston? Be closer to the home office and surround herself with work and things she understood? Because she sure as hell didn't understand people, not even herself. Her mom was a horrible person, even pathological or something, and yet Eileen was looking for a Christmas gift for dear old mom, because that was what daughters did. Eileen was a mess. No wonder Naomi had fled like she did.

The distance had allowed Eileen to ignore her Mommy issues for so many years, but now that she was back in Derby, everything was resurfacing, and she realized why she'd run away. It had seemed a whole lot easier than figuring everything out.

Then her mind grew set on staying and convincing Naomi she wasn't always the asshole Naomi had witnessed. At least. Eileen didn't want to be that way forever. Was it too late for growth or self-awareness? She'd returned home and found the person Eileen now knew she was meant to be with, but she'd blown it. Naomi was constantly on her mind. And it was fucking hell. Pure and simple.

How could Eileen convince Naomi to give her another chance? Would this be the second or third? Eileen knew, if given one final chance, she'd hold on. She had to or her heart would never heal. Had she really just thought that?

Eileen closed her eyes momentarily to pull herself together. It wouldn't suit at all to break down while shopping for a Christmas gift for her mom, the last person she wanted to buy a gift for. The moment she reopened them, a purple and teal object sitting on a glass shelf in front of her snagged Eileen's attention. She picked it up, bringing the turtle eye-level, the little head zagging to the right, left, right, left.

The saleswoman noticed Eileen's interest. "Aren't these cute? Each one is a hand-painted nut with the inside hollowed out. Kids love them. Are you shopping for nieces and nephews?"

Eileen couldn't help but notice the woman assumed she wasn't shopping for her own children. Was it a jab at her sexuality or did she recognize Eileen and knew she was childless? They were roughly the same age and it was highly probable they'd attended the same school.

"I'm shopping for kids spending Christmas in the Derby hospital." Before coming to the store, Eileen didn't have any intention of doing this. But the idea struck her as soon as she spied all the brightly colored and cheerful turtles.

"What a lovely idea."

"Can you set all of them aside?"

"All of them?" The woman's eyes roamed over the thirty-something turtles. "Are there that many kids in the hospital for the holiday?"

"Fortunately, no. But there'll be more in the months to come. Life can be… unfair. These little guys can add color to their bedsides."

The woman's eyes briefly fell to Eileen's rigid arm. "I know what you mean about life… Is there anything else I can help you with?"

"I'm still browsing for a last-minute gift for my mom."

The woman nodded her head as if she understood Eileen's dilemma. "Give me a holler if you need anything. I'll start boxing up the turtles."

"Thank you."

Eileen wandered to the knit section, sizing up a candy-apple red cashmere scarf, which according to the label came from the Aran Islands. Eileen suspected it was true as she inspected the quality of the traditional honeycomb stitch. This was no knock-off, a fact the price on the tag also reflected, but its beauty more than justified the cost. A shame to waste it on her mom.

Her eyes wandered over the other colors, wondering which one Naomi would prefer.

Stop, Eileen. She doesn't like you.

But she wanted to show Naomi she was thinking of her. Was that the best route, though, for another chance?

Buying cute turtles for the kids was fine. Buying Naomi a Christmas gift, and such an expensive one, at that, would that seem—

Someone knocked into her.

"I'm so sorry. Are you okay?" Jane steadied Eileen.

"Uh, yeah. What were…" Stopping herself from saying what she was thinking, she switched gears. "Are you doing some last-minute shopping as well?"

Jane, a glassy look in her eyes, nodded. "For my mom. She's difficult…" she let her words tail off.

Eileen couldn't determine if Jane meant to imply her mom was difficult to shop for or all-around difficult. "I understand." She gripped the red scarf in her hand like it was a neck, twisting it.

Jane glanced about, rubbing her chin. "Maybe I should pick up a gift for Naomi, as well. I bumped into her yesterday at the hospital and she looked down in the dumps."

"Oh, really. Did you volunteer?" A stab of jealousy plunged into Eileen's chest.

Jane shook her head. "No, I can't seem to… it freaks me out. I had to get my yearly blood test, that's all." Her eyes dropped to the floor.

"What kind of gift were you thinking for Naomi? To cheer her up."

Jane stared at the knitted scarves. "Good question. She really likes to bake. A mixer or something."

Eileen stifled a laugh, considering Jane was standing in the middle of a store that didn't sell kitchen supplies unless you counted quirky Leprechaun bottle openers. "Would she like something… so practical?"

Jane laughed. "You got me. I'm admittedly the worst shopper on the planet."

At least she was honest.

Jane's eyes zeroed in on the scarf in Eileen's hands. "Who's that for?"

"I was thinking of getting this for my mom."

"Mind if I steal your idea. Not the actual scarf in your hands. That would be mean. Even for me." Jane chuckled, seemingly aware of her reputation in town. She reached for a sky blue one. "This would make her eyes really pop."

"Sure. I don't have the market cornered on gifts for difficult mothers." Although, this meant Eileen couldn't purchase one for Naomi. Not if every mom in Derby sported one from offspring who didn't allocate enough time or thought to find the perfect Christmas gift. And, Eileen wanted a gift that showed Naomi she cared, not the one that was easy and right before her.

"Maybe this year she won't be so disappointed in me." Jane's expression didn't bank on it. "Oh, hey, speaking of disappointment. I'm sorry I ambushed you that morning in the café. Putting you on the spot for an endorsement." Her glance ping-ponged around the shop. "I'd just read a scathing review of my exhibition and... well... the thought struck me. It was desperate, really." She shrugged one shoulder. "I have to run. But if you ever have time for coffee, I'd love to pick your brain about photography and I promise not to ask for any favors." Without waiting for a response, Jane marched to the register to pay for the scarf. On her way out, she said over her shoulder, "If you would like to meet, Naomi has my number."

The door closed.

Why did Jane assume Eileen was on good enough terms with Naomi to say, "Hey, can I get your ex's digits?" Or was Naomi the Ma Bell of Derby? Although, Jane was way too young to know this reference to the US telephone company.

Back to the Naomi gift issue. Should she buy her something? Was Jane wildly off the mark in suggesting a mixer? She was right about Naomi's obsession with cooking. Any woman with a classic stainless-steel scale to measure flour for simple pancakes took cooking to the obsession level.

Jane, though, outright admitted she was a terrible shopper. And her track record with Naomi wasn't superb. Unless you counted breaking Naomi's heart, which Eileen had accomplished all on her own.

Eileen thought back to one of the gifts she'd purchased for Melissa way back in the day. A coffee mug, simply because days before Melissa had said she needed a new one. And it hadn't even been a clever one, like the one on the shelf proclaiming, "We can't all be Irish... someone has to drive." No, Eileen had bought Melissa a plain white mug and if her memory served her correctly, that was the last gift she'd purchased for her high school sweetheart. Unless she counted the sympathy card Eileen sent when hearing, months after the fact, Susan had died. No, most assuredly that didn't count.

No mixers or mugs. Perhaps best to stay away from any item that started with the letter M.

Eileen started at the shop's entrance, and carefully examined every item in the store. Sometimes when you least expected it, you found something perfect. Like when Eileen had spilled the contents of her change purse in the hospital coffee shop and Naomi had rushed to help her.

A coin purse?

Eileen groaned.

Think, Eileen, what would Naomi like?

Her phone rang, but it wasn't the person she wanted to speak to. On second thoughts, it was the next best person. "Julia, I need your help."

"Are you okay?" There was concern in her voice.

"I'm fine. Just completely at a loss what to buy for Christmas."

"If you're shopping for Mom, I suggest a sweater or something. And, Dad, some nice socks. Warm ones."

Eileen moved to the far corner, hopefully out of hearing of the shop owner. "Not Mom or Dad. Naomi."

"Oh." There was a pause. "Are you asking me to help you buy a gift for a woman you're interested in?"

"I was... Is that weird?"

"Not weird. Totally unexpected, coming from you. But, I've been told it's something most sisters do, but you... oh my God, you must really like Naomi. Like, really *like* her." Julia laughed. "Do you think I can cram another *like* in that sentence?" She giggled as if she was in high school. "I'm just in shock. Total shock."

"I'm starting to remember why I never ask people for help. They lose their frigging minds."

"Oh, shut up and let me enjoy this moment, will ya? My older sister wants me to shop with her. Where are you?" Her voice changed, indicating she meant business.

"The Irish Store on Main Street."

"No, that won't do. I'll swing by with the car in ten minutes and we'll head to Boston for real shopping. Be ready."

Eileen paid for the turtles and scarf, wondering if she'd made a serious mistake calling Julia. She'd never hear the end of it. Especially if she crashed and burned. The thought of knowing she'd tried, though, eased her worry some.

In Julia's car, driving back from Boston, Eileen asked, "Would you like to stop for dinner?"

"Okay, who are you and what have you done with my sister?" Julia eased onto the offramp. "On second thought, don't tell me. I like this version so much better. There's a quaint restaurant just down the road. Their apple cobbler is to die for. I should warn you though, no one there will be under the age of sixty, so you'll fit right in."

Eileen rolled her eyes. "You're taking this sisterly bond a bit too far. Are you sure James and the kids won't miss you for dinner?"

"Are you kidding me?" Julia drummed her thumbs on the steering wheel. "This gives them an excuse to order pizza and not eat any vegetables."

"You force your teenagers to eat veggies. What kind of monster are you?"

"The mother kind."

Eileen closed one eye. "I can't remember; did Mom make us eat healthy?"

Julia handed Eileen her phone. "Can you text James that I won't be home for dinner? As for Mom, I don't remember her ever cooking a meal, but Maggie always included something green, usually your fave brussels sprouts, which I hated by the way."

"It's a wonder you survived." Eileen slowly punched out the text. Within seconds of hitting send, James replied with five pizza emojis. "Does this mean he's getting five pizzas?" Eileen held the phone for her sister to see the so-called message.

"Perhaps. Or he's just that excited for a greasy meal. Michael can demolish a pizza on his own, though. And James likes to keep up with his son, forgetting he doesn't have Michael's metabolism."

Three minutes after five, they pulled into a nearly empty parking lot, in front of a building that looked like a cross between a big red barn and an old western saloon. It even had a wagon wheel next to the door. "Dad would be tickled that we're here for the early bird special." Julia killed the car's engine. "It's a wonder he and mom have stayed married so long."

"Irish Americans can be stubborn." Eileen opened the car door.

"You're living proof of that." Julia dropped her keys into her purse.

The perky blond hostess led them past five tables of older white-haired couples, to a booth near a wall that was formed almost entirely from a massive stone fireplace. Flames danced in the hearth and filled the room with a pleasant warmth. "Will this work?"

The booth was like every other one in the place, with worn vinyl seats and a plain wooden tabletop covered with nicks and scratches. "Yes, thank you." Julia took her seat.

The hostess placed menus in front of each. "Adriene will be right with you."

"I recommend the buffalo chicken cheese enchiladas," Julia said not bothering to open her menu.

"Do they come with brussels sprouts?"

"Nope." She flashed a toothy grin.

Eileen leaned back against the seat. "How much did you hate me growing up?"

"Never did, Ellie. Didn't have to. You were always beating yourself up enough to cover the bases."

Adriene took their drink and dinner order, both sisters ordering enchiladas, and mulled apple cider without the rum.

"Are you ready to spill yet?" Julia asked when the waitress left.

"About?"

"How you messed things up with Naomi?"

"Why do you assume it was me?" Eileen placed a hand over her breast.

Julia fiddled with the silverware, picking up the knife and pointing it at Eileen. "The gift currently sitting in my car is a dead giveaway, which is sweet. But I have a feeling the true gift for Naomi, is the care packages for all the kids in the hospital."

Ignoring Julia's antics, Eileen asked, "Is it too much?"

"It's perfect. And so much better than the coffee mug you got Melissa."

"You knew about that?"

"Women talk," she said as if Eileen was the only person on the planet who didn't understand that simple fact.

"Seems everyone in our town does."

"You want to know why most people talk?"

"Enlighten me, please, oh wise one," Eileen mocked.

"To avoid messing things up with someone they truly care about. So, the way I see it, you can tell me what's going on or never get past it."

Eileen hated the fact that she knew Julia was right. She needed to open up more to Julia and more importantly, to Naomi. Or she'd never be able to set things right.

CHAPTER TWENTY-EIGHT

Naomi peered at the fairy lights she'd hung up in her office only a week ago. They were sagging a bit on the left, but she didn't have the energy to pull up a chair, stand on it, and adjust them again. It was the last day of work before her Christmas holiday started anyway, and she should really be in the break room, drinking eggnog with her co-workers. For a few hours, all of them should be forgetting about the people they hadn't been able to help the past year, and toasting the ones they had.

It was the 21st of December, only four days until Christmas, and Naomi had spent her time—of which she suddenly seemed to have way too much—spreading as much cheer as she could. Mainly in the form of the most elaborate Christmas decorations the children's cancer ward of Derby Hospital had ever seen. But in doing so, it felt like Naomi didn't have any joy left for herself.

The image of Eileen at Tyson's bedside was burned in her mind. No matter how hard she tried to focus on thoughts of the brand-new Christmas sweater she'd bought, or the tree that awaited her at home, or the food her mom would prepare, the prevalent image in her mind remained Eileen giving Tyson that camera. *Eileen. Eileen. Eileen.*

Christ, Naomi wished Eileen *would* leave Derby soon. At least then, she could move on. But what if she really had decided to stay longer? She shook her head. It still didn't make a difference.

With a heavy sigh, she pushed herself out of her chair, and joined the party.

Warmed by a few glasses of eggnog, Naomi swung the door of the hospital wide open. She looked forward to her snowy walk home. By the time she got there, she'd have sobered up, but hopefully still enjoying a lingering buzz. Spending time with the people she worked with, having a chat and toasting the upcoming new year, had transported her mind away from Eileen. She was feeling more ready for Christmas now.

"Fancy bumping into you here," someone said.

Naomi snapped out of her reverie. She'd been so lost in thought, she hadn't seen Eileen coming around the corner.

"I do work here, you know," Naomi said, perhaps sounding a little snippier than she had intended. The truth was that, after she'd run out of Tyson's room last week—literally fleeing from Eileen—she had hoped to run into her at the hospital every day.

"I do know, of course." Eileen stepped a little closer.

Even though she'd secretly hoped for a moment like this— and despite wanting to find out how long Eileen would be staying in town for—Naomi didn't know what to say. She shuffled her weight around a bit.

Eileen ostentatiously sniffed the air between them. "Do they let hospital employees drink on the job these days?" A grin appeared on her face.

"We had a Christmas party," Naomi said.

Eileen nodded. "Good to know… that might tempt me to take advantage of—" They were interrupted by someone else leaving the hospital.

"Hey there, ladies," Mack said. He gave Eileen a quick once-over. "Promise me again you won't neglect your exercises over the Christmas break." He held up his hand. "Come on. Give me a high-five. With your bad hand." He shot Eileen a wide grin and then winked at Naomi. "Always be retraining the pathway," he said cheerily.

Naomi wondered how Mack's bossiness would go down with Eileen.

"You ask too much of me." Eileen's face strained as she tried to lift her right arm. She didn't seem to mind Mack's forwardness about her condition in front of someone else. She turned to Naomi and, almost out of breath, said, "He keeps doing that."

"It's my job." Mack held his hand much lower. "At least give me a low one. Down and dirty, just the way I like it."

Eileen rolled her eyes, but managed to slap her palm against Mack's.

"Thanks for that. Now I have to rush to get some last-minute Christmas shopping done. Just like every year." He tipped a finger to his forehead and walked to his car.

"God, men can be so annoying," Eileen said.

Naomi snickered, then nodded at Eileen's arm. "You seem to have made some progress since, er…"

"Since I asked you to remove that peanut butter jar from my palm?" Eileen arched up one eyebrow.

Naomi nodded. "Are you doing better?"

"Physically, I guess I am." Eileen shot her a weak smile. She breathed in a lungful of air. "Do you think you can ever forgive me, Naomi?"

Naomi wasn't expecting that question. "I didn't know you

were asking for forgiveness," she said, unable to keep a measure of disbelief from her voice.

"I wanted to ask you that day I came to see Tyson. He'd texted me, by the way. I knew you'd be there. But I couldn't really find the words. Not before you left, anyway."

"And now?" Naomi asked, bolstered by the alcohol buzzing in her bloodstream. "Can you find them now?"

Eileen's gaze skittered away and she stared at her feet. Naomi stopped herself from inching closer toward Eileen, even though her whole body was wanting to.

She hesitated for a moment, but then brought her finger to Eileen's chin and tilted it upward.

"I was advised to give you the time and space you needed," Naomi said.

Eileen's green eyes glittered in the glare of the Christmas lights outside the hospital. People were walking past them, going in and out of the main door, but Naomi didn't notice. She only had eyes for Eileen, as though the two of them were frozen inside their own little bubble.

Eileen shook her head and Naomi's finger lost contact with her chin. "Turns out that was the very last thing I wanted. Or needed." Her lips curved into the beginning of a much stronger smile.

"What you did for Tyson was so lovely." Not only for him, Naomi thought. Because it had illuminated Eileen's true nature —the charming, bright, uplifting side of her. "I might have been a bit quick to walk out. I was just… so confused."

"This is *me* asking for forgiveness," Eileen said. "You haven't done a single thing wrong."

"You might be the oldest," Naomi said, still spurred on by how light-headed the alcohol made her feel, "but I'm certainly the wisest."

"Can I take you to dinner? So we can have a proper chat?" Eileen's smile grew bolder.

"How about we cook something at my place?" Naomi asked. "For old times' sake."

"Depends," Eileen asked. "Do we have to go shopping first? Because I'm not sure you're in the right state to drive." She tapped against her right shoulder. "And I might have made progress, but I can't drive us around either."

"I've got plenty of food in the fridge," Naomi said.

"I'd be delighted then." She offered her left arm for Naomi's to slip hers through. "Let's start our journey."

They walked in silence for a few minutes before Naomi drummed up the courage to say, "What you said to Tyson, about looking into photography lessons for kids in Derby. I think that's what confused me most."

"I've spoken to my boss." Eileen's breath turned into little clouds as she spoke. "I can work from Derby for the foreseeable future."

"Really?" A sense of relief washed over Naomi, but it didn't completely erase the unease that had lodged itself in her gut when she and Eileen had last talked. Eileen had been pretty adamant that Derby would never be enough for her.

"I had to take a long hard look in the mirror. And be truly honest with myself. I won't be going to any war zones any time soon. Not with this arm refusing to cooperate. I need more time."

Naomi pressed herself against Eileen's flank. "Will you become the new full-time photographer for *The Derby Gazette?*" she joked, when what she really wanted to ask was what would happen once Eileen's arm was better.

"Not quite. I won't be doing my best photography work for a while. I'll be doing some writing instead."

"Writing?" Naomi's voice shot up in surprise.

"Indeed." Eileen turned to her. Her nose had turned a dangerous shade of red. Naomi wanted to plant a kiss on the tip of it. But they were just walking home together. They'd have dinner. It was too soon. Nevertheless, Naomi felt the desire for it course through her, keeping her glowing with warmth inside.

Eileen was staying. For now, at least. Suddenly, all the Christmas spirit Naomi hadn't been able to muster came rushing to the surface. Yet, she still refrained from kissing Eileen.

"I'm a bit rusty, but my boss has got my back." Eileen's voice softened. "It's so reassuring to know that people have your back."

"I'm glad you're staying," Naomi said and stopped in her tracks. They had reached the town square, where Derby's big Christmas tree stood. "I don't suppose you've bothered putting up one of those yet?"

"No. Someone offered to help me with that but I recklessly squandered my chances." Eileen unhooked her arm from Naomi's and curved it around her waist.

"If we work fast, we can still make it happen. And with my connections in this town, I may be able to get you a good tree, despite it being four days until Christmas."

Eileen turned to her fully. "I'm glad I'm staying too," she said, and gazed deeply into Naomi's eyes. "I'm sorry for the things I said to you. I didn't mean any of them. My mom got to me, the way she does so easily. I took it out on you." She brought her hand to Naomi's face and caressed her cheek with the back of her fingers. "I feel more secure now that I know I still have a job. And that I know I can stay here. Close to you."

They stood staring at each other in silence for a few moments. Naomi knew so much more needed to be said and she could not dismiss the doubts she still felt. But she could not deny a little bubble of hope was growing inside her with every passing second.

It was Naomi who leaned in and bridged the last of the distance between them. She lightly pressed her lips against Eileen's, in the light of the Derby Christmas tree.

CHAPTER TWENTY-NINE

"Hold on one second, let me turn a light on." Naomi reached inside her front door with one hand. "It's such a tricky switch. Not where you'd expect it at all."

Eileen, bemused by the way Naomi contorted her body, asked, "How long have you lived here?"

"Oh, a few years. You'd think I'd have this mastered by now. Ah ha! Got it." Naomi swung the door all the way open. "I hate walking into a dark apartment."

"Didn't you tell me Jane hated it when you forgot to lock the door?"

"Uh, yeah. She did. And, this may seem like an inconsistency, but I'm a woman, so I'm reserving the right to change my mind whenever it suits me." Her smile was stunning. "Besides, it's possible I've watched one too many episodes of *Criminal Minds* the past few nights..." She shrugged.

"Do you check behind the shower curtain now?" Eileen joked.

Blushing, Naomi nodded.

"And, if there was someone there, what would you do?"

"Scream my head off, I suppose. Or completely freeze. Either way, I'm dead."

"When this"—Eileen pointed to her right arm—"is in better shape, I can teach you a few moves. Over the years, I've met some interesting people. The type who can kill you just as easily as saying hello."

"Should I be worried to have you in my apartment?" Naomi's eyes glowed with what Eileen hoped was desire not fear.

"In my state, I should be the one that's worried."

"What state is that?" Naomi's voice was tender.

"Compromised," Eileen whispered, moving closer to Naomi.

"Because of your arm?" Naomi inched even closer.

"That's part of it."

"The other part? Or are there more than two?"

"More than two in all likelihood, but the only other part that comes to mind is convincing you I'm not the asshole you witnessed that one day." Eileen cupped Naomi's cheek. "I was terrible that day."

"You were."

"Thank you for not excusing the behavior."

"I believe in absolute honesty."

"What about second chances?"

"Most definitely. Didn't I give you one already?" As if suddenly becoming aware they were still standing in the entry-way, Naomi said, "Shall we get dinner going?"

Eileen motioned for Naomi to lead the way, but neither budged, both staring deeply into the other's eyes.

Naomi offered a timid smile, toed off her shoes and headed down the hallway to the kitchen.

Eileen kicked off her own shoes and trailed her. The kitchen was slightly messier than the other times she'd been here. "Have you been baking?" She ran a finger through the flour sprinkled over the small kitchen island. Maybe Jane had been right about getting Naomi a mixer.

"I was up late last night making cookies for the staff party and the last thing I wanted to do this morning was clean." She leaned down and pulled out wet wipes from under the sink. "Care to make yourself useful while I gather things for dinner?"

"I can be talked into it, I guess."

"Oh, really. What kind of persuasion are you referring to?"

Eileen's cheeks burned with the beginnings of a blush. "The nonverbal kind would be much appreciated."

"You think you can waltz in here after an apology, sweep me off my feet and into bed?"

Eileen raised her left hand. "Clearly not." She added, "Not until I help you clean at least. What other penance do you have in mind?"

Naomi's lips pressed together, seeming to mull over certain options. "I hate cleaning the toilet."

"Doesn't everyone?" Eileen wiped the island, her eyes on Naomi and not the task at hand.

"Does that mean you won't?"

"Is this the time to explain I'm injured and in recovery?" Eileen looked down at her arm.

Naomi laughed. "Now it's okay for you to talk about it?"

"It's an emergency situation. And, honestly, if you had this excuse to get out of cleaning a toilet, wouldn't you use it?" Eileen moved her arm back and forth showing that, even though she'd made progress, she was still limited.

"Shall I kiss it better?"

"Was that an option all along?"

"It would have been weird if I started kissing your arm when we first met, doncha think." Naomi arched one eyebrow.

"True, although, it would have been an epic first impression. Even more impressive than when I first looked into your face and peered into your smoldering dark eyes. Long lashes."

Eileen closed the space between the two and ran a finger down Naomi's cheek. "Soft lips."

"How'd you know my lips were soft?" There was a hitch in her breath.

"Because there's no way someone this beautiful doesn't have the softest lips." Eileen licked her own, finding it hard to resist shoving Naomi up against the wall.

"I wasn't so sure about yours."

"Aren't you the one who said you prefer hands on experience?" Eileen's head dipped closer to Naomi.

"We're supposed to have dinner," Naomi didn't sound all that enthused about dining.

"Truth be told, I'm not that hungry... for food, that is."

"What are you hungry for?"

There was less than an inch of space between their faces. Eileen could feel Naomi's warm breath on her skin. "I know you're younger and bolder, but I'm going to go out on a limb. I want you. Here. Now."

"And how do I know you won't do a runner again?" Naomi crossed her arms.

"I'm so tired of running." Eileen sucked in a breath. "I said terrible things to you. I let my mom get inside my head with the same old shit she's always controlled me with. Her guilt trip about having to give up the life she wanted to have when she got knocked up—"

"But you had no control over that, Ellie." Naomi seemed horrified a mother could suggest such a thing.

"I know that's true." Eileen patted the top of her head. "In here, though, it's so much harder to sort through all the thoughts and emotions. I still haven't figured out a tenth of it. I need you to understand that part. The self-realization I've been experiencing lately is only just starting. And, I've been burying shit for decades." She stopped to look directly into Naomi's eyes. "I know this, though, I want to stay put and work on me.

On us. You are the most amazing woman I've ever met. I love the way I feel when I'm around you. Your thirst for life is refreshing. I've been surrounding myself with pain and suffering because it made the way I felt about myself easier to bear. How could I feel sorry about my upbringing when witnessing children being blown to pieces by landmines? My mom made it clear all my life she resented me. As much as I hate to admit this, it did a mind fuck on me that I'm only really confronting now."

"Why now?" Naomi's voice was supportive.

"Because I messed everything up. I've been thinking a lot about this. I'm like Bitsy."

"Jane's doll?" Naomi asked, incredulity etched into her brow.

"Yeah. My life is scattered from London to Derby and I need to put the pieces back together. I want to be whole, maybe for the first time. My first step was letting my London flat go to focus on my life here. And, I'm hoping you'll want to be a part of my new life. Even if you only want to be friends for now. You're the key piece of the puzzle—what I've been searching for, but I was too stubborn to realize it until I lost you."

"What about your recovery? You've been so stubborn about admitting anything about your stroke." Naomi leaned against the counter.

"That's how I was raised. Never to show weakness." Eileen sighed. "That day when you came over and I was a brute. Before you arrived, my charming mother straight up told me you'd grow to resent me. Just like she resented me being born."

Naomi slapped a hand over her mouth.

"And, I believed her." Eileen's voice was barely a whisper.

Through her fingers, Naomi said, "I would never feel that way."

"I don't think you have that in you, but hearing it from my

mom—I'm going to say this aloud to you: I have mommy issues." Eileen stood straighter.

"Why didn't you let me in sooner?" Naomi's expression wasn't accusatory, but sad.

"I hate myself for hurting you." Eileen cupped Naomi's cheek. "So very much. I asked earlier, but I want to ask again. Do you think you can forgive me?"

"Oh, Ellie. If I'd known you'd been dealing with half of the stuff you just shared, I would have done more to get you to see how evil your mother is."

A tear fell from Eileen's eye, followed by another and another. Naomi wrapped her arms around Eileen, pulling her close.

"Please tell me I haven't blown my chance to be with you?"

Naomi didn't reply. Instead she loosened her embrace of Eileen and took hold of her left hand, leading her in the direction of the bedroom.

"Good God, that's the biggest tree I've ever seen!" Eileen exclaimed.

Naomi laughed. "I bet you say that to all the girls."

Eileen, with a shy smile, goggled at the tree. "No. Only to the special ones. One, rather." She eyed the base of the tree, where one long branch stuck out blocking half of the bedroom's entrance. "How do you not trip on that?"

Naomi's eyes followed Eileen's. "I've been sleeping on the couch, bathed in the light from the tree." Naomi plugged the tree in. "I thought it'd help perk up my Christmas spirit, which has been severely lagging this year. I blame you, completely." Naomi jabbed a teasing finger into Eileen's chest, leaving her hand on the swell of her breast.

"Allow me to make amends." Eileen stripped the thick comforter off the couch and tossed it on the plush carpet in front of the tree.

Naomi helped her spread out the comforter, standing in the

middle, beckoning Eileen with a come-hither look in her imploring eyes, the pupils expanding with longing.

Eileen moved closer. Naomi placed her hands on Eileen's belt, and undid it, lowering the pants' zipper one tooth at a time. When she reached the end, Naomi eased them off Eileen. She bent down to dispense with one sock. Then the other. Still squatting, Naomi planted a sensual kiss on the inside of Eileen's calf, her mouth working its way up the inside of Eileen's leg. Naomi bypassed Eileen's hot zone, and stood upright, yanking off her own sweater in the process and flinging it across the room.

Naomi captured Eileen's mouth. Her soft lips brushed Eileen's gently. The sweet kisses quickly gave way to hunger, Naomi clearly wanting to possess Eileen's mouth. Her tongue urgently jabbed to seek entrance and Eileen welcomed it. Naomi's entreaty clarifying in Eileen's mind how much she worshipped the woman. Craved her. How each stroke of Naomi's tongue, touch of her fingertips, and lustful moan healed a snippet of Eileen's soul, bridging the divide between their two minds and bodies. Eileen threaded her fingers into Naomi's thick dark hair, pulling her as close as humanly possible, never wanting to let her go. Needing Naomi in her arms, where she belonged. She nipped Naomi's bottom lip, sucking it into her mouth.

Naomi moaned, assaulting Eileen's mouth with determination.

"I'm so sorry," Eileen said in between kisses. "So, sorry."

Naomi rested her forehead against Eileen's, her eyes smoldering.

Eileen planted a soft kiss on Naomi's forehead. Above her eyebrow. On the tip of her nose. Arriving back where they'd started.

Naomi kicked up the heat factor of the kiss from hot to

scorching. Both hungrily grabbing at hips, hands roving over each other feeling the other's curves.

Breathing heavily, Naomi's mouth wandered to Eileen's ear, leaving a trail of sensual caresses. Naomi tugged on the earlobe with her teeth, and whispered with throaty desire, "Show me, how sorry. I need to feel it. You. I need you." Holding each side of Eileen's face, Naomi stared into her lover's eyes as if compelling Eileen to prove everything she'd said earlier.

Eileen's hand started to unbutton Naomi's shirt, but Naomi ripped it over her head, mussing her hair in a sexy way. Naomi unclipped and shed her bra, then tossed it over her shoulder where it landed on the octopus centerpiece. Laughing, she said, "Good thing the candles aren't lit."

"No need with all the lights on the tree. I love how the reflection dances in your eyes." Eileen ran a finger down Naomi's face.

"Keep talking like that and I may just forgive you entirely."

"That would be a shame if that's all it took. I'm eager to prove to you... how I feel... all night."

"Let's get you out of these." Naomi freed her from the baggy red cardigan, moving on to the buttons of the silk blouse, starting at the top. After undoing each one, Naomi kissed the exposed skin. Slowly she eased one sleeve off Eileen, her mouth exploring the muscles of Eileen's good arm. When it came to removing the shirt from the other side, Naomi questioned Eileen with her eyes if she was ready.

Eileen nodded.

Naomi undid the bra, and slipped both the shirt and strap off her shoulder, once again covering Eileen with kisses as the fabric revealed the flesh. Maneuvering the articles past the elbow was surprisingly easier this time around, allowing Naomi free rein to Eileen's body. "One last thing." Naomi slid her hand down Eileen's backside, her fingers gliding under her panties, tugging them past Eileen's firm butt, letting them fall to the floor. "It's kinda hot, undressing you slowly."

"Maybe you missed your true calling." Eileen breathed in her musky scent.

"Undressing women?" Naomi took Eileen's nipple into her mouth, sucking it gently until it hardened, allowing her to bite down.

Eileen's head dipped back, her breath hitching as she managed to say, "I had one particular woman in mind."

"If it's the one I'm thinking of, she's already undressed. Ready for the next step?"

Eileen quirked a brow. "I didn't know there was a step-by-step process."

"Oh, it changes, but right now, I need you on the floor so I can have my way with you."

The two lowered to the floor, Naomi climbing on top of Eileen. "The thought of not feeling your body against mine..." Naomi didn't finish the sentence, opting to kiss Eileen slowly and passionately. Their bodies moved in sync as if they'd been waiting for the other like two swans forming the shape of a heart with their necks.

Naomi snaked down, tracing the outline of Eileen's areola with her tongue, edging closer to the nipple with each completed swirl. Eileen's breath came more rapidly the closer Naomi came to the hardening peak. Tiny gasps. In and out. Eileen's body writhed under the weight of Naomi's.

She took Eileen's nub into her mouth, biting harder this time. It seemed Eileen's nipple had a direct connection to her clit, and the tingling sensation intensified, causing Eileen's buttocks to momentarily levitate over the down comforter as if by magic.

Was this what love felt like? Light. Trusting. Surprisingly easy if you let it in. Or was the heady scent of sex clinging to the air muddling Eileen's thoughts?

Bypassing the other nipple that hadn't quite come out to play yet, Naomi's tongue licked Eileen's skin as she continued her trek down south. Seemingly not wanting to ignore the nipple completely, Naomi tweaked it with the thumb and forefinger of one hand, much to Eileen's satisfaction. Naomi's other hand kneaded Eileen's derriere.

Her cheek grazed Eileen's coarse pubic hair. Once. Twice. Three times. "This feels so good." Naomi buried her face in Eileen's mound. "And I can smell how much you want me."

Eileen sucked in a deep breath when Naomi's tongue split her folds, lapping in the desire. Naomi matched Eileen's eagerness by burying her face into the wetness, sampling Eileen from within, diving in as far as possible.

"I love the way you taste. If I wasn't the jealous type, I'd encourage you to find a way to market it."

Eileen admired the view of Naomi's face between her legs. "You young people today. Always thinking of ways to make an extra buck."

Naomi plunged a finger inside triggering Eileen's backside to arc off the floor yet again.

"This is the type of bucking I like." Naomi winked. "Watching you react when I do things like this." Her tongue flicked Eileen's clit, initiating a full-body shudder.

Naomi added another finger inside, plunging in and out with more force. Eileen's juices were intensifying according to the slapping sounds that came with each deep thrust.

"Oh, Naomi..."

Naomi penetrated deeper, her tongue circling Eileen's bud.

A euphoric wave started, roiling inside Eileen. Her legs bent at the knees, her thighs tensing around Naomi's head. Eileen's nether regions gyrated with urgency. Her panting came out in ragged spurts. Naomi's fingers dug into the flesh of one of Eileen's thighs, as she continued stimulating Eileen's engorged bud, each flick spurring Eileen further over the edge of bliss.

Seconds passed. Or was it minutes? Hours? Naomi's fingers and tongue never tired. As if sensing Eileen urgently needed the final trigger, Naomi hammered three fingers inside, her tongue unrelenting on Eileen's pulsing clitoris. Eileen lurched upward, circling an arm around the back of Naomi's head. Eileen's legs spasmed.

She tossed her neck back. The ripple of her orgasm pinging all her nerve endings. "Oh... my... God..." Eileen's legs clenched tighter around Naomi's head, the tremors transforming into a full-on convulsion.

Naomi didn't stop. Not until two more spasms came and went, leaving Eileen completely limp and spent.

With Naomi snuggled against her, Eileen said, "How am I supposed to show you how sorry I am if you wear me out and I can't reciprocate?"

"Do you want me to take the orgasms back?"

"No take backs." Eileen planted a kiss on her forehead.

Naomi cuddled closer, her arm draped over Eileen's stomach. "It doesn't always have to work that way, you know."

"What way?" Eileen mumbled into Naomi's hair, inhaling the fresh cucumber mint scent.

"Reciprocating each time. Love isn't—" Naomi sucked in a breath as if trying to reel the word back in, burying her face into Eileen's side.

"Go on. Love isn't...?"

"What?"

Eileen laughed. "I love you too."

Naomi's head popped up. "I'd feel better if you'd said it without laughing."

"I'd feel better if you didn't accidentally say it." Eileen grinned.

Naomi's eyes blazed with true emotion. "On the count of three."

"Really?" One side of Eileen's mouth tugged upward as if she was willing herself not to show amusement.

Undeterred, Naomi said, "One."

Eileen added, "Two."

"Are we going on three or after three?"

"I adore you, Naomi Weaver."

"You cheated." Despite her words, Naomi's face lit up. "I love you, Eileen Makenna Callahan."

"Was I supposed to say your middle name? Did I mess it up for good?" Eileen teased.

Naomi, on top of Eileen once again, shook her head. "What am I going to do with you?"

"Can I make a request?"

"Will it be a wiseass one?"

Eileen chewed on her bottom lip. "It doesn't fit my description, but it may be a bit bold."

"This I've got to hear."

"Love me. Tonight. Tomorrow. And all the days after that."

"Oh, is that all?" Naomi gave a lopsided grin.

"Do I get to ask for more?" Eileen's eyes brimmed with hope.

"It is almost Christmas and I'm in a good mood now, so why not."

"I seem to be getting a second wind." She waggled her brows.

"Did you think I was really going to let you fall asleep?"

CHAPTER THIRTY

Naomi opened her eyes and broke into a smile. It was her favorite day of the year and, when she turned on her side, Eileen was sleeping next to her. For the longest time, it had looked like this year's Christmas was going to be one of the worst she'd had in her entire life, but things had definitely taken a turn for the better.

The usual butterflies that somersaulted in her belly on Christmas morning were magnified by the sight of Eileen Makenna next to her. Eileen, who wouldn't be leaving Derby any time soon. Eileen, who had asked Naomi for forgiveness. It hadn't taken Naomi very long to forgive her.

Because their reunion had only taken place a few days before Christmas, Naomi had to hustle to find a present for Eileen. Eileen had claimed that Naomi had already given her the best present by getting her a last-minute Christmas tree and decorating her sparse apartment with enough baubles and Christmas lights to actually make it look cozy for the first time since Eileen had moved in. But, of course, Naomi didn't feel that way about it at all.

Even though Naomi had always been a firm believer in

physical gifts, the past few years she'd grown more into giving the gift of an experience. And she believed she knew exactly the experience to make Eileen have the best Christmas ever. Well, apart from taking her to the Weaver Christmas party instead of spending all day with the Callahans.

Impatience stirring her, she brushed a loose curl from Eileen's cheek. She told herself she didn't want to disturb Eileen, just feel her skin against hers, but of course she wanted Eileen to wake up already. This was their first Christmas together. Naomi felt, deep in her core, that it would be one of the best Christmases ever.

So she let her finger skate over Eileen's cheek again. Even though she understood why Eileen would still be fast asleep. It had been early in the morning when they'd been able to break apart enough to get some much-needed sleep. And Eileen was older. Naomi smiled at the thought. She was also still in recovery, which had led to a few bouts of extreme inventiveness in the bedroom since they'd gotten back together. At the thought of that, Naomi couldn't contain herself any longer. She leaned in and kissed the spot on Eileen's cheek she'd been stroking. Eileen still didn't wake up. Naomi would have to resort to more drastic measures.

She brought her lips to Eileen's ear and whispered, "This is Santa. Wake up now if you want presents today."

Eileen blinked her eyes open.

Naomi's smile widened. Looking into Eileen's gorgeous green eyes, no matter how sleepy they seemed, was always a treat. And a moment of knowing that they—inevitably—belonged together. Naomi couldn't explain it better than that. She just knew.

"What did you just say?" Eileen groaned.

"It's Christmas, sleeping beauty."

"I could have sworn I heard the word *Santa*." Eileen smiled back at Naomi.

"I had to use some special wording to rouse you from sleep." Naomi scooted closer to Eileen.

"How about you use some special actions instead." Eileen was awake enough to waggle her eyebrows.

"I need you awake for that."

"I'm wide awake now." Eileen bridged the last distance between them and slipped a leg in between Naomi's.

"About time." Naomi kissed Eileen fully on the lips now. "It's very naughty to make me wait for anything at all on my favorite day of the year."

"Naughty, you say." Eileen pressed her leg a little higher. "Does that mean Santa won't have brought me any presents?"

"I guess you'll just have to wait and see." It took all Naomi had to not tell Eileen what she had planned for her.

"Please remember that we're spending Christmas with your family," Eileen said. "If it's a present that's going to embarrass me in front of your mom and your many siblings, then please give it to me now." Eileen's eyes sparkled in the morning light.

"I promise you won't be embarrassed." Naomi pushed herself against Eileen's leg. "And I have another present in mind first." When Naomi kissed Eileen next, she slid her tongue between her lips. It was the first Christmas in a long time, perhaps in all of her life, that she didn't want to jump out of bed and start the day.

"Why are we rushing?" Eileen asked. "Your mom's only expecting us at six, isn't she?"

"That's right." Naomi watched how Eileen got dressed. She'd become very adept at doing it one-handedly. Almost as adept as she was at stripping Naomi of her clothes with just the use of her left hand. "But we have to make a stop on the way."

"Do we now? I suppose I'm not allowed to ask where?"

"Nope." Naomi grinned. "The more you hurry, the more time we'll have."

"I can't hurry if I don't know what I'm hurrying for. For all I know, you've been in cahoots with my mom and you have some sort of Callahan surprise planned."

Naomi shook her head. "It has nothing to do with your mother or your family, I swear."

"Good." Eileen pulled the Christmas sweater Naomi had given her over her head, pushing her right arm through the sleeve first with a determined grimace on her face, quickly followed by the left one. "*Voila*. Ready to go."

"I always knew you'd look scrumptious in that sweater."

"If memory serves me well, I've never worn a Christmas sweater in my life."

"What did you wear last year on the big day?"

"This time last year I was in Nauru. Taking pictures of refugees trying to get to Australia. Trust me, it wasn't sweater weather."

"Were you working on Christmas day?" Naomi asked.

"I wasn't meant to be, but… I don't know. When you take pictures of people's desperation on a day like Christmas, it gives a different result. More acute. More piercing, I guess. It could just be my impression, of course."

Eileen had started writing op-ed pieces, but Naomi knew how much she missed photography. Not because Eileen kept repeating how much she did—she wasn't that kind of person. Naomi had only known Eileen a short while but she could tell something important was missing from her life. Something vital.

"I'm sure it's not just your impression." She held out her hand. "When it comes to your craft, you follow your intuition, which is what makes the results so amazing."

Eileen took Naomi's hand in hers. "Let's go then." She found

Naomi's gaze. "Do I need to take my camera to wherever it is we're going?"

"No, everything's taken care of."

Naomi watched how Eileen narrowed her eyes. She might try to put two and two together but she'd never guess where Naomi was taking her.

In the car, Eileen kept peppering Naomi with questions. Luckily, the drive wasn't far and when they turned into the street of their destination, Eileen recognized it immediately because she'd been there before to deliver the pictures Tyson had taken with the disposable camera she'd given him on Thanksgiving.

"We're going to see Tyson?" Eileen asked. "On Christmas day?"

"I arranged it with Deborah. He doesn't know you're coming over to give him an impromptu lesson on that antique camera you gave him. It'll be the best Christmas present he has ever had."

Eileen shook her head. "You," she said. "You're unbelievable." She reached for her purse. "Before we go in." She reached inside and produced a small gift-wrapped box. "I want to give you this."

Naomi's cheeks drew into an involuntary smile. "For me?"

"Who else?" Eileen leaned over and kissed Naomi on the lips.

Naomi studied the box, then tore off the wrapping paper. It was clearly a jewelry box. Slowly, she opened it. Naomi grinned from ear to ear as she clapped eyes on the two sterling silver turtle stud earrings.

"You're not a turtle, though," Naomi said as she took one in her hand.

"I don't mind being your turtle. As long as I'm the only turtle in your life," Eileen replied.

"I love them." Naomi looked up from the earring in the palm of her hand. "And I love you."

"I love you too." Eileen slanted forward to kiss her again.

"We'd best stop making out in the car now," Naomi said in between lingering kisses. "Deborah might not want us in her house anymore." Naomi carefully placed the turtle earrings back in their box. "And I want to see your eyes light up the way they do when you talk about photography." Naomi found Eileen's gaze.

"Your present for me is so quintessentially you," Eileen said. "It's all the things I love about you."

"Plus, I'm making you work on Christmas day again." Naomi winked at Eileen.

"But this year, thanks to you, I will only encounter joy in everyone's eyes." Eileen drew her lips into the widest smile Naomi had ever seen on her.

CHAPTER THIRTY-ONE

E ileen audibly sighed and gripped Naomi's gloved hand.
Naomi squeezed back. "We can still cancel. Get back into my car and go back to bed. Not sure how much sleep we'll get, though."

Eileen laughed. "If last night, or the string of nights since the twenty-first, is any indication, no sleep at all."

"It's hard to sleep when there's a hot cougar in my bed." Naomi latched onto Eileen's arm and let loose a tiny growl into her ear.

Eileen sighed again. "I have considered canceling, but since I only made a brief appearance on Christmas Day, it doesn't feel right not to show up for New Year's brunch. I'm not fond of my mom by any stretch of the imagination, but I want to see Julia and my dad."

They stood in the entryway of Eileen's childhood home, neither of them making a move to cross the threshold.

"Did you want me to take you behind the outbuilding, again? Relax you some?" Naomi waggled her eyebrows.

Eileen placed a tender kiss on Naomi's cheek. "Tempting, but the foot of snow may freeze certain body parts."

As if Mother Nature was eavesdropping on the couple, a slashing wind cut right through Eileen.

"Come on. Let's get this over with so I can take you home and have my way with you." Eileen opened the door, the sound of muffled laughter greeting them.

Naomi helped Eileen out of her coat, placing it on the bench by the door, and planting a kiss on Eileen's cheek. Not satisfied with a peck, Eileen wheeled about to properly kiss Naomi, taking advantage of having their relationship out in the open.

"Geez, Smelly Ellie, way to make a guy feel uncomfortable."

Eileen pulled her face away from Naomi, but kept her arm around Naomi's waist. "I thought men loved to fantasize about lesbians getting it on."

Philip's eyes grew three sizes. "Oh, we do. But not when it comes to my cousin who's more like a sister. Awkward." He exaggerated a shiver, slipping and sliding in his red socks on the tiled floor. Laughing, he gave Eileen a one-armed hug. "Happy New Year, cuz." He proceeded to give Naomi a hug. "We're in the library. Join us."

"Who's we?" Eileen trailed Philip.

"The usual suspects. Your folks, Julia, and James. The rest of the guests aren't expected for an hour or so."

"Why did Mom say ten sharp if she meant eleven?" Eileen groaned, not really asking either Phil or Naomi.

"Got me. Not like I had anything to do, though. New Year's Day is always a letdown and ushers in another slog to survive. And in all likelihood, the new year will be just as disappointing as the last."

"I see you're a glass half-empty kind of guy," Naomi joked. "Is that a Callahan trait?"

"Yes," both answered simultaneously.

In the library, her mom sat in a wingback and her father slouched in a matching one all the way across the room.

"Look who I found loitering in the foyer." Phil swept up a Champagne flute from the refreshment table by the door.

Everyone exchanged hugs and happy New Year wishes.

Julia said, "Naomi, it's so good to see you." She gave her a heartfelt hug. "Why'd you bring the wet blanket?"

"She wasn't needed to gain entry?" Naomi bantered, offering Eileen a brilliant smart-ass smile.

"It's not too early for me to take a nap upstairs." Eileen yawned.

"You'll do no such thing," her mom said. "Have a seat, dear."

Eileen wondered if she was about to receive a tongue-lashing like the good old days. She met Julia's eyes for a hint but only received a *who knows* shrug.

Her mom studied Naomi, who sat next to Eileen, with a look that wasn't entirely polite, but could be considered barely passible for welcoming. So far, both Eileen and her mom had opted not to even hint at the dustup.

Philip sat next to Julia, wrapping an arm around her shoulders. "It's like old times, except we're all old."

Julia elbowed him. "Speak for yourself."

Eileen yawned again, followed by James who sat on the other side of Julia.

"See, Smelly Ellie can barely stay awake." Philip laughed.

Julia whispered something in his ear, causing Philip to slap his knee, laughing even harder.

Eileen threw serious shade at her baby sister. Julia stuck her tongue out. Her mom scowled and their dad appeared to be dozing.

"Eileen, when are you leaving?" Her mom spoke loudly to commandeer the conversation.

Eileen made a show of consulting the clock on the fireplace mantel, not wanting to rehash the conversation they'd had in private, when her mom had shown her true colors. "Is brunch over before it even started?"

Her mom's thin lips puckered and she crossed her legs. "I mean, when are you going back to work, now that the holidays are almost over?"

"Oh, I'm staying put for a while and working from Derby." Eileen reached for Naomi's hand, needing her touch to get through what she was about to say. "You seem in an awful hurry for me to leave, but not everyone feels that way. Most importantly, Naomi."

There was a silence in the room, but Eileen sensed from the supportive expressions on everyone's faces aside from her mom, they were on Eileen's side.

Finally, Julia broke the spell. "Did you extend the lease?" Julia asked as if she'd already known this was the plan, but wanted to make it clear she hadn't shared the news with their mother.

Eileen nodded.

"Guess that means I have even more reason to visit," Philip said.

Julia swiveled her head to him. "You barely visit now."

"You aren't as fun as your sister. Just look at her—the life of the party."

Eileen was smothering yet another yawn.

"Good grief, I can never win in this family," Julia joked.

"What will you photograph in Derby? There won't be another Christmas tree lighting until next December." Her mom seemed to appear flippant, a fake smile on her lips, but there was a biting edge to her tone. Her expression darkened, "I can't believe you're willingly giving up your career for this... town." Her gaze landed on Naomi.

"Mom!" Julia gasped, digging her nails into James's thigh. "When will you get it through your thick head that Eileen had a stroke."

"What's this about a stroke?" Philip questioned Julia, but his eyes soon found Eileen's. "Is that true, Ellie?" He spoke with tenderness.

Eileen nodded, her eyes dropping from his gaze.

Eileen felt Naomi's hand on her back.

Finally, Eileen said, "Yes. That's the real reason why I came home."

"Why didn't you call me?" Philip's forehead puckered.

"I... I didn't want people to know," Eileen stuttered, realizing how this would affect her cousin.

"I'm not people. I'm your Philip. That's what you used to call me when we were kids." His wounded expression spoke volumes, solidifying the guilt in Eileen's gut.

"I'm sorry, Phil. It was my stupid pride." Eileen squeezed Naomi's hand tighter.

Phil leaned forward. "What can I do to help? Just name it and I'll do it."

"I don't... just, be there for me, I guess. It's going to be a long road until I'm back to what I used to be."

Philip nodded as if he'd never leave her side and Eileen wondered if he'd literally do that.

Julia leaned into James.

Naomi casually blotted her left eye with the sleeve of her sweater.

"But don't let it beat you," her mom said.

Julia started to speak, but Eileen motioned for her to stop. Stiffening, she turned to her mom. "Beat me? How is it beating me, Mom?"

"By not going back to work."

"I am working. I'm writing op-ed pieces and tomorrow, I'm starting my memoir."

"What about your career, though?" Her mom folded her hands primly in her lap.

Her dad bolted upright in his seat. "Jesus, Trudy. She's won prizes. Traveled to more countries than all of us put together and you're acting like she hasn't accomplished a goddamn thing." He swatted the air as if brushing everything aside. "And the daughter sitting before me doesn't look beaten at all." His eyes landed on his wife's. "She could have died. Can't you get that through your brain? She could have died!" He emphasized each word in the last sentence.

Julia stifled a sniffle, Philip wrapped an arm around her shoulder.

"But she didn't—" Her mom's voice cracked, the first chink in her armor, but it was difficult to pin down the source of the emotion: frustration or sadness. "Is it wrong that I only want the best for my daughter?"

"Then let her get well without pressuring her to hurry the hell up." Her dad's nostrils flared. "Besides, I like having her here and not in harm's way. I'm proud as hell, Ellie, but you've given your old man so many potential heart attacks over the years. Whenever I heard where you were and how close to the action…" He raked a hand over his thinning gray hair. "It's more than most parents can take."

"Are you implying I never had a sleepless night?" Her mom bristled. "What mother wants their child on the front line?"

He stared as if unsure he believed her words or stiffening shoulders.

"That was the life she chose. I've only wanted…" Her voice wavered and she left the rest unsaid.

No one spoke for several moments.

"If you'll excuse me, I need to check with Maggie about brunch." She rose and made for the exit, her eyes glistening.

"Well…" Julia looked to Phil as if wanting him to complete her sentence.

He took a deep breath.

Her dad left the room.

"And that's how prim and proper Massachusetts families hash out decades of family strife," Eileen joked, although she didn't find any of this humorous.

"I don't think she means to be so... cold." Julia's words came out stilted. "She's just... different."

Eileen still hadn't found the courage to tell Julia everything that had transpired that day when her mom had come to Eileen's apartment.

Philip wiped his eyes. "I need a refill. Julia help me get drinks."

"What?"

Philip jabbed an elbow into her side and jerked his head to Eileen and Naomi on the opposite couch.

"Oh, yes. Of course. Drinks. We should leave and get drinks. Come on James." James stood, putting a hand out for Julia to get up.

After the door closed, Naomi whispered, "Rome wasn't built in a day."

"Good thing I paid my rent upfront for a year."

Naomi blinked. "A whole year. You're really staying?"

Eileen laughed. "Did you think I was pulling a fast one on you? Or were you secretly hoping I'd dash off on an assignment? A long-distance relationship may be easier with the likes of me. I mean, you just witnessed how my family deals with things. If that doesn't scare you off, I don't know what will."

Naomi let out a puff of air. "You're insufferable."

"That's my point. And I was raised by an expert on how never to show emotions. Or love, for that matter."

"I hate to break it to you, but you don't have to be anything like your mother. You've already shown great strides. She'd never volunteer at the hospital and give Tyson a camera. Or contemplate starting a photography class. Not to mention the care packages you handed out on Christmas morning to all the

HARPER BLISS & T.B. MARKINSON

children in the hospital. All those cute turtles. You are insuffer-able, but in an adorable way because you try so hard not to show how much you care about people, but you can't stop yourself from caring." Naomi linked an arm through Eileen's. "I'm not letting you go."

"That seems to be the case, given the lock you have on my arm."

"Will you just shut up and kiss me."

Eileen complied.

Pulling away, Eileen flicked one of Naomi's silver turtle stud earrings.

"Don't even say you're a turtle again," Naomi said with exasperation.

Eileen tilted her head back and laughed. Recovering, she said, "Like I said, I don't mind being a turtle, as long as I'm your turtle. God knows I could use some saving."

"Did you just propose marriage?"

"Trust me, if I do, you'll know. I'm not letting you go either, Naomi Weaver."

"If you do?"

Eileen playfully groaned. "Should I have said when?"

Naomi smiled. "I think it's funny you think you'll be the one who proposes first."

"Did you just propose to me?" Eileen cupped Naomi's cheek.

"Trust me, when I do, you'll know."

"What if we do it at the same time?"

"That would be a miracle." Naomi inched closer to Eileen's lips.

"It seems to be the time of year for them." Eileen's mouth moved even closer.

"There's always next year. No need to rush now that I know you're staying."

"If I wasn't staying, would you propose?" Eileen pressed her forehead to Naomi's.

"You're insufferable. Kiss me like you never want to lose me."

"Easily done, because I don't."

Their lips met and neither pulled away.

ABOUT THE AUTHORS

Harper Bliss is the author of the *Pink Bean* series, the *High Rise* series, the *French Kissing* serial and many other lesbian romance titles. She is the co-founder of Ladylit Publishing and My LesFic weekly newsletter.

Harper loves hearing from readers and you can get in touch with her here:

www.harperbliss.com
harper@harperbliss.com

T.B. Markinson is an American living in England. When she isn't writing, she's traveling the world, watching sports on the telly, visiting pubs, or reading. Not necessarily in that order.

Her novels have hit Amazon bestseller lists for lesbian fiction and lesbian romance.

She also runs I Heart Lesfic, a place for authors and fans of lesfic to come together to celebrate and chat about lesbian fiction.

You can get in touch with her here:

lesbianromancesbytbm.com
tbm@tbmarkinson.com

Made in the USA
Middletown, DE
19 December 2020

29259509R00161